SHADOW

THE THREE LANDS

BOOK 2

A fantasy novel by

D. R. Evans

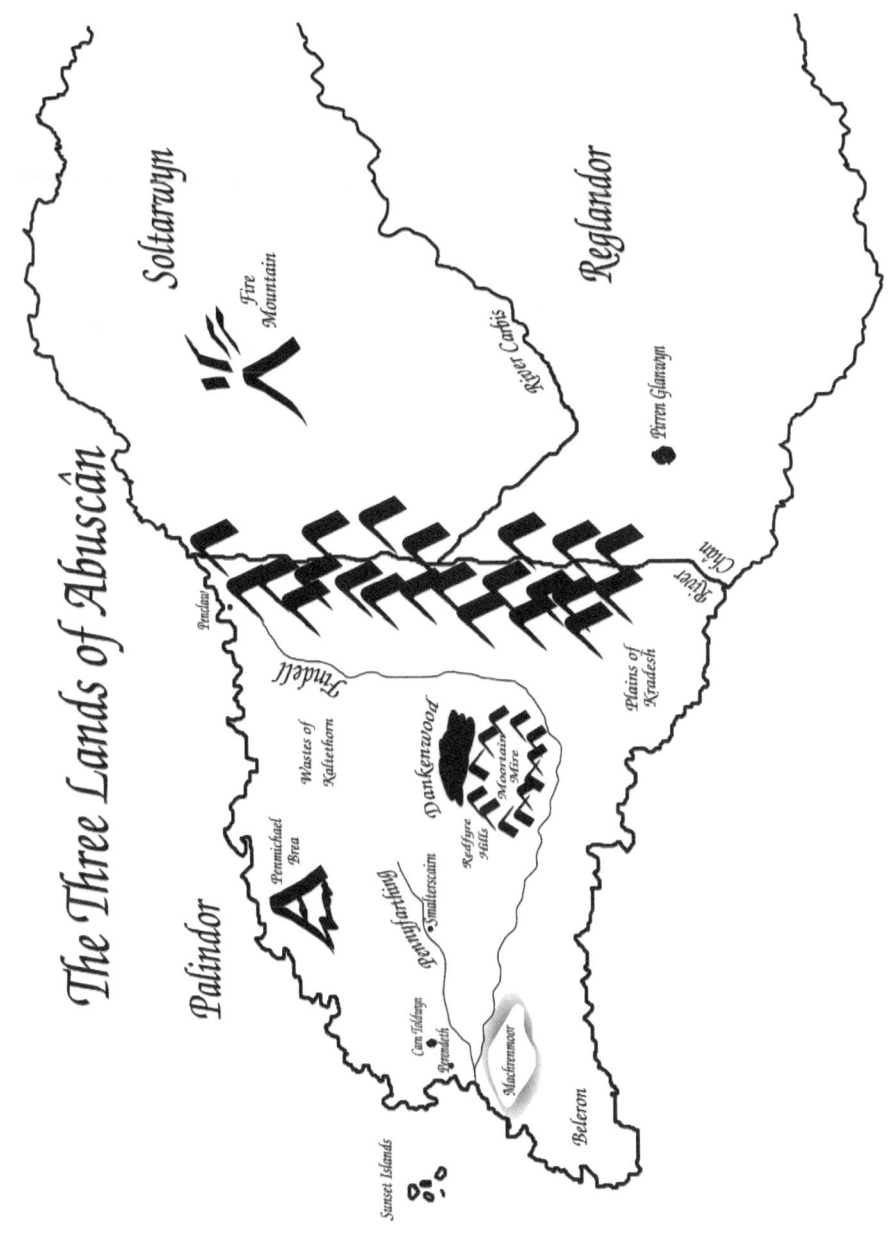

The Three Lands of Abuscán

Palindor

Soltarwyn

Reglandor

Sunset Islands

Cwn Feldenyg
Brendath

Mackrenmoor

Beleron

Pennyfarthing
Smilterscairn

Redfyre Hills

Carn Felderig

Wastes of Ralletthorn

Permichael Brea

Darkenwood

Mountain Mire

Tindell

Pradaw

Fire Mountain

River Corbis

Pirren Glanwyn

River Chan

Plains of Kradesh

i

CONTENTS

MAJOR RACES OF PALINDOR
(only the races important to our story are described here)

Dwarves. Originally underground dwellers, most dwarves now live above ground. Slightly taller than gnomes and somewhat shorter than humans, dwarves are the strongest and most belligerent fighters in Abuscân. The pride of each dwarf is his (or her) battle-axe. Female dwarves are only slightly less strong than males, and either would make short work of a human in combat.

Elves. There are many different types of elf, and each type is named after its most distinguishing quality. The most common elves are wood elves, who live in villages deep in woods and forests; there are also fisherelves (who live on the coasts) and even mountain elves (although these are now rare). Most elves are slightly shorter than gnomes, but are considerably leaner and more spry. They are sociable amongst others of their own kind, but considerably less so with other elves, and rarely interact with the non-elf races. Almost all elves share two great fears: tunnels and water. Only fisherelves are taught how to swim; all other elves are terrified of drowning. Only mountain elves would willingly enter a tunnel or a cave.

Gnomes. The most bookish of the races, gnomes are a rarity except in Palindor. In Carn Toldwyn, Palindor's capital, they are the majority of the population. Not generally of much use in battle, gnomes are slightly shorter than dwarves but, unlike the latter, male gnomes almost always grow long white beards. In the past, particularly intelligent and studious gnomes took an oath at a young age to become Holy Gnomes, the keepers of the ancient books.

Humans. The tallest of the common races. In the earliest times, humans usually led other races into battle, and so it was decreed that only a human could be a monarch.

Hunters. Not really a distinct race, the Hunters are humans who live in the forests of Palindor. They are especially tall and strong; Rarely seen, they prefer to live solitary lives, but their skill with their longbows is unmatched throughout the Three Lands of Abuscân.

Wizards, Sages and Necromancers. In ancient times, there were sages and necromancers. In most portions of Abuscân, including Palindor, the distinction between these has long been lost, and now members of the race are known generically as "wizards." A race not unlike humans in appearance and gnomes in inclination, wizards can command magic, but only of the common kind. No mortal race has the power to control the kiriàl* that lies at the heart of the Three Lands. Originally, sages concentrated their skills on spells of learning and what we would call "goodness." The two main characteristics of sages were their dress (a habit with a large, deep hood) and their reluctance to voice their thoughts. Necromancers used their skills simply to obtain power, and were uninterested in whether the source of that power was good or evil. Wizards vary widely in their prowess, depending on their individual talents and the length and depth of their studies.

---

* A Palindoric word with no good translation. Kiriàl is the name given to the fundamental spiritual realities that underlie the Three Lands of Abuscân: Reglandor, Soltarwyn and Palindor.

Major Characters

Anderskerrin. A fisherelf originally from the village of Penclaw in Palindor. He has settled in Soltarwyn and is married to Hervân.

Catherine. The first High Queen of Palindor. An adult from the world of humans who first visited Palindor as a young woman.

Drefynt. The last of the Holy Gnomes and a friend of Queen Catherine on her first visit to Palindor. Now old and nearing the end of his days, he remains endowed with enormous wisdom and much knowledge, especially regarding the ancient times.

Hervân. The wife of Anderskerrin; a wood elf from Fire Mountain Meadow in Soltarwyn.

Malthazzar. The Lord of Evil and Master of Sheol. Defeated once by the High Queen Catherine, he intends to control Palindor through his servant, Shadow.

Michael. A visitor from the world of humans and the son of the High Queen Catherine. A verse from the ancient times prophesies that the second High Monarch will be called Michael, and he will be known as the High King of War.

Olvensar. The High Lord of Palindor.

Qivir. The chief minister of King Glendour IV of Reglandor.

Shadow. The most ruthless and powerful of Malthazzar's generals, he is entrusted with bringing about the destruction of the Ruling Council of Palindor and bringing Catherine, Michael and the whole of Palindor under Malthazzar's sway.

Sherna. Known as Sherna the Traveller, she is the daughter of the Holy Gnome Drefynt. She has travelled widely through the Three Lands of Abuscân.

Treadlong. A traveller and storyteller with immense knowledge of the Three Lands.

Prolegomenon the First

The garden, normally full of the sounds of life, is ominously quiet. The colors, usually vivid, are tinged with gray. Even the clear, warm light of the golden sun seems watery and lacking heat. The animals, instead of conversing, brood silently. Along a wide, grassy path through the trees walks the gardener, his steps heavy and slow as he converses with the tall, dark, menacing figure of Malthazzar. They pass a young doe, who, from her place in the trees, watches and strains to hear their words even though she feels an oppressive mælstrom of emotions engendered by the presence of the Lord of Evil.

The gardener shakes his head. "No. I know my people. They will not war."

Malthazzar speaks, his cold tones cutting through the air like a sharp winter breeze. "Ha! Only because you protect them. If you withdrew your presence they would soon fall into my ways. You give them no freedom of choice, that is why they follow you: because they can choose no other way."

They take several more steps before the gardener halts abruptly and looks his enemy in the eye. "That is not true. I have faith in my creatures. If I were to leave them, still they would not come under your dominion."

Malthazzar's mouth opens in a hideous, yellow smile. "Then I have a proposition for you. Let neither of us be present in the Three Lands. Let us each send only a few emissaries to do our bidding.

Let us make a pact, you and I, that our chosen instruments shall be given free reign, and then let us see which of us the creatures of Palindor choose for their master."

"You would challenge me, Malthazzar? What right have you?"

"No right, Lord Olvensar, save that you know that your creatures are weak, and that without you they would quickly become my servants instead of your own. It nearly happened once before, if you remember."

The gardener nods slowly. "I remember, but then you and I were both abroad in the land. This time we will be absent?"

Malthazzar nods his assent.

"Then I agree. You are wrong. My people are strong. You can fool them for a time, but ultimately their love will win through. This is what I'll do: I will send two creatures from the world of humans. No harm is to come to them, or I will seek you to the very ends of the worlds, and you will wish that you had never been created."

"There is no need to threaten me. It is their weakness that will undo them, not my strength. For my part, I will instruct carefully the one whom I choose. No harm will come to your... humans" — he sneered as he said this word — "unless they cause harm first. And you will not permit any harm to come to the one I send?"

"Agreed. You have your pact. Now, go!"

The ground trembles and the air fills with loud, sneering laughter. "I leave, Olvensar. But when I return it will be as victor." And with a thunderclap and a burning stench in the air, Malthazzar is gone.

Slowly, the colors return, the air feels clean again, the garden reverts to normality. But the nearby doe sees the gardener shake his head and say under his breath: "And so the test begins...."

PROLEGOMENON THE SECOND

It is night in Sheol.

The burning, blood-red sun has set, its place taken by the black of utter voidance. There are neither moon nor stars; the sky is black with the nothingness of death. Yet there is light of a sort: an evil, burning light cast by the pools of smoldering brimstone that pockmark the dark land and exude their acrid stench over the landscape.

It is night in Sheol.

We stand, formless, shallowly breathing the rasping air, and peer into the depths of a valley. Here, at the very heart of Sheol, is the castle of its lord and master. Here, but a short distance from where we stand, is the castle of one whose name is rarely spoken in this, his kingdom. Here, its dark rock reflecting the burning sheen from its moat of molten sulphur, stands the castle of Malthazzar.

It is night in Sheol.

Trembling, we enter the castle, our senses barely surviving the assault. Worse than the aching black redness that greets our eyes, worse than the foul odor of living, rotting meat, worse by far than the hideous cacophony of the beasts that serve the master of this place, is the sense of loss, of despair, of hatred, of unalloyed evil. For here, this night, Lord Malthazzar has called together in one place his most trusted generals, his most powerful soldiers, his most deceptive spies.

Together, they have eaten and drunk until sated, gorged with the black, nameless, undead meat and drunk with the dark, oily liquid contained in their goblets. If these were mortals, they would now be sleeping off their excesses, but for these minions of darkness there is no rest, merely a dragging, loathsome tiredness, a fatigue from which there is no relief. For it is true that there is no rest for the wicked, and here, gathered together in one place, are the most wicked of creatures ever to serve the Lord of Evil.

But there are two here tonight who stand apart even from this loathsome crowd. The first is obvious: Malthazzar himself, the Lord of Sheol, seated at the head of the immense table at which the meal just concluded took place. Tonight he appears in all his diabolical glory, the red light from the torches in the sconces on the walls of the Great Hall seemingly swallowed by his black form. Slowly, he looks around the table, his eyes reflecting the red light. Creature by creature, he weighs what he sees before passing on to the next of his minions.

His soldiers, his generals, his spies do not observe their master. They are too busy talking and arguing amongst themselves, some still drinking of the fruit of the bitter dark vines that grow in the parched, baked soil of Sheol. Here and there, arguments have broken out: who is the greatest of Malthazzar's army? for what reason have they been summoned? Contemptuously, Malthazzar's eyes pass over these creatures, searching for the one who will do his bidding, the one on whom he must depend to bring his plan to fruition.

It is night in Sheol.

His eyes settle on a single creature unlike the others gathered before him. This is the second one who stands out from this gathering: a small creature, shorter than a man, taller than dwarf.

Yet, even as we look at him — if, indeed, the creature is male — we find that we cannot be sure even of his height. His shape seems indeterminate: one moment he appears as a short, dark mouselike creature, the next a tall, well-built human. But even as he undergoes these metamorphoses, one thing remains constant: black as his companions around the table are, this creature has an altogether different quality of blackness. His blackness seems, surprisingly, less complete — perhaps, we may hope, less evil — a dark grayness rather than a complete blackness, a mere absence of light rather than a destructive swallowing of it.

But there is something else about this creature, some other quality that causes Malthazzar's eyes to cease searching. Alone of his subjects, this creature is not engaged in conversation; alone of his subjects, this creature has not touched the goblet before him; alone of his subjects, this creature is looking fixedly towards the head of the table, meeting the eyes of his lord.

Malthazzar stands hugely to his feet. He bellows a command: "Cease! Be quiet!" Silence descends on the chamber as all eyes now turn toward him. "Begone, all of you, back to your dominions. I have no further need of you." The stones of the castle reverberate with the power of his voice.

For a few moments, there is confusion as the creatures make for the room's exit. Soon only two creatures remain in the hall. For a long moment, they lock eyes, then one lowers his head in submission.

Quietly now, Malthazzar speaks to the remaining creature. "You! Shadow! Why did you not leave when I bid everyone depart?"

The creature's head rises again. For a moment, Malthazzar seems unsure whether there might not be a touch of haughty arrogance in this creature's bearing, but even as he watches, the gray shadow flickers and becomes smaller, the eyes that momentarily locked with his own dropping submissively to gaze at the dark, slimy flagstones.

"Did you not desire that I remain behind, my lord? For so I thought I saw in your eyes."

"Indeed, it is so. You may raise your eyes and look on me, for I have chosen you for a task. You will be the instrument through which I gain my greatest victory. You, Shadow, have been chosen from all my generals to be the one whose name shall be revered throughout the ages as the greatest of all those who serve me. Because of you, the minions of the hated High Lord will be destroyed and deliver Palindor to me. Come closer, and I will explain your task."

The gray body lifts itself from the crude bench on which it has been seated. Without hesitation, the creature walks towards his lord, ignoring the movement and the muffled sounds coming from the remains of the half-alive, half-dead meat that formed their meal.

Shadow bows his head in supplication and drops to one knee before Malthazzar. "I am honored above all others this night, my lord. Tell me thy will and it shall be done."

Malthazzar smiles to himself. He has chosen well; he has chosen well indeed. This time, Palindor will be his.

Truly, it is night in Sheol.

I Reverie

Katrin Fowler was dying, the inoperable tumor in her head robbing her ineluctably of her life-force. Her time would soon be at an end.

If it were not for her son Michael, she would not mind so much. After all, even though thirty six seemed far too young to die, death held few fears for her. Ever since her husband, Ben, had been cruelly taken from her in a car accident three years ago, there had been little except Michael to live for.

Her thoughts wandered to Michael, and she found herself dwelling on the past. Michael had been such a beautiful, well-behaved child when he was little. His teachers had commented on how intelligent he was, what a pleasant child he was to be around, and what great potential he held. But all that had changed after the accident.

Looking out the window at the drizzle that lay heavy on the sea, Katrin's thoughts returned, as they did several times a day, to that moment when the telephone had rung.

It was a Tuesday; for some reason that fact remained burned in her mind, as if it were somehow important. Michael had just arrived home from school and was eating a snack. It was her tenth wedding anniversary, not that Michael was aware of the fact. Ten years since she had ceased being Katrin Taylor, unemployed college graduate, and started a new life as Katrin Fowler, wife of a promising young

7

doctor who had just become a junior partner in an established practice in town.

For neither Ben nor herself had there ever been anyone else. Within seconds of their first meeting, they had both known that they wanted to spend the rest of their lives together. What neither of them had foreseen was that that time would be so short.

They had married, and within the year Michael had been born. There had been no other children, much though Ben and she had desired them. Perhaps they had spoiled Michael when he was little; but who, Katrin wondered in self defense, could have blamed them? Michael was everything that anyone could want in a child. Indeed, she remembered thinking not long before the accident that she did not deserve such a happy life: a loving, caring, successful husband, and an intelligent, thoughtful, hardworking son. She could not help wondering sometimes if her illogical guilt at her own happiness had somehow been the cause of the accident that had destroyed that happiness. But no, that was impossible....

Still the drizzle hung like a cloud just beyond the glass. Her mood matched the grayness of the drizzle as her thoughts continued inexorably onward, replaying the events of three years before.

The telephone rang. She glanced at the clock on the kitchen microwave: nearly four o'clock. Ben had told her that he hoped to be home before now — his shift at the hospital was over at three. But she was not worried. Long ago she had come to accept the fact that talented surgeons like Ben could not keep regular office hours, and it would not be the first time that an emergency at the hospital had caused him to change their dinner plans at short notice.

She picked up the telephone at the first ring. "Hello?"

A woman said, "Hello, Mrs. Fowler?"

"Yes."

"This is the hospital." So Ben was going to be late. It must be a real emergency, she thought; Katrin could not remember the last time Ben had not called personally to apologize that he wouldn't be home on time.

There was a pause before the voice at the other end of the line continued. "I'm afraid I have some bad news, Mrs. Fowler." Even then, Katrin had not suspected what was coming, although the tone of the other's voice should have warned her. "Dr. Fowler was in a traffic accident on his way home this afternoon, not a hundred yards from the hospital. He was rushed here and Dr. Wentworth operated immediately. But I'm afraid there was nothing he could do, the internal damage was too great. Your husband is dead, Mrs. Fowler. I'm so sorry."

She could remember little of what happened next. She had tried, many times, to reconstruct the exact sequence of events, but she could never quite fit her memories together in a pattern that made sense. The next thing she remembered clearly was sitting on Michael's bed, trying to comfort the child whose face was buried in his pillow, screaming "No! No! No!" at the top of his lungs.

For a while, Katrin and Michael had seemed to adjust well to their loss. The first warning sign hadn't come until about six months later, when the principal of Michael's school called to tell her that Michael had been caught beating a boy with a tree branch. The boy had had to go to the hospital to receive stitches, and Michael was suspended from school for the rest of the week. The parents of the injured boy decided not to press charges, but that was of little comfort to Katrin, who had been unable to discover from Michael why he had set on the boy. The injured boy also refused to talk about it, and the school officials confessed to having no clues as to what might have precipitated the fight.

Katrin never did discover what the fight had been about; but it was only the first of many scrapes that Michael got into. Three years later and now in middle school, Michael had become part of what Katrin thought of as "a bad crowd": he often played truant, and was suspected, although he had never actually been caught, of bullying any student who crossed him.

Katrin began to think about moving away, perhaps to the country, where Michael would be removed from the growing influence of street gangs. While she was pondering this possibility, she noticed that more and more often she was feeling tired, and sometimes her limbs stiffened inexplicably. She began to experience episodes when her left side went numb. For several weeks she ignored these symptoms, putting them down variously to a virus, then simple fatigue, then worry over Michael. Eventually, after an entire day when she was so tired that she was barely able to get out of bed, she at last went to her doctor.

9

A barrage of tests carried out over the next month had brought her the news: there was an inoperable tumor in her brain. Although medication could be prescribed, there was nothing that science could do to save her. She should get her affairs in order; if there was ever anything she wanted to do, she should do it now, because she would be lucky to survive more than a few months.

Katrin had no living blood relatives except Michael, but Ben's brother, Kenn, was married and had a son a year older than Michael; Kenn and his wife agreed that they would gladly accept Michael into their family when Katrin could no longer cope. Her son's future settled, Katrin and Michael sat down and had a very grown-up conversation about how to spend the time that remained.

"I'm open to any ideas," said Katrin, "except sitting at home waiting for the inevitable."

Michael shrugged. "I don't care."

"I have some money saved. If ever there was a time to spend it, I guess that time is now."

Michael seemed suddenly interested.

"You mean we could do something really cool, like travel around the world?"

"Sure, if that's what you want."

"Anything to get away from here."

So she sold the house, placing most of the proceeds in a trust fund for Michael, took Michael out of school, and then used the remainder of the funds from the house for their journey around the world.

Travelling from east to west, they had started with visits to several states, crossed the Pacific to Japan, then worked their way through Singapore, several stops in Australia, then on to India, Israel, through eastern Europe and were now at their last stop: the tiny duchy of Cornwall, in the southwest of England.

At first, Michael had been a perfect travelling companion. His sullenness and rebellion had disappeared, and he had taken as much interest as she in the sights and sounds (and sometimes smells) that had greeted each stop.

But since they had arrived in Europe Michael had become more withdrawn and morose; now he spent much of his time alone, walking the streets of the towns in which they stayed. As far as she could tell, he was causing no trouble, and she decided that the change was simply because their journey was nearly over, and the reality of what would happen once they left Cornwall for home had begun to weigh heavily on the boy's mind.

The trip had done Katrin good. She felt much better — until, without warning, two days ago, she had suddenly blacked out. It was late, and Michael was already asleep. She was walking across her room in the cozy bed and breakfast, when the next thing she knew she was flat on her back, the clock on the wall showing that several minutes had passed. Scared, she said nothing to anyone. The incident had not repeated itself, but for the last couple of days she felt more tired than at any time since leaving home.

But along with the tiredness was something else. For the first time in nearly two decades, Katrin found her mind dwelling on the extraordinary events that had occurred when she was a teenager.

There had been a car accident involved that time as well, although she had no memory of it. In fact, more than one of the doctors whom she had consulted in the past six months had expressed the opinion that her tumor might have been caused by the long-ago accident. Her brain had been starved of oxygen for several minutes, and it was possible that she had received a blow to the head that had gone unnoticed at the time. Afterwards, her parents had told her that she had lain for months in a coma, unmoving, never conscious, barely alive. And yet, to the astonishment of the doctors, who had been unanimous that she would never again open her eyes (much less live any kind of a normal life) she had eventually recovered from the near-fatal accident.

She never told the doctors what had happened to her during those months in which she had lain in a coma.

She had tried to tell her parents, though. They, loving her, had never contradicted her story, but her father had sown the seeds of doubt by explaining: "Katrin, you know that dreams sometimes seem very real; well, when your brain has received a trauma like yours did, it is very possible to have especially vivid dreams. They might easily seem real at the time, but really they only happened inside your head. If I were you, I wouldn't tell anyone about your dreams. Just be thankful that you're back here with us."

11

Even though she had wanted to argue with her parents, she knew that she had no proof that there really was a place inhabited by dwarves and gnomes and goblins and trolls. Besides, it would have sounded childish for her, a young woman of nearly sixteen, to have insisted that such a place existed. She never again tried to tell anyone about Palindor. Even Ben had died not knowing. It was only after the doctors' diagnosis of her tumor that something had happened that had made her begin to wonder about Palindor....

It was a small, almost inconsequential, incident.

One day, hurrying to put some clean clothes in a drawer, the drawer had somehow closed heavily on her left thumb. In pain, she examined her thumb to see if she had broken it. Unbidden, her thoughts crossed two decades. Into her head flashed an image of her left thumb extending toward the edge of a dark blade. She felt the sword cutting into her flesh, and then the terrifying darkness that followed as the power of the sword entered her body.

The flashback had lasted only a moment, but its results stayed with her to this day. When she examined her thumb after trapping it in the drawer, in exactly the place where the sword had cut her, there was now a small scar of raised tissue, lighter than the surrounding skin: a healed wound from long ago that had not been there moments earlier.

She hadn't thought much about Palindor for many years. But now she found herself wondering, over and over again: did Palindor really exist, or was it, as her father had insisted, just a trick played by her brain?

Could such creatures as elves and wizards really exist? It seemed impossible. It *was* impossible. Yet the mark on her thumb testified that, even though it made no sense, there *was* such a place, and she once, long ago, had been its High Queen.

She found herself thinking of Olvensar, the strange High Lord of Palindor. Was there really such a person? An old man in dirty gardening overalls whose eyes seemed to hold a power strong enough to create worlds? Several times recently, she had caught herself thinking out loud: "Olvensar, please show yourself. If you are real, please come and do something about this lump inside my head." But of course nothing had happened.

Until yesterday.

Cornwall was a wild, rural, remote part of England. During the summer, this part of the country was inundated with tourists, but now the holiday season was over and there were few visitors. Lying three hundred miles west-south-west of London, Katrin and Michael were in the extreme western part of Cornwall, where once Celts had lived and traded with the Romans who later came to occupy the rest of the country that would one day be known as England. But here the wild Celts, surviving in the harsh environment where the land confronts the Atlantic Ocean, had continued their strange, mystical existence for many hundreds of years before finally succumbing to occupation.

Katrin had known little of this when they had arrived. To her and to Michael, this was merely their last stop, the westernmost part of England, with only the Atlantic Ocean separating them from America. Yesterday they had arrived at the bed and breakfast, planning to stay for a few days before returning home. Feeling strong enough for a walk, she had accompanied Michael into the nearby small town: a tourist trap in the summer, a fishing village in the winter, and now resting uneasily between seasons. As had become her custom on their round-the-world trip, Katrin had gone to a bookshop to buy a guidebook to the area.

Her heart had nearly stopped beating. There was a book: *Guide to West Cornwall* it was called. But on the cover, underneath the title, was a photograph: a picture of a large slab of granite held aloft by three tall, crudely-shaped granite pillars. Her hands shook as she picked up the book. "I know what that is," she heard herself saying. "It's a quoit."

"Indeed 'tis, ma'am," said the shopkeeper in a Cornish burr. "That's Lanyon Quoit. It's easy to find. Just take the back road to Penzance. It's near a village called Morvah. Can't miss it."

But Katrin was not listening. She repeated the words over and over again. "A quoit, a quoit...." She had seen a quoit but once before, more than twenty years ago. But that quoit wasn't near a village in Cornwall. It stood alone on the highest point of Machrenmoor, south of Carn Toldwyn.

In Palindor.

II The New Star

It was a moonless night, perfect for hunting in the eerie darkness of Dankenwood.

The trees stood silent, unmoving and black around the clearing in which stood the ramshackle hovel that was the residence of the master of Dankenwood. Not far away, a noise, a disturbance as of a creature being dragged along the ground, was drawing slowly closer.

After a while, Fayorn came into sight of his home. He was short, squat, obese and ugly, his yellow teeth bared with the exertion of pulling the deer's carcass. Renewing his efforts, he pulled the dead animal, which would last him a week or more, into the clearing that surrounded his hovel.

He rested for a few moments, then recommenced dragging the animal towards his home. As he reached the door, perspiration dripped from his brow to the ground, creating invisible damp patches on the sterile, friable soil.

Suddenly, the patches were invisible no more, as a light blazed high in the western sky.

Fayorn turned toward the light, nearly toppling as his ugly, ungainly body struggled to keep its balance. For a moment he stared at the sight that greeted his bloodshot eyes. To the west, high above the forest, a bright new star had appeared in the heavens.

Flaring brilliantly yellow, it was as bright as a full moon, bright enough to throw his shadow against the uneven wall of the hovel. He blinked his heavy eyelids several times, hoping that the vision would disappear as suddenly and as quickly as it had appeared. But the new star remained in the sky, silent, still, and brilliant.

"No!" he shouted.

Dropping his burden, Fayorn scrabbled at the ancient wooden door of his hut, desperate to open it and escape the brilliant yellow light.

He slammed the door closed behind him. But it was not enough: the light from the star entered the hut through the cracked windows. The ugly creature rushed around the room, pulling thin drapes across the windows. But still the light came in.

"No! I will not do it!" he shouted into the empty room, a desperate look in his eyes.

———————

Several days' journey to the west, an old gnome was strolling meditatively through the thick trees that grew close to his house on the edge of Carn Toldwyn.

Drefynt, last of the Holy Gnomes of Palindor, was old now, and becoming more frail with each passing moon. He could walk but a short distance without the aid of the stout cane that he now held firmly as he took his slow steps.

In recent months, Drefynt had grown into the habit of taking an evening walk in the woods near his home. His eyes were no longer what they had been even a year ago, and after scribing all day he could no longer see clearly enough to read in the flickering light from the candles of an evening. So he had begun to walk instead. He never went far, nor for very long, just half an hour or so in which he could be alone with his thoughts.

He turned to make his way back towards his home. As he did every night, he thought lovingly of his wife, Lorin, her physical beauty now gone, but her spirit as warm and loving and caring as ever. How lucky he was to have found such a one with whom to share his days; he was blessed indeed. Quietly, almost whispering, he said: "Thank you, Lord Olvensar, for bringing Lorin to me."

15

His thoughts were interrupted by a sudden change in the forest around him. What had been until this moment a dark and perhaps slightly ominous environment was suddenly lit by a bright light. The dark shapes of the trees and their shadows receded, to be replaced by the gray-brown and green of the trunks and needles themselves.

Astonished, the gnome stopped.

He peered around, trying to discover the source of the light. For several seconds he was at a loss, then he craned his head upward, towards the starry, moonless sky. The intertwined branches of the trees high above his head intervened, cutting off his view of the sky, but there could be no doubt that the light came from somewhere high above. Hurrying as best he could, he made for the edge of the forest so that he might see more clearly the sign that the heavens had sent.

The knock came on the door, as Fayorn had known that it would. It seemed like he had been waiting for hours, the light of the hated star shining unblinkingly through the loose weave of the ancient, dirty drapes that hung across the windows. Here in Dankenwood, time was not always as simple as in other places, and to an observer it would have seemed a matter of mere minutes since he had entered the hovel, breathing deeply and shouting out his rejection of the light in the sky.

The knock was gentle, yet it rang around the simple, dirty, earth-floored room with an urgency that could not be ignored.

For the first time in four thousand years, Fayorn regretted that there was no lock on the door. The thought of a lock had never occurred to him before; after all, was he not Master of Dankenwood? Nothing could enter this part of Palindor without his knowledge; no creature could threaten him here in his domain, where he was the undisputed master of all. But he realized, too late, that he had been too sure of himself. For there was one indeed who could come and go as he pleased. And doubtless it was an emissary of this one who now stood unseen and unbidden on the far side of the unlockable door.

Fayorn looked at the door, his breaths coming in short, loud, terrified bursts as he waited for the knocking to be repeated. But there was no second knock. Instead, the door was silently pushed open to reveal a creature standing on the doorstep.

Where Fayorn was ugly, this creature was beautiful. Where Fayorn sucked in his breaths in sharp, jagged inhalations, this creature breathed gently and evenly, sure of itself and its purpose. Small, no larger than the master of the wood in which he stood, but mouselike in appearance and with fur that shone golden with a supernatural light in the glow from the star, the creature eyed Fayorn. The creature made no movement to enter the hovel; instead he spoke quietly and firmly from the threshold. "Master Fayorn of Dankenwood. I am the dablik. The time has come."

"No!" shouted Fayorn. "I will not do it! I will not!"

For several seconds, there was no movement and no sound apart from the noisy heaving of Fayorn's chest. Gently, the creature spoke again. "But it is time. The sign has come, and I have been sent."

"No!"

With a final scream the Master of Dankenwood came to life. He ran across the dirty floor of his hovel and, closing his eyes against the force of the impact, threw his full weight at the creature that stood in his doorway. But there was no collision; instead, there was only a soft thud as Fayorn flew through the air to land on the carcass of the deer. Scrabbling crazily to his feet, Fayorn looked around, but the dablik was gone.

Drefynt emerged from the forest and stood on the damp grass that surrounded his secluded house. Looking up, he gasped at the sight that met his old eyes. High in the heavens, directly above Carn Toldwyn, a single dot of light shone yellow, outshining by far the dim, twinkling lights of ordinary stars which could now barely be seen, obscured as they were by the brilliant glow.

"A new star," he said to himself in awe. "But what does it mean?"

His wife of half a lifetime found him several minutes later, still leaning against his staff at the edge of the forest, not a dozen steps from the house, just gazing up at the bright new light in the sky.

"Drefynt, my dear. What is it? Do you know?"

Drefynt tore his eyes from the star. For several seconds he could see nothing, his eyes dazzled by the glare at which he had been gazing. Slowly, he made out the form of his beloved wife standing next to him. He shook his head. "Nay, Lorin. I know not. It is a sign, of course. But what it portends, I cannot say."

"But if Drefynt the Wise knows not the meaning of a sign, then who in all Palindor will know?"

Drefynt shook his head again. "That also I know not. But it is not a sign meant for me, otherwise I would know its meaning." Falling silent, he gazed at his wife as she stared at the bright star. He shivered, then continued. "But I am uneasy. Such a sign can only be the doing of the Lord Olvensar. Which means it must be a grave matter indeed. We would do well to meditate on this, good wife."

Lorin tore her eyes from the star. "Aye, well, you'll be meditating in bed if you catch cold out here. Come on inside; the fire is warm and the hour is late. Perhaps you can investigate this sign in the castle library in the morning."

Drefynt looked unconvinced, but with a final glance at the new star, he took his wife's hand and together they went indoors.

The door was barricaded now with the table and chair that were normally the only furniture in the dirty room. Fayorn was confident that if the golden-haired creature returned he would no longer be able to open the door. The deer, its blood still sticky on the floor, lay in the middle of the room. Fayorn eyed it appraisingly. He could make it last for ten days, perhaps even two weeks if he was sparing. He would not starve. With another glance at the doorway, he nodded to himself, his yellow teeth flashing in the light that trickled through the drapes. He had done all he could. All he could do now was to hope for the best.

He laid hold of the deer to drag it into the hut's only other room, the kitchen, where he could begin to hack at the carcass with a knife.

A movement in the kitchen doorway caught his eye.

He looked up, and all hope drained away. Standing in the low doorway, hunching over slightly, stood an old man.

The man's garb, such as could be seen in the filtered yellow light, appeared to be an indiscriminate gray-green-brown color, as if once, long ago, it might have been green, but was now spoiled by a long period of use in a particularly dirty garden. In one hand, the man held a stout staff, against which he leaned.

His face was partly hidden by a white beard and mustache and unfashionably long hair. But Fayorn could only wish that the face were entirely hidden. Especially the eyes. The old man's eyes were fixed on Fayorn, and there was no mistaking the meaning in them. Tired and careworn though the man's face appeared, his eyes were alight with an angry fire.

Fayorn bowed his head under the gaze. For a while, there was neither sound nor movement. At length, Fayorn lifted his eyes to meet those of the old man.

Anger had left them now, replaced by a look of compassion that spread across the man's face; then, wonder of wonders, it seemed to suffuse outwards from the man himself, crossing the space between them and filling Fayorn himself.

Fayorn relaxed as a wave of compassion swept over him. And after the compassion, another emotion, one that the small, ugly creature could not for a moment place, so long ago was it that he had last experienced it. His mind groped, trying to recall the name of this feeling that enveloped him. At last, with an audible cry of discovery, the memory returned: this was *Love*.

Who can say how long these two stood thus? It seemed like forever, but perhaps it was only a few seconds. Gradually, Fayorn lowered his gaze once more to the ground, ashamed now of his behavior to this man's emissary.

The man spoke. His voice was gentle, deep and, most of all, filled with love for the one whom he was addressing. "You are sorry, are you not?"

Fayorn nodded. Quietly, he said, "I am; I am indeed."

"Good. That is enough. Now, lift your head and look at me. The time has come, as you knew it must. For four thousand years you have been confined to Dankenwood, master of all you survey, just as you once desired, but unable to be free. This evening I set you free. But first you must perform the task that I long ago entrusted to you. Do that, and then you will be free. But I compel you not, for you know that such is not my way. Stay here, or be free. What is your decision, sage?"

Fayorn knew that he could not refuse the one who stood before him. He nodded. "It was part of our agreement. I shall perform the task you set me those long years ago."

"Good. Then I shall be gone."

"Wait! Will I see you again?"

The old man's face broke into a caring smile before covering itself with a look of infinite sadness. "Indeed, good Fayorn, you will see me again if you perform your task, but not before you have faced the very Prince of Evil. But when we meet, you and I shall talk, and you shall learn many things. Now, go about your task. There is no time to delay. Every moment is precious."

Fayorn lowered his head. When he raised it again, he was alone but for the carcass of the newly killed deer and the pitiful dirtiness of his pathetic hovel.

There was no one to watch as the squat figure wended through the black trees. The figure waddled clumsily on its short legs and every now and then stopped momentarily to cast its eyes heavenwards to the bright new star. Taking a breath as if drawing sustenance from the bright yellow pinprick of light, it shifted the weight of a rectangular, cloth-covered object that it carried beneath its arm; then it continued westward toward the perimeter of the forbidding black wood.

Other stars circled overhead as the night wore on, but the new star hung stationary high in the western sky.

The figure reached the edge of Dankenwood.

At the boundary, it was as if a line had been drawn on the ground. On Fayorn's side the trees were black, the air was heavy, and a dull oppression pervaded all. On the other side lay the forest of Palindor, dark evergreens swaying in a slight wind, the occasional hoot of an owl disturbing the silence, and the air filled with the scents of late autumn.

Fayorn halted. Standing under the very last tree of his domain, he looked out into the forest beyond. The light from the star made the trees of Palindor shine, while those behind him remained black, swallowing the star's light.

For several minutes, Fayorn stood motionless, gazing into Palindor. "Four thousand years, and now it is over. Released from my prison, but only to die...." The words were barely audible, even to himself. He looked at the star, took a deep breath, then purposefully stepped across the unseen line.

For a second, nothing happened; then there was a slight shimmer in the air around the once-Master of Dankenwood. Gradually, the air steadied. Where the squat, ugly, figure had stood was now a taller creature, clothed in a gray mantle, a large hood hanging over his head, hiding the features of his face in shadow. The figure shifted the weight of the cloth bundle under his arm and strode forward. Behind him, the new star began to light the trees of Dankenwood.

It was the fifth night since the new star had appeared.

Drefynt could recall no mention of the star in any of the Holy Books that he had seen when he was a youth. But this was no great surprise: after all, it had been so long ago, and he had been merely a novice, with no access to the most holy and mysterious volumes.

He had searched the library of Dynas Carn Toldwyn without any expectation of success. Most of the volumes in the library were relatively new, scribed since the liberation of Palindor by Catherine, the First High Monarch. The library held no more than a dozen books of the Old Days, books that had been scattered throughout the land at the time when Cerebeth, her spirit under the evil dominion of Malthazzar, had caused the destruction of the libraries at the Holy Barrows of Perendeth.

Although these old books spoke of interesting and important matters, they were all histories, for none of the prophetic and holy works were ever permitted to leave the Barrows, and hence all had perished. So it was with disappointment but no great surprise that Drefynt replaced the last of these volumes on the shelves without having found any reference to the sign that now burned in the heavens over Carn Toldwyn each night.

But still he wondered what the sign might mean. He was unable to concentrate on his work during the day, and the evening hours found him wandering in the forest behind his home longer than usual. And so, late in the evening of the fifth day since the star appeared, he was standing in a small clearing near the edge of the forest, staring up at the star, asking himself yet again: "But what do you mean? What are you trying to tell us?"

There was a disturbance in the trees on the eastern edge of the clearing. Startled, for he had heard no one approaching, Drefynt turned, and a figure stepped into the clearing.

Drefynt knew instantly what kind of creature this was, even though (and partly because) its face was hidden in the shadow of a large hood. The creature halted, not six paces distant. It wore a gray habit which covered the length of its body from its head almost to the ground. Even its feet were hidden under the hanging gray garb. Only the hands were visible. One hand hung free by its side; the other supported a rectangular object under the creature's arm.

Slowly, Drefynt executed a grave, respectful bow.

"Drefynt, humble gnome of Carn Toldwyn at your service, Wise One."

There was no response other than a slight movement of the hood, as if the creature had inclined its hidden head slightly.

For several seconds, nothing happened; Drefynt had the uncomfortable feeling that he was being examined for worthiness. Then the creature unbent its arm and held out the rectangular object towards the aged gnome. Drefynt could see now that the object was wrapped in a protective cloth. Gingerly, Drefynt stepped forward and accepted the cloth-covered article.

"I thank you," he said. He looked up at the bright star and then at the figure. "Does this have anything to do with the sign?"

There was no response.

"I see," said the gnome. "I thank you again for this." He hefted the object he had been given, intrigued by the weight under the cloth. He bowed slightly towards the silent figure, whose only response was to turn away and return to the shadows; within moments, the sage was gone.

Drefynt stared for some time at the place where the sage had disappeared, then looked at the object in his hands, then at the star. "I suppose this is the answer, isn't it?" he apostrophized the star.

Tucking the object under his arm, he made his way thoughtfully back to his cottage.

III The Traveller

Sherna was used to the stares. Her attire identified her as being from Palindor, and, because travellers from the Third Land were few in Pirren Glanwyn, it was a rare creature that did not let its eyes rest on her for several seconds before passing on its way. But in earlier visits to the capital of Reglandor, she had been subjected only to simple looks of curiosity. Now the eyes did not rest on her just for a few moments, but they kept watching, cold and hard. And surely it was not her imagination that behind those eyes was no longer mere curiosity; now they seemed filled with a barely veiled animosity.

The gnome shivered.

Back home in Carn Toldwyn she was known as Sherna the Traveller. And she deserved the name, for alone of those now alive had she not travelled to Soltarwyn? throughout Reglandor? even to Valguard? Had she not seen sights unknown to any of her compatriots? And had she not met creatures whom others believed to live only in myth? Yes, she had travelled widely and seen much in her two hundred and fifty years. She had risked her life countless times, been thrown into dungeons, nearly died of exposure on mountains, known hunger and thirst, yet never had she known such a sense of almost tangible distrust as now, walking the streets of Pirren Glanwyn, trying to maintain a steady stride, attempting not to acknowledge the belligerence that surrounded her.

She had heard rumors: whispered conversations, abruptly ended when she drew near: talk of how the land claimed by Palindor belonged rightfully to Reglandor. It was hard to believe that war might erupt between Palindor and Reglandor after so many lifetimes of peace. Still there was no gainsaying the fact that the glances cast in her direction were far from friendly.

She glanced up at the sky. The position of the sun told her that it was not yet midmorning. She would be through the city and on the road to the border by noon. Within the week, she would be back home in Carn Toldwyn. Perhaps then she would find an explanation for the belligerence that filled the air.

Sherna hurried on through Pirren Glanwyn. Her longest journey, to the golden spires of Valguard on the shores of the Eastern Ocean, was nearly over. Just a few more days now before she was home.

No other Palindoric creature within living memory had seen the Eastern Ocean, although her father Drefynt had told her that it was mentioned several times in the books that he had seen in his youth in the Barrows of Perendeth. All those books had been destroyed by Queen Cerebeth, part of the story of Cerebeth, Malthazzar and the High Queen Catherine that Drefynt had scribed long before Sherna was born. She was proud of the fact that her father had scribed many of the books that formed the basis of the teaching in Palindor's schools.

His books had inspired his daughter to explore the lands beyond Palindor, to discover for herself how many of the old tales that her father had scribed referred to places that actually existed, to see with her own eyes the creatures and lands that featured in her father's stories.

But now she was anxious to return to the home she had not seen for many months. That night, she saw for the first time a puzzling yellow star, far away in the west. It seemed to be drawing her onward, toward her home.

The final few days passed uneventfully, and at last, toward midnight one evening, she arrived at the cottage where her mother and father lived. She was surprised to find them both still awake (though dressed for bed), finishing mugs of hot cocoa.

Glad though they undoubtedly were to see their daughter, it was clear to Sherna that her father was preoccupied. His greeting, far from the expected emotional reunion, was halfhearted; and it was impossible not to notice how anxious and careworn he looked. At 750, Drefynt was a good hundred years older than was the common span of life for a gnome. His days were surely coming to a close.

She said nothing that evening, for they were all tired, but she went to bed with a heart heavy with worry for her aging father.

When she awoke, the sun was already high in the sky. Downstairs, she found her mother dusting the living room. Her father had left for his office in the castle on the hill hours before. Sherna, full of tales from her travels, was anxious to begin the pleasant task of regaling her father with them so that he might scribe them, adding them to the hundreds of tales he had already committed to paper. But her mother wanted to talk too, and it was early afternoon before she left the cottage on the eastern edge of Carn Toldwyn to make her way up the hill towards the castle.

As she was leaving, Sherna asked about the yellow star that filled the night sky with its light, but the only response from her mother was: "You'll have to ask your father about that," accompanied by a worried look.

When she had been a child, the castle on the hill at the north edge of town, Dynas Carn Toldwyn, had astounded Sherna. It was hard to believe that something so large and so grand actually existed, right here in Carn Toldwyn. Long ago, so her father told her, the castle had been home to the kings and queens of Palindor. It had been built when Palindor was first founded, at the conclusion of a war with the kingdom of Reglandor, by the army of the first King Yndlarn, and from that time until the end of the kings and queens, the reigning monarch had lived in the castle overlooking Carn Toldwyn. Once the Ruling Council was established, the castle was put to uses that were more mundane.

Now it served principally as the place in which the Ruling Council met and deliberated. Some of the rooms were still decked out grandly and served as large reception rooms in which visiting dignitaries could be greeted. There were rooms in which balls were held. There was the grand library, which housed the largest collection of books in the land. What had once been the rooms of the monarch's ministers were given over to judges, artists and scribes (of whom her father was the most celebrated). The rest of the castle was maintained but rarely used.

As Sherna climbed the hill, she could not help comparing the building rising before her with the castles and palaces she had encountered in her travels. Far from being the great and magnificent edifice that she had considered it when young, she now recognized that of the three lands of Abuscân, Palindor boasted the weakest, smallest and most insignificant of castles. Indeed, as she entered the stone courtyard, she felt almost shamed that the land of her birth was so pitiable. Of one thing only was she glad: because Carn Toldwyn was so remote, standing as it did isolated on the western shore, decades would pass between visits by princes and kings from other lands, so that at least the lack of grandeur was not as humiliating and embarrassing as it might have been.

She made her way directly to her father's office, her footsteps echoing noisily from the bare walls which, had they been in any other castle, would have been decked with banners and tapestries. Her moodiness was only magnified when she pushed the door open to find his room empty.

"Excuse me."

Sherna turned to see a middle-aged dwarf standing in the corridor. Sherna bowed slightly and introduced herself. "Sherna, known as the Traveller, gnome of Carn Toldwyn and daughter of Drefynt, known as the Wise."

The dwarf bowed lower, acknowledging her as worthy of respect. "Polthern, dwarf of Carn Toldwyn, at your service. If you are looking for your father, I am afraid he left shortly after he arrived this morning. He said he was going to visit the Barrows at Perendeth."

Sherna could not keep the surprise off her face. Such a journey was a long one for a gnome as frail as Drefynt had become these past few years. And it was odd indeed that he had mentioned no such journey to her mother.

"Did he give a reason for his journey?" she asked.

"Nay, he did not. But if you would permit me to say it, I have never seen such a look on your father's face. He seemed both determined and fearful. But what concerned him, I know not."

"Thank you, good dwarf. He left here early, you say?"

"Yes. I was here as the sun rose this morning. I am a composer, you see, and I could not sleep for worry. The Ruling Council has asked me to compose a piece to celebrate the arrival of the emissary from Reglandor four days hence, but I have been unable to complete the piece and time is short. Drefynt passed by my office this morning perhaps an hour after sunrise and, as usual, he greeted me and we chatted for a short time before he began his work. But it was not more than ten minutes before I heard the sound of his cane again in the corridor. I came to the door to ask him where he was going in such a hurry. 'To the Barrows at Perendeth. The time is at hand,' was his reply. Then he was gone. Do you understand it?"

Sherna turned the words over in her mind. "The time is at hand." What did that mean? What could possibly cause her father suddenly to leave his office and make the long journey to the Barrows? At his age, walking infirmly as he did, it would take an entire day to reach the Barrows and return, and no doubt he would feel the effects of the unaccustomed exertion for many more days. She thanked Polthern, then turned her attention to Drefynt's desk, hoping to find some clue as to what might have caused his sudden departure.

On his desk lay a book, presumably from the castle library. It was an old volume, a book from the Old Days, perhaps even a Holy Book, although it could not have been stored in the Barrows, otherwise it would have perished alongside the others.

Sherna walked around the desk, the better to examine the aging leaves. She was afraid to lift the book: the parchment was yellowed and brittle and could be easily damaged. Beside the book was a short stack of sheets of new paper, recently scribed.

She looked carefully at the old book. The ink was so yellowed that it was almost the same color as the parchment. With difficulty, she could make out the characters on the page, but could make no sense of what she saw:

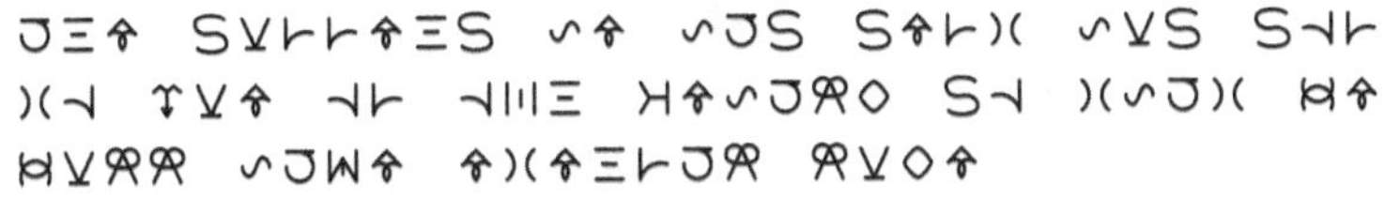

Carefully, she lifted the book to try to examine its title page, but as she did so there was a brittle snap, and several pages shattered irretrievably into small pieces. Guiltily, she replaced the book on the desk and turned her attention to the stack of papers.

She recognized her father's scribing immediately on the top sheet, and although the words were written in the old style, the characters themselves were modern. There was only a fragment of a sentence on the page: *And the sign of the coming of the red one....*

The sheets underneath were written in her father's hand in the same style. He must have been translating the old book into modern script. She turned to the bottom sheet, which should be the translation of the start of the book. In Drefynt's shaking hand was written: *The History of the Third Land as it Will Be.* Then, in smaller letters underneath: *scribed originally by Matím, of the Order of Holy Gnomes, who knew Toldwyn himself* and then, in smaller letters yet: *translated from the old tongue by Drefynt, last of the Holy Gnomes.*

Her hands began to shake as she understood the enormity of what she was reading. Her father had found a book — not just from the Old Times, but from the time when Palindor was founded. Indeed, perhaps the book was even from before that time, for the book's title referred to "the Third Land," rather than using the name of the country. She continued reading on the next page.

> *The land, it will be born in blood. Red will flow the rivers, and red will burn the sky. In cries and pain and blood and death will the land be birthed. And this shall be its birth. And in its birth shall be the death of the one who gives it life. For the price of life is death. And death begets life.*

She flicked through the pages impatiently. She stopped at a passage that spoke of something that had happened within her father's lifetime:

> *The white Queen from afar will come and to that distant place will return. That place we know not; neither is it in us to have knowledge of that place. For it lies both near and far and this is a mystery to those who dwell in the Lands. The Monarch shall destroy the Monarch. Not utterly, for the Monarch cannot be killed by such as the Monarch. But for a time, the Monarch and the Monarch shall depart this place.*

She skipped some more pages, until she came to the final sheet that had been completely translated.

> *But one shall remain, and he shall be caused much pain and sorrow and he will wail and cry out for relief, but relief shall not come; and distress will be his; and despair will come to him at the loss of his child; and he shall end his days in grief. But his dynasty will remain, and the child of his child shall be great and saving.*

There the page ended, to be continued on the single sheet with its mystifying unfinished sentence: *And the sign of the coming of the red one....*

Carefully, Sherna replaced the pages on the desk where she had found them.

Glancing out the window she could see, in the distance, the cliffs at Perendeth, near which the Holy Barrows stood. What had suddenly caused her father to leave this work to undertake a journey so hazardous to one of his age?

She looked again at the ancient book. She wished that she had been a better student when she was younger; perhaps then her father would have taught her some of the old letters.

She had seen similar marks on her travels; the characters were reminiscent of some of the old scripts in the Crystal Hall of Soltarwyn, but those scripts were now unreadable, the meaning of the characters lost forever. As it would be in Palindor with the death of her father, she now realized, for he had never taught anyone the old letters and the words of earlier times — presumably because until now everyone had assumed that no texts had survived from the very oldest days.

30

But what had he read? What terrifying words completed the sentence that he had started to scribe? There was only one way to find out.

For a young gnome in good condition, it is not far from Dynas Carn Toldwyn to the deserted Holy Barrows at Perendeth. For Drefynt, frail and needing the help of his cane, the journey would have taken the better part of a day had he not had the good fortune to be passed by a human on horseback soon after leaving Carn Toldwyn.

The human, a man dressed in the garb of a Hunter, passed without a word; but after his steed had continued a few steps past Drefynt, he pulled the horse around and looked more carefully at the old gnome.

"The gnome Drefynt, is it not?" the human asked.

Drefynt raised his eyes from the road and, shielding his eyes against the bright, late-autumn sun, looked up at the strong young man before him.

It was hard to say which was the more perfect specimen: the horse or the man. The man's status as a Hunter was marked by the small white cross traditionally worn by such on his green tunic. Exceptionally tall, even for a Hunter, the man towered over the diminutive gnome. The man's horse stood, flexing its muscles, as if aching to be off at a gallop, carrying his rider in the chase as he hunted down a deer in the Palindor forest. Even here, on the treeless road winding up to the Perendeth cliffs, the creature seemed completely at ease, as if it knew that none could possibly challenge its magnificence, here or anywhere else.

"It is indeed, Master Hunter."

"'Master Hunter'? Do you not recognize me?" A pause and then, "No, there is no reason why you should. I was but a child when last you saw me, and though it is fifteen years since then, fifteen years is but little to a gnome, and where I have changed much, you have changed hardly at all."

"Nay, good Hunter, your words are false." Drefynt smiled as he spoke, aware that the compliment, although untrue, meant that this man was polite and chivalrous. "I have aged much these past

31

fifteen years, and will not see fifteen more. Yet I do admit that I have changed perhaps less than you. Let me see now, surely it cannot be.... Why yes, now I see you more clearly, you must be Anthelron, whom I last saw as a little child learning to shoot blunt arrows at a tree."

The Hunter looked pleased, knowing that this distinguished gnome had paid him a compliment merely by remembering his name. "Indeed, good gnome, it is I. And you will be pleased to know, I am sure, that I eventually mastered the art of releasing my arrows true."

Drefynt laughed. "I doubt you not. For even as a child your arrows struck the tree more often than those of this poor elderly gnome. But tell me, what of your father and mother? Are they still well? It is long indeed since I have seen them."

"You forget our ways, good gnome. I am a Hunter, as are my father and mother, and thus our paths rarely cross. But yes, the last time I saw them, they were both well and still strong, although I fear that my mother will soon be growing weak and will be taken from us."

"That time comes to all of us, Master Hunter, even gnomes."

"And so, good Drefynt, where is your destination this day?"

A frown crossed Drefynt's face as he recalled the reason for his journey. "To Perendeth; to the old Holy Barrows."

"But that is a long journey for an aged gnome. What is so important about the Barrows? I have never been there, although I have occasionally passed by on this road; I believed there to be nothing there now, just some of the old tunnels that the Holy Gnomes constructed in the old days."

"Aye, you are right. But it is long since I have visited the home of my childhood, and I have a fancy to see them one last time."

"Well then, old gnome, that's enough for me. My path takes me close by. Let me help you on to my horse, and he will carry you to the Barrows."

Anthelron slid out of his saddle and helped the gnome into the seat. Climbing on to the animal behind Drefynt, the Hunter took the reins, wrapping the gnome in a cage of arms to protect him from falling.

Glad to be urged forward once more, the horse recommenced the climb towards Perendeth.

Sherna hurried down the hill on which the castle was perched, passing through the town and then taking the road southwest towards Perendeth. The long climb winded her, and she was tired and panting when finally she reached the mounds that marked the entrance to the disused Holy Barrows.

She looked around, searching for her father, but at first there was no sign of him. Then she saw Drefynt, standing alone some distance away across the sward, near the edge of the cliff, the sea breeze blowing his long, thin hair wildly as he leaned against his cane and gazed towards the distant horizon.

As she walked toward him, she could not help but notice how frail and yet how wise he looked: weak in body but strong in knowledge and wisdom. She realized that she was terrified that something was about to befall her father, that whatever had brought him to the cliff might also be about to take him forever away from her.

He did not acknowledge her presence until she reached his side.

She followed his gaze out to sea, and as she did so, the wind dropped as the sun fell toward the horizon. The ocean churned against the granite cliffs far below. Out to sea, beyond the horizon, lay the Sunset Islands, the only land to the west of Palindor. She had never travelled across the sea, and she was suddenly grasped by a desire to cross it once in her life, so that she might see for herself what the islands were like.

She wondered what her father was looking at.

"The future...." Whether he was answering her unspoken question or merely giving voice to his own thoughts she could not tell. With a deep breath of the salt-laden air, he turned from the ocean and regarded his daughter.

"Now, why would you be coming all this way?"

"Father, I was worried about you. You should not exert yourself too much. The dwarf in the office next to yours, Polthern, he told me what happened this morning. He said that soon after you arrived, you left again in a great hurry, telling him that you would be coming here. What is it, Father? What's the matter?"

He did not answer, instead looking into her eyes with an expression that she could not read.

"Is it something to do with the book you're translating?" she prompted.

"Book? Oh... aye, the book. You looked at it then?"

"Yes, Father. I was concerned to know what might have driven you all the way out here."

"But you did not discover the answer?"

Sherna shook her head. "No. I looked at the book, but I couldn't understand the script. So I looked at your translation. Father; where did the book come from? It's so old, and it speaks of things in a strange way — things that have been and things that are to be."

"No, my daughter. The book speaks only of things that are to be. And as for where the book came from, I do not know. It came into my care but recently, and I have been filled with a sense of doom ever since I laid my hands on its ancient pages. Come, Sherna, take my arm and accompany me to the Barrows."

He held out his arm, she intertwined her arm with his, and slowly they walked away from the edge of the cliff towards the grassy mounds.

Wordless, he halted in front of the tallest mound, which rose above them to some three times his height. The entrance to the labyrinth below was before them: a dark hole in the grassy hillock.

For some time he contemplated the entrance in silence. Sherna gazed at her father, wondering what he was thinking about. Slowly, almost imperceptibly, a tear formed and then trickled erratically down the old gnome's face to be lost in the tangles of his unkempt beard. Sherna took her father's hand and squeezed it. With a sniff, he turned from the mound and looked at his daughter. He returned the squeeze.

"Come! The past is the past, and what will be will be. Let's return together. It will be very late by the time we get home, and there is much to prepare for...."

Sherna became aware of a sound that had been growing in intensity for some time: the urgent, rhythmic thudding of a horse's hooves on the hardpacked road. Her father heard it too, and stopped speaking.

They turned toward the road and a horse galloped into view, breathing noisily, a tether attaching it to a second horse which followed close behind. Only the first horse was ridden, by a brightly dressed dwarf, a brilliant scabbard hanging from his side, catching the fire of the low sun. The second horse, riderless, breathed deeply but with less urgency.

The dwarf reined in his horse, and the second horse slowed to a walk. The horses and the rider crossed the grass to the place whence the gnomes watched them.

Still seated in the saddle, the dwarf bowed. "Good Drefynt. Mistress Sherna. Trenegar, dwarf of Carn Toldwyn, at your service. Begging your pardon for interrupting you, but the Ruling Council desires the advice of the gnome Drefynt the Wise with all due speed. They dispatched me but half an hour since, and they await your coming with trembling and expectation. If you would do me the honor of accompanying me?"

The two gnomes looked at one another, a question in Sherna's eyes, a grimness in Drefynt's.

"I had not expected it so soon." The words were quiet, almost a mumble, as Drefynt spoke not to his daughter but to himself.

Sherna wondered what her father could mean, but there was no time now for discussion; the rather inappropriately dressed Trenegar was clearly anxious to begin the return journey to Carn Toldwyn.

The dwarf leapt heavily from his saddle. Sherna and Trenegar helped Drefynt on to the second horse; then Sherna climbed, unladylike, into position behind him; Trenegar, in a single bound, leapt on to the back of his horse (which shuddered visibly at the sudden imposition of the dwarf's weight). The tether joining the horses was untied and then the riders turned the horses and began the journey back toward the town.

Sherna's head was swirling with questions. Her father still had not divulged the meaning of the words in the book; neither had he explained his sudden journey to Perendeth where, as far as she could see, he had done nothing more than stand on the cliff and look out to sea. Then there was the matter of the tear she had observed while he stood outside the Holy Barrows: what could have caused her father such grief? And to cap everything there was this urgent summons to advise the Ruling Council. What could possibly have precipitated such an urgent request? The Ruling Council was not even supposed to be in session; what could have happened in the short time since she left Carn Toldwyn to cause them to meet and then to seek out Drefynt the Wise with such haste?

But there was no opportunity to ask her questions as they were carried towards Carn Toldwyn. Behind them, the sun set. Almost immediately, the bright light of the new star shone forth above the town. Uneasily, Sherna could not shake the feeling that the sign in the heavens was somehow related to the questions that burned in her mind.

IV The Antique Shop

The rain seeped through her clothing as Katrin hurried through the narrow cobbled streets of the small town. Michael walked quickly by her side, sullen and bad tempered. "You shouldn't go out in this kind of weather. You know it's bad for you," he had almost shouted at his mother in the bed and breakfast. The words he had wanted to say — "It might make you die sooner" — had remained unsaid.

Since yesterday, his mother had been acting strangely.

It had something to do with the guidebook she had bought in the bookstore. Ever since she had seen the ancient stone construction on its cover, she had seemed to be somehow lost inside herself, as if not fully aware of what was happening around her.

He was scared: his mother had never acted like this before, and he was frightened that this sudden change in mood signalled the beginning of the end. Last night she had stayed up late reading and rereading the guidebook. This morning she had woken up with the crazy idea that, despite the miserable weather, she wanted to go out to buy a history book of the area.

She knew as well as he did that the medication for her tumor made her prone to sickness, and it would be so easy to catch pneumonia from the cold rain that poured relentlessly from the low, leaden sky. But she had insisted, and so now he found himself almost running to keep up with her as she navigated the ancient narrow streets that led to the shops.

He was angry at everyone: at himself, for letting this happen; at his mother, for insisting that she was going out in this kind of weather; at his father for dying and leaving them alone; at the doctors for being unable to remove the tumor inside his mother's head; at everyone for this being such a miserable, unhappy world.

They came to the junction of two narrow streets, and his mother looked uncertainly at the choice before her. Michael knew which way they should go, but in his sullen mood he took a perverse pleasure that his mother, after hesitating for a few seconds, chose the wrong street. *Now she'll get lost and have to ask me for help*, he thought with a self-righteous inward smirk.

He hurried after his mother. Faced with more choices, she became ever more confused, and she soon became completely lost. *She'll have to ask soon*, he thought as they passed a chapel and then turned sharply to the left into the smallest street they had taken so far. Houses with strange names abutted the cobbled street, the sidewalk nonexistent: names like *Chylowen, Chyandour, Burnwithian, Lamorna*. Geraniums, weighted by rain, grew forlornly in a window box, the only splash of color in the entire street.

They passed a shop in the middle of the row of houses. A dirty green signboard hung over the small window. In ornate, faded letters the word ANTIQUES ran the length of the board. Underneath, in smaller script, was the legend MEMORABILIA FROM NEAR AND FAR. In one corner, in letters no more than an inch high, was the name of the proprietor: H. L. OLVENSAR. A few steps past the shop, a sudden thought gave him an idea how to get them out of the wet street.

Katrin stopped, an insistent pulling at her sleeve intruding on her thoughts. Michael was saying something. "Back there. We just passed an antique shop. Maybe they would know something about the history of the area." Katrin looked around helplessly and was forced to admit to herself that she was lost. Even if they were of no other help, at least the people inside would be able to tell her how to reach the other shops.

Michael opened the door, and there was a cheery jingle from a bell overhead as he stepped into the gloomy interior. He turned to see his mother, still standing in the rain, staring at the board over the shop window. The color had drained from her face, and the rain ran unnoticed in rivulets down her upturned face.

"Come on," he shouted.

For a moment she didn't move. Then, with an odd look on her face, she followed him inside.

The shop was small, cramped and dingy. Around the walls were shelves filled with bric-a-brac: vases, colored glass floats, horse bronzes and the like. In the center of the shop a table ran from the rear almost to the window. Against the rear wall was a small counter on which stood an old-fashioned cash register. Behind the counter was a narrow curtain, presumably hiding a doorway into an area behind the shop which was forbidden to customers. There was no sign of the proprietor,

Michael began looking at the shelves without any obvious interest. His mother, seeing that they were alone, began to do likewise while she waited for the shopkeeper.

"Wow, Mom, look at this!"

Michael unsheathed a sword from a dull leather scabbard. The sword glistened in the gray light from the window; it looked new, sharp and ready for use.

Katrin began to scan the shelves. She didn't know what she was searching for, but somehow she was sure she would know it when she found it. Michael scanned the table in the center of the store while he idly withdrew and inserted the sword in its scabbard.

"Hey! Cool!" He picked up an old leather belt. He threaded the scabbard on to the belt, and tied the belt around his waist. The buckle, large and dirty with age, carried a strange design, like letters in some foreign script. In the center of the buckle was a dull red stone.

"What are you doing?" Katrin turned to see what mischief Michael might be up to, but she stopped in the midst of turning as an object on the table caught her attention. Stretching out her hand, she was surprised to see that it wasn't shaking.

She picked up an old, dusty belt. The buckle had a design of raised characters, with a white stone in the center. She ran her hand along the length of the belt. There! Her hand caught in the deep nick, exactly in the right place — where a dagger had caught the belt she had been wearing twenty years ago near a quoit on a high moortop in Palindor.

She wrapped the belt around her waist and buckled it tight. She looked up, suddenly aware that someone had joined them. On the far side of the table stood an old man — a man whom she had thought never to see again. She could not help herself: tears began to trickle down her cheeks. Suddenly all the worries and difficulties of the last twenty years melted away, to be replaced by a joy she had last felt when she was a teenager, lying in a hospital, comatose after a car accident that could so easily have taken her life.

"What is it, Mom?"

The old man, his dull clothes accentuating the gloom of the shop, turned toward Katrin's son.

"Michael, your mother and I have met before, a long, long time ago. Now, tell me, are you a brave warrior with your sword buckled by your side?"

Michael looked embarrassed, as if a grown-up had caught him playing a silly, childish game. He shuffled his feet and blushed, looking from the old man to his mother, unsure how to answer.

The old man smiled. "It's all right. I was just thinking that you looked as if you were born to wear that sword." Katrin looked at Michael. The shopkeeper was right: there was something about the way Michael carried himself when he was wearing the belt and sword....

The shopkeeper continued, "Which is to the good. For shortly you will have a chance to prove that you are worthy. I leave you with only one word of advice: the sign of a true warrior is a strong heart and a strong mind, not a strong hand. A true monarch is one who knows how to refrain from using his sword in anger or fear."

He turned to Katrin. "And now you, dear child...." He addressed Katrin just as he had done more than twenty years before, as if the intervening years had been swept away. "You have been calling for me, and now I am here. The time has come for you to be tested once more, only now a graver and more difficult task lies before you. The words I had for your son are for you too. Violence is not the way. True strength lies in the ablility to refrain from using your sword, not from using it. Remember that my strength is in you.

40

Use your talents wisely, and remember always that I have faith in your ability to complete the task you have been set."

The words meant little to Katrin. As was so often the case, Olvensar seemed to be speaking in riddles. She opened her mouth, but Olvensar raised his hand for silence. "Hush! There is no time to answer your questions, nor to prepare you for what is to come. I have made an agreement and I am bound by it, and already Malthazzar's minions are at work. We can delay no longer. Now, go with my blessing. Remember: true strength lies in the heart and the mind, not in the sword."

There was no overt gesture, no pounding of a staff on the floor. Yet suddenly the room swirled indistinctly. The shop, already tenebrous, seemed to waver around them and become even grayer, as if enfolded by a heavy, whirling fog. The mist shrouded Olvensar and then hid him. Katrin turned to Michael just in time to lose sight of him in the fog.

For a few seconds, Katrin's universe was confined to gray tendrils floating against an equally gray background only inches from her eyes; then the fog began to clear. She looked around anxiously. The gloomy interior of the antique shop had been replaced by granite stones. Olvensar was gone. Looking around desperately for her son, she realized that Michael too had disappeared.

She was alone.

V The Reason for the Summons

As they approached Carn Toldwyn, Sherna and Drefynt eyed an
ominous storm gathering in the north of Palindor.

Usually, the peak of Penmichael Brea*, the solitary mountain in
northern Palindor, could be seen long after sunset, its snowcapped
peak reflecting the reds and oranges of the sun still shining on
the tall, majestic peak. But this evening a line of dark, wintry
clouds filled the sky to the north. Not just the peak, but even the
mountain's lower slopes, were hidden by the clouds as they were
battered by the first storm of the season.

It was unusually early for a storm of such ferocity. If it continued
southward to Carn Toldwyn and then moved on to Beleron, it
would kill many of the late-autumn crops which were not yet ripe
for harvest, presaging a difficult winter. Drefynt muttered a quick
prayer that Olvensar would guide the storm away from the fertile
lands of the south, giving the farmers time to finish bringing in
their crops before the weather worsened for the winter.

As the road turned northward into town, the distant cloudbank
was hidden by the hill atop which stood Dynas Carn Toldwyn.
Drefynt's thoughts turned from the storm, and he began to speculate
about the reason for the Ruling Council's summons.

---

* The word *Brea* is pronounced as if it were *Bray*.

As their horses climbed the slope to the castle, everything in the town looked peaceful and normal. Behind the colorful drapes covering the windows of the houses, candles were burning, casting odd-shaped shadows as the houses' occupants moved around inside. Here and there creatures were hurrying home. More than once, Drefynt smiled as they passed pairs of young creatures holding hands with eyes only for one another.

And high overhead, shining more brightly with every second as the twilight darkened into night, hung the burning yellow star.

His reverie was broken as the horses reached the castle courtyard. Dismounting, he looked around the courtyard, which was empty save for two gnomes hurrying out through the main gate and a single dwarf on sentry duty in the shelter of the huge front door of the castle.

He recalled the time when he had escaped (with Olvensar's help) from the dungeons, now unused, that lay deep beneath the castle. He remembered looking around the corner of the castle to see an army parading, ready for war, in this very courtyard. On that occasion, *he* had been the enemy, and the army would have captured him and turned him over to Malthazzar had he been caught. This time, the Ruling Council was seeking his opinion on some pressing matter. *How times change*, he thought with a grim smile.

He refused to be hurried up the steps, although Trenegar's impatience was obvious. He walked slowly, his cane rhythmically tapping the echoing stone floor of the corridors, until he was shown into the chamber where the Ruling Council met. The two humans who guarded the doorway let him pass, but they closed the doors behind him, barring Sherna and Trenegar from following.

Drefynt looked around the chamber. Once, the reigning monarch of Palindor had used this as a judgment room, and the chamber retained something of its old splendor, with gold and purple banners decorating the walls, interspersed with weaponry from the Old Days. Even Scalmyùt and Scelberon, the High Queen's sword and scabbard, hung on the wall. Once a week the room was still used as a kind of courtroom in which the Ruling Council settled legal disputes.

Six pairs of eyes were on Drefynt. Ymyr, the current spokesman for the Ruling Council, stood as he entered, and the other four members of the council, including Drefynt's own son Benglubber, followed his lead. Ymyr gestured to a comfortable chair that stood alone on one side of the chamber, near the fire which burned in the hearth. Some distance from the chair was a large oval oak table, behind which were the five members of the council. On the other side of the fire was a second chair, on which perched a youthful Huntress whom Drefynt did not recognize.

"Pray be seated, good Drefynt," Ymyr said.

Drefynt lowered himself into the empty chair. He eyed the members of the council as they sat down. Three of the councilors he knew well, the other two he recognized only by sight.

On the extreme left, and closest to him, sat his own son, Benglubber, in the seat that had once belonged to Drefynt himself. Drefynt sometimes wondered about his son. He had never shown much aptitude for study or scholarship, and it was many years before he had settled on a career as a gardener. Benglubber had married late (although not as late as his sister, who was still unmarried) and had fathered a son only ten years ago.

Drefynt was under no illusions that under ordinary circumstances a plodding thinker such as Benglubber would ever have been appointed to the Ruling Council. It was obvious that Benglubber owed his position entirely to the fact that he was the son of Drefynt the Wise. Even so, Benglubber had given a good account of himself in the council's deliberations and Drefynt was proud of what his son had achieved.

Next to Benglubber was Gwyndoor, an immensely strong dwarf originally from a village in the east of Palindor, but now an established blacksmith in Carn Toldwyn.

In the middle of the five was Ymyr, a bookish gnome of middle age from a good family, whose ability to see both sides of an issue made him a popular leader.

The remaining two members of the council were Verrin, a wood elf from Smalterscairn, who, like most elves in the presence of other races, seemed ill at ease in the council chamber, and Parma, a graceful human female whose husband farmed several large fields in the area known as Beleron, in the extreme southwest of Palindor.

"I apologize on behalf of us all for this imposition," began Ymyr, "but we are faced with an emergency, and cannot agree amongst ourselves what is to be done. We have decided to put the case before you, as the last of the Holy Gnomes and one who has himself sat on this council, so that we can hear what you have to say before we make a final decision."

Drefynt nodded slightly, acknowledging the respect that was being paid him. "I shall do what I can to assist you."

Ymyr gestured towards the Huntress, who had remained silent and motionless throughout the introductory comments. "Anthlea, perhaps you would be so good as to tell Drefynt what has brought you to Carn Toldwyn."

"Drefynt the Wise, I bring you greetings from the house of Aramis, from whom I have the honor to be descended."

She nodded in Drefynt's direction, showing as much respect as a Hunter ever gave any other living creature. Drefynt returned the nod, offering his own respect to the house of Aramis.

Anthlea continued, "My mission is urgent, for I fear the consequences of what I have seen. I hunt in the far east of Palindor, not far from the Mountains of Mourn, between the River Findell and the Plains of Kradesh. About two weeks ago, I was hunting at the very edge of my domain when I observed a small caravan of humans crossing the plains moving westward, as if they had come from Reglandor and were heading for Carn Toldwyn. Their route took them for a while near the forest, which is how I came to notice them, but I paid little attention to them at the time.

"I came across them again the next day. I had chased a stag into a small glade not far from the edge of the forest. In the glade were five humans, the same ones I had seen the day before. They were all dead. A fire still smoldered in the center of the glade, and the remains of the humans were scattered around the clearing. Each of them was lying face down, with blood splattered over the nearby grass.

"They were all men, and one was dressed in finery, showing him to be a man of rank and distinction. Not one of them had drawn his sword, although the sword of the man of rank was pulled half way out of its scabbard. Food was spilt near the fire; it seemed clear that the men had been disturbed while preparing a meal and had been overcome too quickly to defend themselves.

"Naturally, I scoured the ground for tracks. A group of three creatures, two-footed but heavier than any such creature in Palindor, had struck them, attacking the glade from all directions.

45

"I examined the belongings of the slain humans and I discovered that" — she gestured towards the table at which the council sat, and Ymyr lifted a leather pouch for Drefynt to see — "on the body of the man of rank. I must apologize, learned gnome, that I know little of reading and nothing at all of writing, but the style of the letters on one of the documents in the pouch seemed of such importance that I felt I would be derelict if I did not bring the news of these events to the attention of the Ruling Council.

"But at first, I must confess, I was undecided, for although I knew what I *should* do, I set my mind against it. Carn Toldwyn is a long journey from the eastern forest. And I have never entered a town before, and felt no desire to see how creatures might live, confined to cells of block and stone, instead of living free under the stars.

"So for several days, I did nothing, but one night, as I tossed and turned in my sleep, a bright star flared high in the western sky, and I knew that the star was meant for me, telling me I must bring my news to the Ruling Council.

"For several more days, though, I tried to ignore the sign in the sky, for I had set my mind against this journey. But the star did not dim, and each night I felt it accusing me of failure. At last I realized that I would know no peace until I brought my news to Carn Toldwyn, no matter how inconvenient the journey might be. The next morning I set out, and I arrived this afternoon." She concluded her story with a glance at the Ruling Council.

Ymyr nodded. "Thank you, Huntress Anthlea. Your story is well told. Good Drefynt, perhaps you would be so good as to read this?" He passed a sheet of parchment to the gnome. "It is the writing of which Anthlea spoke; it was inside the pouch."

Drefynt took the single sheet and examined it. The letters were formed grandly and importantly, as if to lend weight to their message. The writing was Palindoric, although the style was that of Reglandor.

> Let it be known to all those present that the bearer of this document is our emissary. He is to be treated with the respect due to my own person. He is empowered to entreat with the Ruling Council of Palindor in all

46

respects as if he were monarch of Reglandor. If harm
should befall the person of my emissary, or those with
whom he travels, the Ruling Council of Palindor will be
held justly responsible and our vengeance shall be swift
and sure.

The signature was the single word: Glendour.

For days, Drefynt had been wondering how the war was going to
start; now he knew.

"You understand our predicament," Ymyr said to Drefynt. "The
King of Reglandor will hold us responsible for the deaths of these
humans, and he is not a man who will simply pass it off as an
accident. What do you advise?"

"What is your own advice to yourselves? Surely you do not need
me to assist you? Surely the Ruling Council is sufficiently wise
that it need not seek the words of an aged gnome to determine its
actions?"

The words were unexpected and caused a stir in the chamber.
The council members looked first at one another and then away from
each other, as if embarrassed. Ymyr answered for them. "Good
gnome, your words hurt us. But they do so justly, for indeed we are
responsible for Palindor and we should be able to make decisions,
be they easy or difficult. But on this matter we cannot agree, and
we would prefer your counsel before proceeding further."

Drefynt nodded. For a moment he had hoped to escape responsibility for what was to happen, but now he knew that that would not
be possible. He turned to Anthlea. "Tell me about the creatures
who killed these humans. You are surely a skilled Huntress. Did
you not attempt to track them into the forest to discover what
manner of creatures they were?"

"Aye, I did. And that is perhaps the most strange of all. Although
their marks were clear on the grass of the glade, in the damp earth
under the trees there was no sign of the creatures' passage."

"You searched all around the perimeter of the glade, but there
were no marks? As if perhaps these beings had been spirited out of
nowhere to perform their ghastly deed, and once they had finished
they vanished back to the place whence they had come?"

Now it was Anthlea's turn to look embarrassed. "Aye; I know it is hard to believe, but so it seemed to me. I swear it on the name of Olvensar: in the forest itself there was no trace of the creatures."

"And these creatures, they made tracks like humans, only heavier?"

"Aye. The creatures were not tall, I could tell that from the spacing of the tracks. That is to say, they would not have been considered tall had they been Hunters. Perhaps ordinary humans would regard them as taller than is usual."

"And let me ask one more thing. Could you tell from the tracks what manner of footwear was on the feet of these creatures?"

It seemed a strange question, and evidently not one that the Huntress had considered before. She thought for some time before answering. "I cannot be sure, for, as I told you, there were no tracks in the damp soil underneath the trees where a firm impression would have been left. But I would say that the creatures were not barefooted; neither were they wearing sandals. More than that I cannot say."

"Could they then have been shod for war?"

The Huntress' eyes opened slightly at the ramifications of the gnome's question. "You are suggesting that they might have been wearing armor?"

The gnome nodded.

"Aye... that could certainly be. And it would explain the heaviness of the footprints in the grass. Aye, I should have thought of that before; certainly they might have been wearing armor."

Drefynt nodded, his fears confirmed. But now, what to tell the Ruling Council? How much of what he had surmised should he tell them, and how much was it better to keep to himself? For to tell them that Dark Knights were once more abroad in Palindor would create consternation and panic when perhaps even yet there was a chance that battle could be prevented.

He made his decision. Even though it was probably futile, an attempt at peace had to be made. Palindor was not yet ready for war, although if he understood the book correctly, the one who would lead them was already abroad in the land.

He addressed the Ruling Council. "Those responsible for the killing will not be found. I beg you, do not ask me how I know this, for my knowledge is of the Old Days and would bring only distress. But I assure you that no mortal creature can apprehend them. We must turn our attention, instead, to making amends to King Glendour of Reglandor for the wrong that has been committed on our soil.

"I urge you to consider the only open and honest course available to you: that the facts as we know them be made known to the king, and we trust that he will not hold us accountable for actions over which we had no control."

The five members of the Ruling Council eyed him, wordless and grim. They exchanged glances with one another. Finally, Ymyr spoke. "Drefynt, we thank you for your counsel on this matter. You may leave."

The Ruling Council debated long into the night.

At first, only Benglubber supported Drefynt's advice; the others wanted either to ignore the entire fiasco and hope that the disappearance of the emissary and his party would remain a mystery, or to try to appease the King of Reglandor by sending him some valuable gift. But one by one all those gathered around the table came to the conclusion that there was no simple and obvious solution. Drefynt's plan certainly had merit; but was it the only choice?

To hope that the truth would not be discovered was probably to hope for too much, and to attempt to bribe the king into silence might anger him and lead to open conflict between the two nations. But if they sent a message to Glendour, how would it be received? Should they send just one person with the message, or should it be carried by a distinguished party, perhaps including one or more members of the Ruling Council?

As Verrin pointed out, the king perhaps would feel that since he had lost an entire party in Palindor, it would be no more than common justice that the entire party from Palindor be detained and, perhaps, killed. None of them knew much about King Glendour, and none was willing to trust that he might not want to exact precisely this form of retribution.

And so the discussion continued.

They came to no agreement that night. All of them were aware of the stakes: if they chose wrongly, they could plunge Palindor into a war that it could not win. And perhaps there was no right choice. Maybe war was inevitable.

They broke up soon after midnight, agreeing only to continue the discussion the following evening.

VI Blizzard

Michael was too confused to speak or to move. He listened as the strange old man, whose eyes seemed to bore through him to his very soul, spoke in riddles, first to Michael himself and then to his mother. Strangely, his mother seemed not only unperturbed by the peculiar man, but even to understand him. The old man had said that he and Michael's mother had met before, but it must have been long ago, before Michael was born; but even that seemed unlikely: his mother had never been to Cornwall before, and it was obvious that the man had owned this shop for a very long time.

But suddenly, his confusion turned into surprise and amazement. From nowhere, a fog rolled into the shop, obliterating from view the shelves, the antiques, even his mother and the old man.

For a few moments the fog swirled around him, and then he felt an intense, biting cold. The fog became thicker and whirled around him heavily. White patches flashed past, standing out against a dark background. The biting cold intensified. Even through his sweater and raincoat the cold cut like a sharp knife. Within seconds, Michael was stamping his feet to keep warm.

But the ground had a peculiar consistency, not at all like the hard wooden floor of the antique shop. Looking down, his mouth dropped open as he saw that he was standing on a white, squashy substance that could only be snow. Closing his mouth, he felt the cold liquid of melting snow that had been driven into his mouth by the blustering wind. He had no time to think about what might have happened or to be amazed at the sudden change in his surroundings. Only one thing was important: he had to get out of this blizzard, and quickly.

He began to stumble around. The snow was deep; he thrashed around at random, but quickly realized that this was no way to escape the deadly cold. Wind drove snowflakes into his eyes. He could barely see, and he was getting colder by the second.

Michael began to shiver. He tried to find some constant feature among the whirling whiteness, from which he might get his bearings. But the snowstorm was too intense: he could see nothing clearly. All he could tell was that it looked like the snow was slightly less thick towards his right, where the sky seemed a little darker.

He stumbled forward to the right, plowing through knee-high drifts, holding his hands under his arms for warmth, until he tripped and fell face forward into the snow. The cold bit into him with a new intensity. For the first time, he began to be afraid that he might be about to die. The thought spurred him to his feet, and he stumbled onward.

After a few more yards, he began to be sure that the wind here did not whip around quite so violently, and the snow was falling a little more gently. The way before him was definitely darker than where he had just come from. Continuing forward, at the last moment he thrust his hands out to prevent himself walking straight into a rock wall that had appeared out of the shimmering whiteness before him.

He looked back the way he had come, and then at the wall in front of him. There was no doubt: he was in the lee of some kind of cliff, which was protecting him from the worst excesses of the storm. But even so, he was still freezing. He could not stay long even here without succumbing to the numbing cold. He began to walk along the base of the cliff, keeping the wall on his right. He had no idea what he was looking for: perhaps a cave in which to shelter, or maybe some sign that there was someone else nearby who might help him before it was too late.

He tripped and his face fell heavily against an outcrop of rock. For several seconds he lay in the snow, suddenly too tired to press forward. With a great effort, he lifted his face clear of the snow, and saw a large red mark against the whiteness where his head had lain. He put his hand to his cheek and felt warm wetness. Withdrawing his hand, he saw that it was covered in blood. He got to his feet, but his legs wobbled precariously under him. He took five more steps, then collapsed exhausted in the snow.

I'll just rest here for a few seconds, he thought. *I'll just regain my strength, and then I'll be able to go on.*

His thoughts made little sense, but he was past caring. The blood began to congeal on his face. He laid his head comfortably in the snow and closed his eyes. *Funny how this cold snow feels so nice and warm. Yes, I'll just rest here a while. Maybe I'll go to sleep....*

———————————

Michael moaned as he flickered into consciousness and then went back to sleep. Time passed. Several times he opened his eyes momentarily, only to close them once more. At last, his eyes opened and stayed open.

Where was he?

He tried to remember. At first, he could recall only patches, and in no particular order: a snowstorm; a gloomy, rainy day; walking through narrow streets; an antique shop; a terrible, lethal cold. Gradually, the events ordered themselves into a sequence. But the sequence made no sense; there were still aching gaps in the chain of events, and, try as he could, he could not fill these gaps. Most obvious of all: how had he gone from the antique shop to the frigid snowstorm?

He could not remember. All he recalled was standing in the antique shop with his mother and a strange old man dressed in shabby clothing; then there was a fog, and the next thing he knew he was in the blizzard.

Giving up, he began to wonder where he was.

He tried to look around, and the right side of his head lanced with pain, reminding him that he had fallen and hurt his head on a rock.

Cautiously, he examined his immediate surroundings. He was under several layers of blankets, with more blankets under him to protect him from the hard rock of the floor. He seemed to be in a cave of some sort, but of a rock unlike any he had seen before. It glowed dimly, so that although no entrance was evident, still he could see quite clearly. The air against his face was chill, although the blankets kept his body warm. There didn't seem to be anyone else in the cave.

Slowly, afraid both of making a noise and of making his head hurt, he cast off the blankets and rose unsteadily to his feet. He patted himself down; he was dressed as he had been when he left with his mother to find the shops, in a warm sweater and trousers. For a second, he was at a loss to explain a sword hanging from a belt around his waist. Then he remembered how he had tied the belt in the strange old man's shop. His shoes were no longer on his feet: they were placed, along with his raincoat, neatly at the foot of the blankets.

He raised his hand to his head. He could feel blood congealed along a long, narrow wound high on his cheek and which wound around his eye and across his temple. When he had felt his face in the snow, the entire side of his face had been covered with blood; someone must have cleaned the wound while he slept. He put his shoes on, then began to look for a way out.

The chamber was perhaps ten feet high and twenty five feet in diameter. There were two obvious passages leading out of the chamber, more or less opposite each other. It was impossible to distinguish the two passages, except that the first was narrower than the second. He chose the wider one. Making as little noise as possible, he clambered over a rock and entered the passage.

It turned once to the right and then to the left, and then the dim glow of the rock was eclipsed by a burning bright light. Ahead, the end of the passage glared with a whiteness so bright that it was painful to look at. Squinting against the glare, Michael made his way towards it. The air here felt fresher, and Michael realized that the light was coming from beyond the entrance of the tunnel.

He halted at the entrance. The sun was shining out of a clear blue sky. He couldn't remember the last time he had seen such a bright blue sky, with nowhere a cloud to be seen. Covering the ground was a thick layer of pure white snow, perhaps a foot and a half deep: the blinding whiteness he had seen in the tunnel was caused by the sun reflecting off the snow.

He blinked several times. Of one thing Michael was absolutely certain: he had never been in this place before. In front of the cave entrance, the thick layer of snow extended for about twenty feet. Beyond that the ground fell away steeply; in the distance and far below was a great forest of dark green trees. There was no trace of snow on the ground below, and it was obvious that Michael was looking down on the forest from a great height.

Beyond the forest was a coastline, and beyond that a blue sea glistened, sun pennies reflecting the sunlight. Nowhere on the vast sea which stretched to the horizon was any sign of movement.

He breathed deeply; there was a chill in the air, but its coolness was invigorating rather than painful. With every breath he could almost feel himself getting stronger. He stepped away from the mouth of the cave and into the snow, and sank nearly a foot before it supported his weight. Carefully, he stepped towards the far edge of the snow.

The edge of the snow was clear and sharp, and beyond it the ground fell away precipitously to the treetops far below. Turning around, he saw a mountain towering above him, and the cave in which he had woken was revealed as a small tunnel in the mountainside.

He looked at the narrow ribbon of snow, and then at the near-vertical wall of the mountain. However he had got here, it was a miracle that he had not stumbled over the precipice to his death. Without thinking, the words "Thank you" escaped his lips, although he had no idea whom he was thanking or even, exactly, for what he was thankful.

Suddenly, there was a sound, and he realized that until now the mountainside had been utterly silent. There was not the slightest breath of wind, and no sound of birdsong or machinery reached this high on this mountain from below.

But now there was a sound. It came from his left as he looked at the mountainside, where the narrow ribbon of snow on which he was standing veered around a wall of rock some distance away. He hesitated, wondering whether he should hide in the cave. He waited too long: before he had reached a decision, a figure appeared around the rock. Somewhat taller than himself and dressed in some kind of heavy fur coat, the figure was too distant to be seen clearly, but the soft thud of its boots crunching against the snow carried clearly over the still air. The figure saw Michael and waved cheerily. Michael waited while the figure approached.

He was a short man with long, dark hair and a wrinkled face of indeterminable age, clad in heavy clothes. He carried a large pack on his back. Hanging on one shoulder was a small bow; a half-full quiver hung easily on the other shoulder. He smiled as he halted in front of Michael. But there was something disconcerting about the smile, as if the man was smiling with his mouth but not with his eyes.

The man spoke. "Greetings to you, good sir! It is not often that I see a stranger in these parts, although I see that you are a warrior and mayhap capable of defending yourself against the creatures of the mountain." The man nodded towards Michael's waist, indicating the scabbarded sword that hung at Michael's side.

He began to feel anxious again. Why could he not remember how he had got here from the shop? And still he wondered: where exactly was "here"? He was still certain he had never been in this place before. But the man was still talking, and Michael had no time to ponder the questions that flooded his mind.

"I apologize, stranger. Permit me to introduce myself. My name is Qivir, and I am bound for Pirren Glanwyn, in Reglandor. If you'll forgive me saying so, it's getting late and will soon be dark, and, mighty warrior though you may be, this mountain is no place to be after sunset. Come! If you are going my way, let's travel together. I find that journeys are shorter and more enjoyable if one has company."

Michael was too confused to speak. Obviously, this man was not the one who had saved him from the snowstorm — for Michael had now decided that someone must have rescued him from where he lay in the snow and taken him to the safety of the cave in the mountain — but he was not at all sure he liked the implications of the man's words. Why was the mountain no place to be after dark?

"Come, come, young man. You look as if you have seen a spirit! I won't harm you. I am merely an adventurer who is anxious to complete his travels and return home before winter sets in. You see, apart from my bow I carry no weapon save this" — the man withdrew a small but dangerous-looking knife from the folds of his coat; it glinted ominously in the sun — "which I use merely for protection and the killing of small animals. It is, you will readily admit, no match for your sword."

Still Michael was speechless, unsure how to address this stranger. Of one thing he was sure, though: despite the man's words, the knife, small though it was, would make short work of him if Qivir chose to use it.

Qivir continued, "So, my friend, what say you? Will you join me and afford me companionship? Surely you don't intend to stay on the mountain all night, and we must be on our way if we are to be off its slopes before night falls."

Michael looked back towards the opening of the cave. He had no idea who had saved him from the blizzard, nor where that person might now be, but as he looked around, the awesome loneliness of the place impressed itself upon him and, before he was quite sure how it happened, he found himself saying: "No, you are right. We should be getting down before nightfall."

"Then come with me, young man," the furclad stranger said, and he began to move away, heading in the direction in which he had been travelling before he stopped to speak with Michael.

Michael fell in behind him, placing his feet in the holes in the snow made by Qivir. "My name's Michael, by the way," he said, but the stranger made no response, although Michael was sure that he must have heard.

Qivir travelled quickly, and it took all of Michael's energy to keep up with him. The path become narrower and steeper as they walked. For a while, it seemed like they were making little progress, but after an hour Michael could tell that the forest was definitely closer and the snow much less deep than it had been near the cave.

Still, nightfall came before they had reached the shelter of the trees. With the darkness came a new, biting cold. If he had not been walking so quickly, Michael would soon have been shivering, for the cold seemed to make its way effortlessly through his clothing.

There was no moon, but the sky was clear and full of stars. Michael had no time to look at the sky carefully, but he realized uneasily that he did not recognize any of the usual constellations;

in their places were seemingly random patterns of stars that shone brightly and without twinkling in the still, clear air. In the direction of the sea was a single bright star, brighter even than Venus at its most brilliant, but with a yellower color and in the wrong part of the sky. Michael began to wonder where he could be that even the celestial signposts were unrecognizable.

Then, quite suddenly, they reached the end of the snow. In the space of a few hundred paces, it went from being several inches deep to being no more than a light powder to being completely absent. And now, not far below, in the light of the bright star, Michael could see the forest rising to meet them. A wind sprang up, and the soughing of the trees rose through the air to meet them.

A few minutes later the path widened and suddenly Michael found himself walking through a greenwood forest, the trees dense overhead, blocking out much of the starlight. Michael wanted to ask when they would stop to rest for the night, but Qivir kept hurrying silently forward, and several minutes passed before, without any warning, he stopped, looked around, and said: "All right, this will be as good a place as any to spend the night." Without waiting for a response, Qivir dropped his pack to the ground next to a tree.

Now that he was no longer moving, Michael shivered. Qivir searched through his pack and withdrew a small brown object. Turning to Michael, he held it out.

"Here, try this on; it will keep you warm."

Michael took the tightly wrapped object and shook it open to reveal the furred skin of some animal, shaped to make a long tunic. Placing it on over his sweater, it stretched nearly to his knees, and he immediately began to feel warmer.

Qivir continued, "I have food enough for two tonight, but tomorrow we must hunt. Now, we have travelled hard these past hours and you look tired. Let's eat, then sleep. Tomorrow our way will be easier and we can begin to get to know one another."

From his pack Qivir withdrew two small loaves of bread and a massive hunk of cheese. Ripping the cheese in two, he offered one half and a loaf to Michael. Michael wolfed down the food. Then, exhausted, he lay on the pine needles that covered the forest floor and, in seconds, was asleep.

Qivir looked at the boy at his feet, and smiled.

Terafin the Hermit was worried. Increasingly desparate, he followed the tracks down the mountainside, the yellow star lighting his way. He had to catch up with the boy.

It was gone midnight when he reached the end of the snow. No Hunter, he knew that without the marks in the snow to guide him, he had lost the boy's trail.

What to do?

He had to do something. With a grunt of resignation, he turned toward the yellow star. It hung over Carn Toldwyn, where the Ruling Council met. He had no choice. He had to go there, for the buckle worn by the young human who had gone missing could be worn by but one person in the whole of the Three Lands.

The young human who had disappeared was Michael, High King of Palindor.

VII Reunion

It took only a moment for Katrin to realize where she was.

Overhead was a dark mass of rock, blocking out the light of the sky. The slab was supported by three pillars: massive, lichen-covered granite columns that were aged and immovable. Looking down, she saw that she was standing atop a small, squarish rock that was set level with the ground.

She was inside Toldwyn's Quoit, high atop Machrenmoor, in Palindor; and under the slab beneath her feet, so it was said, lay the body of Toldwyn, first warrior of the Land, waiting in repose for the day when Palindor would face its greatest danger and he would lead the High Monarchs into the final battle.

She breathed deeply, looking out past one of the granite columns toward Carn Toldwyn in the distance. The sun was low in the sky and would soon set, and there was an autumnal chill in the air. But Katrin was neither cold nor scared. Rather, a calm feeling of determination came over her — for no longer was she Katrin Fowler, with a tumor bringing death to her thirty-six-year-old body; here she was Catherine, the First High Monarch, and she knew that Olvensar has sent her to Palindor for a purpose, although as yet she had no idea what that purpose might be.

Automatically, her hand dropped to her side, to feel for the reassuring presence of Scalmyùt and Scelberon, the sword and scabbard of the High Queen. She stopped, and then looked down. Her sword and scabbard weren't there, even though she was wearing the High Queen's belt. She looked around, half-expecting to see them lying somewhere nearby, but there was no sign of them.

The sun was already noticeably lower in the sky. She cast a final look around, shrugged, and, without hesitation, stepped out of the quoit and headed north across the moor towards Carn Toldwyn.

The sun set as she approached the Pennyfarthing River, and her attention was attracted by a bright, yellow star that seemed to hang high above Carn Toldwyn.

She stopped, gazing up at the star, and uttered a question — or, perhaps, a prayer — "What do you want of me? I will do whatever you desire, but you must tell me."

She waited in case some kind of obvious reply came, but nothing happened. She shivered and pressed onward. A couple of minutes later she reached the Pennyfarthing and began to cross the bridge. Halfway across, she stopped, her attention caught by a movement in the trees nearby. She peered into the gloom, but she could see no sign of any creature. Whatever it was, it seemed to have disappeared.

She looked ahead, along the winding road to where the glimmering light of candles in cottages could now be seen, and for the first time she wondered exactly what she would do when she reached the town. Go to the castle, she supposed, and announce her presence.

She began to walk again, but as she stepped off the bridge, another movement at the corner of her eye made her stop. She turned quickly, and this time she saw a figure dressed in a gray habit standing in the shadows.

The figure was motionless, watching her. Moving slowly, she began to walk towards it, half expecting it to take fright and dash away into the woods. But the figure did not move, and, as she drew close, she realized that it was probably a human. She couldn't be certain, because its body was hidden by a gray, monkish habit, whose hood drooped down and completely hid the creature's face.

She waited for the figure to introduce itself. After a few moments, she realized that it was not going to.

She wondered how she ought to introduce herself: should she openly declare who she was? Instead, she heard herself saying, "Catherine, human of Carn Toldwyn, at your service."

The other nodded, but did not reply. Intrigued now, in her curiosity Catherine became positively rude by Palindoric standards. "And, stranger, who may you be?" she asked.

For several seconds there was no response. Then the figure turned away, indicating with a gesture that Catherine was to follow. More than a little unnerved by the ghostlike creature, Catherine began to do so.

Wordlessly, the figure led her into the forest and then around the southeastern corner of Carn Toldwyn.

Catherine lost track of time as they trudged through the thick layer of needles on the forest floor. To their left through the trees she could be see the glimmer of lights from the town, so she knew that they were travelling only a few paces from the forest edge. At length they reached a small clearing. The gray figure halted in the center of the clearing. She more than half expected that it would now throw off its hood and reveal itself, but it did no such thing. Instead, it merely stood, as if waiting patiently for something to happen. High overhead the bright star lit the silent tableau.

Catherine began to feel uncomfortable. Just when she was on the point of breaking the silence, she heard a sound: someone was coming through the forest towards them. The gray figure made no attempt to hide from whoever was approaching.

She turned towards the sound and, a few seconds later, an old gnome shuffled with the aid of a cane into the clearing. The gnome had his eyes on the ground in front of him, and placed his feet carefully so that he did not trip over the small, exposed rocks that littered the clearing. He was moving slowly, deep in thought, mumbling to himself and to Olvensar about his worries.

Drefynt stepped into the clearing as he did every night. For a moment, he did not realize that he was no longer alone. Then he raised his eyes as he became aware that someone was watching him.

It was a moment before he recognized the one who now stood before him. She was much older than when he had last seen her — but that should not have been a surprise; after all, four hundred years had passed since the High Queen had left for a walk in the gardens and disappeared. Strangely, though, he realized now that he had always thought of High Monarchs as ageless, and it came as a shock to realize that this was not so.

In the four centuries since her disappearance she had aged by perhaps as many as twenty or thirty human years — he always found it difficult to estimate the age of humans — but there was no doubting the identity of the person standing before him. Even without the belt to denote her rank, he would always have recognized her unique blend of quiet assurance and fire.

But, strangely, she did not seem to recognize him. Then he realized that when they had last seen one another he had been in early middle age; now he was the last known surviving companion of those heady days when the High Queen had come to Palindor, and old indeed.

Humbly, he bowed. "Queen Catherine. It is I, Drefynt, known as the Wise, gnome of Carn Toldwyn, last of the Holy Gnomes of Perendeth, now, and always, at your service."

Catherine could not believe her eyes. Surely this old gnome could not be her Drefynt? Surely this was not the gnome, perhaps the wisest of all the Holy Gnomes, who had been with her at Toldwyn Quoit, when Malthazzar had been banished from the kingdom? Gnomes lived for many hundreds of years, and she had been gone for only twenty.

But with Olvensar, as the Drefynt whom she remembered would have said, nothing is impossible.

The old gnome remained in his bow, his eyes cast towards the ground. "Look at me!" Catherine commanded.

The gnome raised his head, his weight shifting to his cane. For several seconds, Catherine looked past the wispy white beard and into the lined face. Then she broke into a smile and ran across the clearing.

She nearly swept him off his feet as she embraced him. "Drefynt! Drefynt! Truly it is you! I thought I would never see you again! Oh, Drefynt; it is so good to see you again!" As she released him, she was not in the least embarrassed that tears were dribbling down her cheeks.

Suddenly, she remembered the gray figure that had led her to the clearing. She turned to thank it, but it was gone.

"There was a creature, Drefynt," she said, "a creature in a gray habit, who led me here."

63

"Aye. It is a sage; the last of the sages, I suspect. Indeed, I thought they were all gone many generations ago, but perhaps they are merely in hiding. I know not."

"A sage? He said nothing to me. He met me down by the bridge across the Pennyfarthing and then led me here."

"I too have seen this sage, just once, four days ago. Do not concern yourself that he said nothing. Sages rarely speak. They believe there is little point in speech unless you have something truly worth saying. It is, I confess, a belief that has increasing appeal as I age: speech seems to add only confusion to what would otherwise be simple and clear.

"This sage brought me a book, an ancient book of the Old Days, older even than the books that were destroyed in the fire at Perendeth, and the things revealed in that book have brought me much pain and grief. But of one thing I am glad: that events have reunited us, although I wish that the circumstances were more auspicious."

"What do you mean, Drefynt? You sound as if something awful has befallen Palindor."

"No, not quite yet, but it will do so if I read the signs aright, and the events leading to it have begun. Much is written in the book, but much more is left unwritten. I knew not that you would return; I knew only that the Red King would be here."

"The Red King?"

Catherine tried to remember something. Something very important. But it was slipping away from her. It was gone.

"Aye. You remember the rhyme, surely:

> *A White Stone for Catherine*
> *First Queen of Palindor;*
> *A Red Stone for Michael*
> *The High King of War.*

"Well, that star that shines so brightly overhead appeared nine days since, and five nights later the sage gave me the book. The book was written in an ancient script, and since I received it I have been busy translating it as best I can into the modern tongue.

"Just this very morning, I read that the time of the Red King will be signalled by a bright star in the sky, a sign sent by the High

Lord. There will surely be bloodshed of some kind, for he is the High King of War, and I am sure that he is already here, although I have as yet heard no news of him.

"The rest I can only surmise. I have come just recently from a meeting of the Ruling Council, and they tell me that an emissary and his party from the king of Reglandor has been found dead in the eastern forest. Although no one else suspects it, I believe that they were killed by Dark Knights" — Catherine shivered; how well she remembered her confrontation with those inhuman creatures — "which means that the power of kiriàl is at work once more in Palindor.

"We are gripped by forces that we do not comprehend, my queen. That there will be bloodshed, I am sure. That the Dark Knights' massacre of the emissary from Reglandor somehow marks the beginning of that spilling of blood, I am almost equally certain. But what will happen, who will be involved, and what will be the outcome, I cannot guess."

"Then my returning to Palindor must have something to do with these troubles?"

"I know not. The book does not mention the White High Queen. But it can hardly be a coincidence, can it?" He smiled at her.

"No, it cannot." She returned his smile. For, no matter what the future held, at least one of her friends from the old days would be by her side.

Drefynt continued, "Now, tell me. Apart from the sage, has anyone seen you since you returned?"

"No, not that I know of."

"Good. I think perhaps it is best if as few creatures as possible know you have returned, at least until we are more certain what your rôle is to be. Now, come. You must stay at least this one night with me. There is so much to discuss. Much has happened since you were last in Palindor."

The aged gnome held out his hand and together the two friends headed for Drefynt's cottage.

VIII Attack

Michael and Qivir journeyed together for several days.

They quickly settled into a routine. During the hours of daylight, Qivir led the way through the forest in a roughly south-easterly direction. He moved quickly and quietly, and at first it was difficult for Michael to keep up without making a great deal of noise. Eventually, Qivir solved this problem by killing a deer and spending two hours sewing a pair of strong moccasins from the animal's hide, so that thenceforth Michael's footfalls were almost as quiet as his own. Qivir seemed to know the locations of all the villages and even the lonely houses in the depths of the forest, and he guided Michael around them so that the pair remained unseen.

Once or twice a day, Qivir would suddenly stand stock still, lifting his hand as a signal for his companion to do likewise. At such moments, Michael would strain to hear what had caused Qivir suddenly to halt. Occasionally, he would hear the sound of a creature moving through the trees some distance away, but more often he heard nothing. After a minute or two, Qivir would lower his hand and they moved on.

By the evening of each day, Michael was exhausted. If food was running low, Qivir would disappear for a while into the trees, returning with freshly killed meat for them both. As often as not, Michael was already asleep, curled up on a thick bed of needles under a tree. Qivir would prepare the food, cooking it over a smokeless fire, for Michael to eat in the morning.

Breakfast was the only time of the day when they relaxed and chatted. Qivir told Michael about himself, but Michael did not notice as the days passed that Qivir never asked him anything. So he did not notice that he was forgetting about everything except the trek that had begun outside the cave on the mountainside.

Qivir was the chief minister of his Majesty, King Glendour IV of Reglandor, which was a mighty kingdom to the east. A chain of tall mountains, the Mountains of Mourn, separated Reglandor from the land through which they were travelling, once part of Reglandor but now an independent land called Palindor, which was inhabited by fierce creatures. The only easy crossing between Palindor and Reglandor was at the extreme southeastern corner of Palindor, where the mountains were reduced to a series of grassy hills at the boundary of the two countries, and it was for this region that they were now heading.

The chief minister explained why it was vital that they pass through Palindor undetected: "Our dress identifies us as being strangers. If we were seen, we would be set upon and killed. The creatures of Palindor are warlike. They kill for no reason. It has ever been so. One day, Reglandor will once more march forth and take possession of Palindor, but as yet that day has not yet come, and until then no citizen of Reglandor is safe within the confines of this land."

The fourth day was particularly exhausting, with Qivir pressing on even harder than usual. "We will soon be at the edge of the forest, and from there it is but a single day's journey into Reglandor, where we can be more at our ease," Qivir explained as he pushed relentlessly onward.

At the end of the day's march, Michael could barely keep his eyes open. His muscles ached and his feet were blistered despite the snug moccasins. Hungry though he was, he was asleep within seconds of Qivir declaring a halt in a small clearing.

Qivir watched from the edge of the clearing, and a smile crossed his face as the exhausted human fell asleep.

Qivir strode into the forest a short distance. Placing his hand to his mouth, an eerie, haunting sound sprang from his lips and reverberated around the trees, which shook in resonance with the sound in an unnatural way.

He waited.

After a couple of minutes he heard a snuffling sound not far away. Silently, he walked towards the sound. Peering around a tree trunk, he caught sight of a boar turning over pine needles in search of food. He smiled.

The boar, suddenly aware that it was no longer alone, looked up, directly into Qivir's eyes. It took a moment for terror to register. But the boar could not tear itself away from Qivir's gaze: while it watched, transfixed, Qivir raised his right arm, making a tight fist. Without warning, a silent grayish-black bolt flashed from Qivir's fist to the doomed animal. The boar fell over sideways, dead.

Qivir stood over the boar; and then his attention was caught by the sound of a larger creature making its way through the trees. He cupped his hands to his face and once again the ghostly, ghastly reverberating sound bounced among the trees.

Moments later, a tall human strode into the clearing. He was dressed in a Hunter's garb: all in green, a small white cross embellishing the tunic. Slung over his shoulders was a longbow, a quiverful of arrows on his back. Attached to his belt was a sheath from which a dagger protruded. He strode forward until he was standing at arm's length from Qivir.

Qivir spoke. "Tomorrow morning. We are in a clearing five hundred paces in that direction. Come for us as we breakfast. I worked him hard today, and he will sleep late tomorrow, so there is no hurry."

The Hunter nodded. "It is my honor to obey you, my Lord." He turned to leave.

"One more thing. The dagger is wrong. Hunters carry broadswords at their waists." The Hunter turned to face Qivir; there was a flickering grayness around the dagger that hung from the Hunter's waist. The grayness receded, leaving behind in the place where the sheath and dagger had hung a scabbarded broadsword. Qivir nodded. The Hunter turned and disappeared into the trees.

The sun was already high when Michael awoke. He remained motionless for several seconds, eyes closed, trying to identify the wonderful aroma. Meat cooking! Qivir must have killed a boar last night. He opened his eyes and stretched luxuriously. His muscles began to loosen.

"Come along, sleepy head. Even though we're nearly out of the forest, we can't afford to sleep all day," Qivir chided Michael with a smile as he tended to the makeshift spit on which he was slowly turning a boar's carcass. "Breakfast will be ready in five minutes, and there's a stream about two hundred paces in that direction. Careful; it's very cold."

Michael nodded and got to his feet, then went in search of the water. He returned several minutes later, to see Qivir already helping himself to a second portion of juicy meat. Hungrily, he too tore a hunk from the carcass and began to wolf it down.

"Will we reach Reglandor today?" he asked.

Qivir looked up at the sun, then at the mountains that towered not far away to the east. "Possibly, although we are getting a late start and we are perhaps still an hour from the Plains of Kradesh. But yes, probably with luck we should pass over into Reglandor by this evening."

There was a sound, a sort of swooshing. For a second Michael could not identify it. But as he watched, Qivir suddenly keeled over to one side and lay on the ground writhing. In horror, Michael saw that an arrow protruded from Qivir's left shoulder. Before he could move, the swooshing sound came again and Michael saw a second arrow quivering in the ground within inches of Qivir's head. A tall man clad in green, with a white cross on his tunic, sprang into the clearing.

"I'll teach you to enter Palindor," the man shouted, drawing a deadly looking sword.

The man sprang forward, crossed the clearing at a run, then flung himself on Qivir, who was desperately trying to pull the arrow from his shoulder.

Michael came to life. Without stopping to think, he drew his sword, which glittered dangerously in the morning sunlight. The man looked up, interrupted as he was about to hack at Qivir, to see Michael advancing on him.

A look of alarm crossed the man's face. He drew back his sword and hurled it like a knife at Michael. Michael dodged to one side, but the sword caught his shoulder a glancing blow. In a pain-driven fury, Michael's brought his sword down in a single, fearful blow.

Afterwards, he could not remember how it had happened. He did not think that he had meant to kill the man. He had struck only once, and it had not seemed to him, at the time, that even that single blow had landed with tremendous force. But there was no denying the result.

The sword landed across the man's trunk as he tried to roll out of the path of the oncoming blow. Ignoring clothing, skin and even the bone of the man's ribs, the sword tore a path through the man's body. Blood gushed in an horrific fountain. In only a few moments, life drained out of the man. His momentum caused him to roll over on the ground, the flow from his side turning the grass bright red, his sightless eyes turned downwards.

For several seconds, Michael didn't move as he tried to take in what he had just done.

At first, he thought that the attacker was simply feinting, that he was not seriously hurt. But as he watched the blood that poured out of his body turn slowly to a trickle, he realized that no one could survive such a wound. Michael looked up at his sword, poised high over his head for a second blow. Blood dribbled down the metal blade, across the hilt and on to his hand. With a shout, he dropped the sword.

For a second, he thought that he was going to be sick, but then he was brought to his senses by the pain in his shoulder and the movement of Qivir as he sat up on the grass, a blood-tipped arrow held firmly in one hand, the other hand clasped tightly over his shoulder to staunch the flow of blood from his wound. Qivir dropped the arrow to the ground. "Here, help me up. I must get to the stream. We should bathe our wounds in case his weapons were poisoned."

Aghast, Michael helped Qivir to his feet. Together, they hurried towards the stream where only minutes before Michael had washed. Qivir plunged into the stream and sat down heavily in the center of the icy current. The water came up to his neck. He began to massage the wound, letting the water enter freely to clean it, leaving a red trail downstream of where he was sitting. "Do the same!" he urged Michael. "Wash it out to get rid of any poison."

Michael dropped into the water, like Qivir fully clothed. For a second the ice-cold liquid caught at his breath as it seeped through his clothes, then he too was cleaning out the wound in his shoulder. The trail that swept downstream was narrower and fainter than Qivir's. He saw with relief that the attacker's thrown sword had barely broken the surface of his skin, while Qivir's wound seemed quite deep.

It was too cold to stay long in the water, and after a minute both of them waded out and stripped to let their clothes dry in the sun. They examined one another's wounds: Michael's was little more than a scratch, and Qivir's, while deep and painful, was not life-threatening.

"We should get out of here as quickly as we can, though," Qivir said. "That was a Palindoric Hunter. And if there was one, there are probably others. As soon as our clothes are dry enough to wear, we should get moving again."

"But what about your pack? How will you be able to walk carrying that weight? I know I couldn't carry it."

"Never mind about that. Go back and get your sword; we might need that. But leave everything else. We'll travel light the rest of the way. Maybe we can still reach Reglandor before the day is out."

The clothes were still sopping when they put them back on. Michael returned to the clearing, his clothes squelching uncomfortably with every step. Unable to face the man whom he had killed, he looked away as he bent down and picked up the sword. Blood was already congealed on the weapon. He carried it, unsheathed, back to where Qivir was fashioning a makeshift sling out of a creeper.

"Clean it in the stream, then dry it thoroughly on the grass. Then carry it for at least ten minutes before you sheath it, otherwise it will rust and lose its edge," Qivir said.

Michael helped Qivir tie the sling so that it supported his left arm, easing the pain in his shoulder — he realized that he had already forgotten about his own shoulder — then cleaned the sword as Qivir had instructed.

The two of them set off. This time Qivir headed south instead of south-east. "This is the quickest way to the forest's edge. We'll

71

be more exposed, but once we get on to the plains, we'll be able to travel much more quickly than we ever could inside the forest," he explained.

So it was that little more than half an hour later the trees thinned out and they found themselves standing on the edge of a large, grassy plain. To the south-east was a line of small hills, still several thousand paces distant.

"There's a river on the other side of the hills. The far bank of the river is Reglandor," Qivir said.

They looked around anxiously, but apart from the birds in the sky, there was no sign of any other creature. Keeping close to the edge of the forest, they made their way toward the distant hills.

It was early evening when they reached safety. They climbed a low hill, and the sun was just setting as they reached its summit. Before them, the hill sloped downward to a wide river, a bridge across the river no more than five hundred paces ahead. Michael turned and looked back at the land that they had crossed.

He spat. "Palindor! Good riddance!" He did not see the smile that crossed Qivir's face.

Turning firmly around so that Palindor was behind them, the two marched down the grassy hill and crossed the bridge into the Kingdom of Reglandor.

IX A Journey Begins

Drefynt was more worried than he had ever been before. There was so much on his mind, but how much of it could he share with another creature? Even the High Queen Catherine, who was completely trustworthy — as was Sherna, his daughter — could not be told everything, for surely they would try to thwart the prophecies, possibly with disastrous effect.

Still, he was gladdened by Catherine's unexpected arrival. That meant that when the fighting started, there would be *two* High Monarchs fighting for Palindor, rather than the one he had been expecting. Still, there were other, less promising, signs. Most worrying of all was that no word of High King Michael had yet reached Carn Toldwyn.

Could he be mistaken? Was it perhaps not yet Michael's time? Or was it simply that the High King was in some other part of Palindor? After all, when Catherine had first arrived in the land all those centuries ago the only person to know about it for several days had been his brother Trondwyth.

But something else worried him even more than Michael's absence. Something that he couldn't share with anyone else.

It had happened when he and Sherna had been hurrying back from Perendeth after being summoned by the Ruling Council. He had looked up at the storm swirling around Penmichael Brea, and prayed to Olvensar that the oncoming storm would spare the farmers in Beleron. Praying to Olvensar was something that long ago had become second nature. He was in late middle age before he had realized that Olvensar always heard and answered prayers. The strange thing was that Olvensar's answers rarely came the way that one wanted or expected, which was probably why so few people realized how involved the High Lord was in his subjects' lives. Still, there was always the reassuring feeling when one uttered a prayer that Olvensar had heard and would eventually, in his own good time, get around to doing something about it.

Until now.

Coming back from Perendeth, for the first time in hundreds of years, Drefynt had been left feeling empty as he prayed, as if his words were merely meaningless entreaties. Suddenly, he had been certain that the words would have no effect because — and this was the terrifying thing — *no one was listening*. And ever since that moment, he had felt the same empty feeling whenever he had tried to pray. Olvensar, he could not help thinking, seemed to have forgotten him. Did that mean that the High Lord was no longer interested in Palindor? The thought was too awful to contemplate; but what other explanation could there be?

The last few days had been tense. He had intended to keep Catherine's identity a secret, but his wife's quick-wittedness had thwarted that plan. Within moments of Catherine's arrival in the cottage, Lorin had spotted the white-stoned buckle. Flustered, she had immediately curtseyed and said: "Your Majesty, you do us a great honor." Sherna had overheard the declamation, and so his plan to hide Catherine's identity was instantly shattered.

But all of them agreed that no one else should know that the High Queen had returned. At first, Catherine was prepared to remove her belt and leave it in a safe cranny somewhere in Drefynt's cottage, but the old gnome would have none of that: "There's a power in that belt, and you never know when it may manifest itself." So instead Catherine had taken to wearing a long tunic that draped down and hid the buckle from view.

To dispel any questions, Drefynt, Lorin and Sherna openly escorted Catherine around Carn Toldwyn, introducing her as a friend of Drefynt from "far away."

Catherine was surprised how little had changed in the intervening centuries. Creatures still greeted one another on the streets, and she could not walk more than a few dozen steps without coming across friends good-naturedly passing the time of day. The cottages were still well kept, with bright window boxes, fresh paint and pretty curtains. The Ruling Council was obviously doing a good job.

The only difficult part came when Drefynt took her up to the castle, to show her how it had changed since her day.

Drefynt led her into the Hall of Judgement, and Catherine halted, her eyes fixed on the wall.

"Scalmyùt and Scelberon!" she exclaimed.

"Shhhh," Drefynt said, looking around in case someone had overheard. Fortunately, no one was around.

"What are they doing here?"

"When you disappeared, they were found in the garden of the catacombs. We hung them here in case you ever returned."

"I don't suppose I can have them?"

"Not if you want your identity to remain a secret. Best to leave them here for now. They won't be going anywhere; we can get them if you need them."

"I suppose you're right. Still, I do miss wearing them." She looked at them wistfully, but knew that Drefynt was right.

These were good days. Drefynt and Catherine wandered aimlessly for hours, talking about the times they had spent together, both before the confrontation at the quoit, when they had barely known one another, and then afterwards, when the two had become firm friends.

Catherine saw few changes in the gnome other than that he was now aged and obviously approaching the end of his life. For his part, Drefynt saw that Catherine was quite changed. She was now gentler and more thoughtful: still a warrior queen, but a different kind of warrior. Even though she wished that Scalmyùt and Scelberon hung at her side, it was not because of the power of the weapons, but simply because they were in some way part of her.

Her spirit was, if anything, stronger than it had been before. She seemed confident both of her own abilities and Olvensar's support. "Strength," she said, "is not the same as might, and sometimes the strongest creatures are those that seem the weakest. It often takes more courage to die willingly for your convictions than to fight." Drefynt pondered these words for many hours as he lay in the darkness of his bed, trying to come to grips with his fears for the future.

After a few days, a carriage halted outside Drefynt's cottage and a messenger got out and told Drefynt and Sherna that the Ruling Council wished to see them.

"What do you think they want?" asked Catherine.

"They must have come to a decision about Reglandor. I do hope they've been sensible. Come on, Sherna, I suppose we can't leave the Ruling Council waiting."

A few minutes later, the old gnome and his daughter were ushered into the Judgement Hall.

After a few preliminary exchanges, Ymyr got down to business. "Thank you for coming so quickly. We wanted to tell you that the Ruling Council has decided how to respond to the death of King Glendour's emissary." He held up a scroll sealed with purple wax on which was embossed the great seal of Palindor. "We have decided to follow your wise advice and tell Glendour what we know and to invite him to pay us a state visit. As the most-travelled citizen of Palindor, we would like to ask you, Sherna, if you would do us the honor of carrying the message to the king. Let me emphasize, though, that the mission is not wholly without danger. There is a possibility that King Glendour will react badly to the news that his emissary is dead. Whoever carries this scroll may be risking imprisonment. Or worse."

Benglubber interrupted. "Don't feel like you have to accept, sister. I thought you would be the best person for the job because you have travelled so widely. But Ymyr is right: this could be a very dangerous mission. Think carefully before you accept."

Before his daughter could respond, Drefynt interjected. "If Glendour comes, he will bring troops. Some might say that inviting Reglandor troops to Carn Toldwyn is to invite trouble."

"We know," Ymyr admitted. "But we felt we had no choice. The decision was far from easy. In the end, we felt that this was the minimum that might be acceptable. Otherwise, he might easily bring a much larger contingent of troops into south-eastern Palindor on the pretext of searching for the outlaws who killed his messenger.

And such an army would pose far more of a threat than a state visit."

"I'll do it," said Sherna, cutting off the discussion.

"You don't have to, you know," said Benglubber, looking at his sister with a mixture of pride and sadness.

"I know. But someone has to, and you're right: I'm the obvious choice."

"There is one condition," said Drefynt, surprising them all. "She will take a companion. The human who has been staying with me for the past few days will accompany my daughter on this mission."

"Why?" said Ymyr. "Who is she that she could possibly help Sherna?"

Drefynt shook his head. "That is the condition. Take it or leave it."

For a long moment there was silence. It was obvious that the members of the Ruling Council were displeased by Drefynt's ultimatum. Sherna tried to smooth things over. "She'll help. She, like me, is an experienced traveller. And she is a human; Glendour is more likely to listen to her. Please forgive my father for making his request seem like a demand. But he is right: our chance of success is better if she accompanies me."

"All right, then. We agree," said Ymyr. "Take this scroll. When can you leave?"

"Tomorrow. We should be in Pirren Glanwyn within the week."

Sherna and Drefynt were dismissed with the Ruling Council's thanks. As soon as they were alone in the carriage, Sherna turned to her father: "What was that about? What if Catherine doesn't want to go with me? You don't have to worry about me, you know. I can take care of myself."

There was a long silence before Drefynt replied. "Trust me, my daughter. Something terrible is about to happen. Actually, I think it's already started."

"What do you mean?"

"I don't really know. I wish I did. But it involves Catherine, and somehow it involves Reglandor."

Drefynt refused to be drawn further.

When they got back to the cottage, Sherna explained the situation to Lorin and Catherine, while Drefynt retired to his study to think.

That evening, Drefynt went out and did not return before everyone else had gone to bed.

The following morning, Sherna and Catherine ate a large breakfast and were finishing filling packs for the journey when Drefynt appeared carrying a large parcel. He handed it to Catherine, saying, "I went to a lot of trouble to get these for you. When they find out they're gone, they'll go looking for them. You don't want to be around when they do."

She ripped the package open, and gave a delighted cry when she saw Scalmyùt and Scelberon. She gave Drefynt a hug. "You mean you stole them from the chamber?"

"Nay, of course not. I took them for you, and are they not yours? That is not stealing." Just for a moment, he looked like a young gnome again as a twinkle lit his eye.

Catherine donned the gifts. Sherna appraised her with a frown, then bent down and picked up a handful of dirt and rubbed it into Scelberon's cracked leather. "It didn't look right," she explained. She nodded. "Much better now."

They said their goodbyes and, with the sun climbing toward noon, exchanged final hugs with Drefynt and Lorin. Without looking back, they strode into the forest and disappeared from view.

Drefynt and Lorin remained motionless, holding hands and looking at the spot where their daughter and their friend had disappeared into the trees. Lorin turned to her husband. "You can't hide anything from me. You know something, don't you? They aren't coming back, are they?"

Startled, Drefynt looked at his beloved wife. "Is it that obvious?"

"No, not to anyone else. I'm sure they don't suspect a thing; but you can't hide it from me. After all, I've lived with you for nigh on three hundred years. Surely you don't think I can't see through you after all this time. And don't think you can get away with changing the subject either. I repeat: they aren't coming back, are they?"

"I'm not sure. I didn't want to tell you this until after they'd gone. The prophecy says only that I will end my days in great grief and distress, and that I will lose my child. We have two children, but I feel sure that one of them is to be lost. I fear that my days are few now, and the final grief is beginning. Come, my dear Lorin" — he hugged her — "we must be strong and trust in the ways of the High Lord. Once before I needed him — all Palindor needed him — and he helped us. Surely he will do so again."

He wished he could be as certain as he tried to sound.

X In the Arena

King Glendour didn't know what to make of the stranger.

Qivir, his chief minister, had surprised him three weeks ago by announcing that he was departing on a mission and that the king would be pleased by what he would bring with him on his return. Mystified at the time, the mystery had only deepened when Qivir had returned with a young human, little more than a child. Qivir had presented the young man to the king and requested that he be given a state room in which to stay, as he had saved the minister's life during their travels. Puzzled, the king had agreed. Now he hoped that Qivir was about to explain.

There was a knock on the door of his chamber.

"Enter!" the king commanded, and Qivir walked into the room. Qivir bowed, then accepted the chair that the king offered. "Now, Qivir, tell me about this human. Is this the one whom you sought?"

"Yes, your Majesty, this is the one."

"But he is just a child. What interest do I have in children? My mind is too busy with matters of state."

"By which I assume you mean the problem of how you will invade Palindor?"

The king's only answer was a silent nod.

"Then you should be most interested in the child, Your Majesty, for it is through him that Palindor will be sent into turmoil and then conquered."

"How so?"

"You will see, your Majesty, you will see. All I ask is that you trust me. You know that I have never led you astray. And in this of all matters, which is closest to my heart, I will not fail you."

"But who is the child?"

"I cannot tell you now. But tomorrow if you are at the training arena at noon, you shall have your answer."

"Then pray tell me at least where you have been. Where did you find this boy?"

"In Palindor, your Majesty. Palindor will be brought to its knees by one of its very own."

The king was still puzzled, but he could not resist joining with the wide smile that creased his minister's face.

It was hard for Michael to take it all in. King Glendour's palace occupied a low hill in the very center of Pirren Glanwyn. Everywhere he looked were lavish trappings of gold and purple. In the corridors, guards were posted outside every room: real guards with weapons, guards who looked as if they were ready to use those weapons at a moment's notice.

He had been intrigued by the city as well. Pirren Glanwyn was surrounded by a wall, and the only entrance he had seen was a wide gate on the south side of the city. The gatekeeper and his guards (all four of them) had been respectful as he and Qivir entered the city, but what had shocked him more than the exalted status of his travelling companion was the fact that neither the gatekeeper nor any of the guards were human. And as he and Qivir strode through the city's busy streets towards the palace, he could not help being struck by the wide variety of creatures that lived in this place. Qivir pointed them out: dwarves, satyrs, gnomes (not many of those), nymphs and many other creatures, as well as a goodly number of humans. Most of the dwarves were in armor, as were many of the humans. In the palace itself, almost everyone wore battle dress. He wondered if Reglandor was preparing for war or if this was the normal state of affairs in this kingdom.

On arrival, he had been given a massive state room in the west wing. He had eaten a wonderful meal and then slept deeply on the softest bed he had ever known. He woke late the next morning to the sound of a knock on the door.

"Come in," he called sleepily.

Qivir strode into the room. "You slept well, I trust."

"Wonderfully, thank you."

"And now you are hungry. Food is always on the table in the Great Hall. Just go down and take what you need whenever you want. The servants keep the tables well stocked. But I should caution you against eating too much this morning. It is already midmorning, and you will need to be alert at midday. We are to go to the arena. I have told the king how you saved my life, and he would like to meet you there, and it is always best to be alert when with the king. He sometimes gives the impression that he is confused, but I assure you that it's only an act; he has the sharpest mind of anyone I know. So I'll come back for you shortly before noon and I'll take you to the arena."

"Thank you; I'll be ready."

With a bow, Qivir turned and left the room. Closing the door behind him, he made his way purposefully down two flights of steps and along a corridor at the end of which was a single door, closed and unguarded.

Qivir tapped sharply on the door.

"Enter."

Qivir opened the door and swept into the room beyond. An old, stooped human closed and barred the door behind him.

The room was large and dim. There were no windows. On cluttered shelves scattered around the walls, small globes glowed with a phosphorescent green, lending an eerie hue to the scene.

As well as Qivir and the stooped human, there was a third person in the room. A youngish human dressed in light armor was seated, incongruously, in a wooden chair in the very center of the room. He stared forwards vacantly as if completely unaware of his surroundings.

"Is he ready?" Qivir asked the human who had closed the door.

"Very nearly. Give me one more minute, that is all."

The old man hobbled forward, then spoke to the man in the chair. "Who are you?"

The man answered in a monotone. "My name is Laird."

"Whom do you serve, Laird?"

"I serve the Ruling Council of Palindor."

"And what is your mission?"

"To kill the king of Reglandor."

"And what shall be the sign?"

"The sign shall be when Qivir, the chief minister, touches his finger to the side of his nose."

"Very good. Now, you will depart from this place with the chief minister."

The stooped figure looked across to Qivir for confirmation. Qivir nodded.

"Then go!" commanded the old man, loudly snapping his finger.

The man in armor shook his head twice as if trying to clear it of some vague, uncomfortable memory, then looked around. He seemed not to see the old man standing in front of him. His eyes searched the room, then alighted on Qivir. "Ah, good! you're here."

"Yes, but we must leave now. The king will be at the arena at noon, and we mustn't keep him waiting."

The arena was in the northern quadrant of Pirren Glanwyn: a circular area at the bottom of a pit, with a level surface of flattened dirt perhaps a hundred and fifty paces across. Ranged around the perimeter were banks of seats cut into the ground. Here and there on the flat, central area were warriors testing themselves against one another. The clash of swordplay mixed with the loud grunts of wrestling as warriors fought. Half a dozen spectators watched from the benches, entertained by the informal sparring contests taking place below them.

Into the arena strode Qivir, flanked by Michael and Laird. Their entrance caused one dwarf who was in the middle of a dagger match with a human to lose his concentration. The dwarf wondered what had brought Laird, a warrior who surely was not in need of practice, to this place. The human lunged and drew blood, ending the contest.

Qivir and Michael watched the mock battles taking place around them, the minister explaining to the youngster the finer points of some of the matches. Laird looked idly around, bored by it all.

A couple of minutes later, the king entered the arena. He halted and looked around, obviously interested in the contests. Some of the contestants interrupted their sport briefly in order to bow to the king. Qivir began to walk towards his liege, saying gruffly to his companions: "Stay here. I need to talk to the king alone for a moment."

He halted beside the monarch and began to speak quietly. "Your Majesty. I have arranged for the human child to face the warrior Laird in sword-to-sword combat."

"Laird? Surely not! Laird has never been bested in swordplay, and the human from Palindor is but a boy."

"Nevertheless, I think Your Majesty will see the wisdom of the match. But there is something else you should know." Now Qivir spoke even more quietly, in little more than a whisper. The king leant close to his minister to catch the words over the hubbub of the fighting around them. "It's about Laird, Your Majesty. I visited Naomin the Necromancer this morning. He has been watching Laird by means of his magic, and he tells me that Laird intends to try to kill you one day soon."

"Laird? Never!" The king shouted, quite audibly.

His attention caught by the sound of his name, the great warrior turned towards the king, who lowered his voice to complete his protest. "Laird is my greatest warrior. He is utterly loyal. He would never raise his hand against me."

As if he were deep in thought, Qivir's hand rose and rubbed the edge of his nose gently.

The effect was instantaneous. Laird unsheathed his sword, bellowed, "For Palindor!" and began to sprint toward the king, sword raised high.

Without stopping to think, Michael ran after him, drawing his own sword.

As he reached the king, Laird's sword came down in a mighty sweep. The king dodged to one side. There was the sound of ripping cloth, and a red stain began to spread where the king's tunic was torn.

Laird raised his arm for a second blow, then hesitated, confused by a voice behind him: "Stop and face me, you traitor!"

He turned to see the boy, sword held levelly in front of him, regarding him with menace in his eyes.

Michael said, "You would attack a man without warning? You coward!"

The taunt stung, and Laird now turned from the king and advanced on Michael.

With a whistle, the warrior's sword swung down, intending to sweep the boy's sword out of his hand. But the incredible happened. As Laird's sword hit Michael's weapon on its mighty downward sweep, instead of carrying Michael's sword before it, the latter remained level, as if supported by the strength of a hundred men. There was a mighty clang, and Laird's sword was stopped in its tracks.

The force of the impact caused a lancing pain to shoot up Laird's arm. He nearly lost his grip on his own sword. And then Laird watched his own death come to him.

Michael's eyes fixed on Laird's and Laird found himself watching, powerless to move, as oh-so-slowly, Michael turned his sword so that its tip faced Laird.

Laird watched Michael's swordtip coming closer. It moved past his own sword, then paused momentarily, pressing against his chain mail. The forged links shattered and split apart. The swordtip passed through his leather tunic; it broke his skin and passed into his body. Laird was filled with a detached powerlessness as life poured out of him. By the time that he crumpled to the ground, he was dead.

Michael withdrew the sword from the inert form at his feet and looked around for somewhere to wipe the blade clean. The king was shaking as the enormity of what had happened began to sink in.

Qivir said, "Did you hear what Laird said, Your Majesty? He shouted 'For Palindor!' before he struck you. But did I not tell you that the human boy would be a match for Laird? I tell you, Your Majesty, I have seen many warriors, but never have I seen anything like this boy. He is a warrior born like no other. With him in your service, you need fear no one, for there surely lives none who could defeat him in battle."

The king nodded vacantly, part of his mind still trying to absorb the events of the last few moments. Laird! Of all people, Laird! How could he have so misjudged the warrior? But he could not refute the evidence of his own senses. His mightiest warrior had attacked him in the hated name of Palindor, and within seconds had been slain by this mere slip of a boy who now stood before him.

"Clean up this mess!" he shouted to the warriors who had ceased their mock battles. "You and you" — he jabbed at Qivir and Michael — "come with me. We must talk."

The king turned and strode out of the arena, Qivir and Michael — blood still dripping from his sword — trotting after him to keep pace.

XI The Knights Return

It was the evening of the second day after Catherine and Sherna had left Carn Toldwyn. As usual before turning in for the night, Drefynt went into the forest near his cottage for a few minutes to be alone with his thoughts.

The evening was chillsome, and he was ready to go back inside earlier than usual. These past couple of days there had seemed little point to his evening strolls in the forest. With the departure of his friend and his daughter he had become unfocussed and dispirited. He felt old.

Even the work of translating the ancient book no longer held any attraction. It revealed too much; he found that he was no longer interested in knowledge of future events. The events would be painful enough without having to contemplate them beforehand.

And it was no good praying. Praying now just brought an enhanced sense of his aloneness. Somehow, everything seemed so futile, so pointless. He turned to make his way back to the house where he knew that Lorin waited dutifully with a mug of warm cocoa. A nearby sound suddenly attracted his attention.

He turned towards the sound, unsure what to expect — and completely unprepared for what he saw. Looking rather like a large dormouse, with a golden coat that positively shone in the light from the yellow star, a creature stood on its hind legs at the edge of the trees.

The two eyed one another for several seconds before Drefynt approached the newcomer. He looked the creature over for several seconds. For a moment, he wasn't sure. There was no indication of age about the creature's face with its quivering nose and black, twinkling eyes. But who else could it be?

"Drefynt, Gnome of Carn Toldwyn at your service."

"Of course you are. Did you think I wouldn't recognize you?"

Drefynt's smile became a grin. He had been right; this *was* the very same creature, known only as "the dablik," who had helped him escape from the catacombs during Catherine's last visit to Palindor.

The dablik wasted no time in preliminaries. "Now, Drefynt, I came all this way because I need your advice. What would you say if I told you that something strange is going on?"

"I would say, my friend, that we should go somewhere comfortable where we can discuss the matter. Would you come to my house, so we can talk in comfort?"

The dablik's nose twitched violently. "Inside? In a house in a town? No, no, you won't catch me indoors more than can be helped. It was bad enough in Entelred's cottage all those years ago, but at least that was in the forest. Can't we talk here?"

Drefynt sighed, the thought of warm cocoa receding. "Aye, if you wish it. But I must rest these weary legs of mine. Here, sit beside me." He lowered himself on to a small rock. The dablik trotted out from the shadows and dropped gently to the ground at his feet.

"Now, my golden-haired one, what exactly is the problem?"

"There is a High Monarch in Palindor, but he has gone missing...."

Drefynt sucked in his breath. The dablik had most definitely said "he," not "she."

"A High Monarch? You mean King Michael?"

"So it would seem. I have not seen him, you understand, but another has. A human boy was found, trapped on Penmichael Brea during a snowstorm. Only Olvensar knows how he could have got there; anyway, there is a hermit, Terafin by name, who lives in caves high on the side of the mountain. He was watching the storm from the safety of one of his tunnels when he saw a dark shape struggling through the snow. No sooner had he seen it than it slumped to the ground. Terafin hurried out and realized that it was a young boy, from the sounds of it about the same age as the High Queen Catherine was when she visited us.

"Anyway, Terafin dragged the boy into the nearest cave. The boy was terribly cold, and unconscious. Terafin managed to give him some warm smoothberry tea to drink, then put some blankets around the boy and went looking for me.

"As you know, there are tunnels almost everywhere in Palindor, and that's where I can usually be found. These past few decades I have made my home, such as it is, in the tunnels near Penmichael Brea. It happened that when Terafin found the boy I was journeying back from southern Palindor, so he couldn't find me. When he returned to the cave, the boy was gone. But his tracks were clear in the snow. And so were the tracks of another, who seems to have met up with him and then convinced him that they should travel together. The tracks followed the path down the mountain and into the forest, where Terafin lost them. Terafin was so agitated that he set out for Carn Toldwyn with the intention of telling the Ruling Council about the boy. He left me a note, though, and I caught up with him before he was halfway here."

"But you spoke of a High Monarch."

"Aye, I did. The hermit described the boy to me. He was attired strangely, but he carried a weapon, a scabbarded sword, on his belt."

"So?"

"From Terafin's description, it was the belt of the High King Michael. Terafin recognized it: that's why he needed to report the matter to the Ruling Council. He spoke of a metal buckle with strange markings, as if they were letters from the Old Days, and a dull red stone in the center."

Drefynt nodded. "Just like the High Queen's belt."

"Exactly."

"Then I have news for you, dablik. There is not one High Monarch abroad in Palindor, but two. The High Queen has returned."

The dablik's nose twitched in pleasure at this unexpected news. Drefynt quickly told him the story of Catherine's return, and explained the journey she had undertaken with Sherna.

At the end of the gnome's story, the dablik stood. "Then I should be going. We may not know what has become of the High King, but at least we know where one High Monarch is. I should follow her. I feel a shadow over the land, and I would never forgive myself if harm were to befall the High Queen. Goodbye, Drefynt. Until next time." So saying, the golden-haired creature disappeared into the forest.

With a weary groan, Drefynt got to his feet and went in search of his now-cold mug of cocoa.

Catherine and Sherna were in no particular hurry. They travelled carelessly through the forest, unmindful of how much noise they made or attention they attracted. While they walked they talked, finding much to share, Catherine telling of her adventures when she had fought Malthazzar and then travelled around the realm as its High Queen, Sherna telling tales of her journeys in distant lands. Each captivated the other, and their friendship quickly blossomed. Since they made no effort to hide, every hour or two they would encounter creatures travelling either singly or in small groups, with whom they would exchange cheery greetings and a few words of gossip. At night they would make a fire to warm themselves and to cook their food.

It was on the morning of the fourth day that Catherine began to feel uneasy. Several times she stopped and cocked an ear, listening for sounds that were out of place. As the morning wore on, she began to stop without warning and, turning around, she would scan the surrounding forest for telltale movement.

The third time she stopped, Sherna asked: "What is it, Catherine? Do you hear something?"

"No, not exactly. But I feel something, as if we're being watched. Haven't you noticed it?"

"No. But even here in the relative safety of Palindor it is well to trust one's instincts. We must be careful, and hope that whatever creature it is shows itself soon."

But that day neither Catherine nor Sherna caught sight of the creature, if indeed there was one.

It was nearly noon the following day when they reached the border of Dankenwood.

The two companions had already agreed that they would head for the dark wood and then travel around it. It was one of the few places that inspired fear in Sherna, and even Catherine had uncomfortable memories of it, although she was *almost* sure that Fayorn, the ugly master of the place, would permit them passage if they were to find themselves in the wood.

But when they reached the border of Dankenwood, they were surprised. For although the boundary between the greenery of the Palindor forest and the darkness of the wood was still clear, on the far side a change was taking place. Amongst the bleak darkness of the trees, patches of green were showing as shoots sprouted forth. The companions halted at the edge of the wood, unsure now whether they should skirt around it as planned, or whether they should simply go ahead into the wood. Even as they watched, a small mouse ran from the forest across the invisible line and into the wood. They both saw it, and looked at one another in wonderment.

"That would never have happened before," said Catherine.

"No. It's as if Dankenwood has been released from its enchantment."

"I wonder then if Fayorn is still master here?"

"I don't know. But perhaps it would be safe to enter. Certainly it would be faster than having to go around."

"Then let's try, and if Fayorn shows himself, I'll ask him what has brought about this change."

Taking a deep breath, they crossed the line into the wood.

Although the trees were still black, the ground underfoot was moist, and Catherine remembered clearly that last time she was in this place even the rain could not penetrate the darkness of Dankenwood. Now it was obvious that it had rained recently. The sounds of the forest to which they had become accustomed continued more or less unabated as small animals scurried through the greening undergrowth.

They reached the hovel in the middle of the afternoon.

Catherine's concern at entering Dankenwood had disappeared, to be replaced by an increasing certainty that they were being followed.

As they entered the clearing and saw the ramshackle building, she wanted to ignore the hovel and keep going.

But Sherna's curiosity got the better of her. "Surely this must be Fayorn's abode? For no one else calls Dankenwood home. We can at least see if he's in. I've always wondered what he's like. One hears stories, of course, but one never knows what to believe."

Catherine was vacillating, torn between seeing the old master of Dankenwood again and trying to shake off their pursuer. Suddenly the sound of hoofbeats came from the wood behind them: horses, several of them, not far distant and coming closer by the moment.

There was a movement at the corner of her eye, and Catherine turned just in time to see a gray blur disappearing into the shadows. A knot formed in her stomach. The hoofbeats came nearer.

"Quick! Into the cottage," shouted Sherna.

They started to run. But the horses were too quick. Sherna and Catherine had covered barely half the distance to the hovel before the horsemen burst into the clearing. Catherine turned — and was gripped by terror. Transfixed, she watched as three black horsemen drew their equally black steeds to a halt. Led by a halter, a fourth horse, riderless, pawed the ground.

Sherna did not turn around until she reached the safety of the brokendown building. She pushed the door open and tumbled inside. Only then did she realize that Catherine was not with her. She turned to watch, aghast at the scene that unfolded in the clearing.

One of the horsemen detached himself from the other two and walked his horse slowly forward until it stood only an arm's length from Catherine. The grim, black horseman looked down at the High Queen.

Catherine returned the horseman's gaze, awaiting his next move. Slowly, he drew his sword from its scabbard, exposing a black blade that, instead of glinting in the late autumnal light, swallowed the light as if it had never existed: the sword was a darker and more pitiless black than even the horseman himself.

Catherine's hand moved toward Scalmyùt, but then she remembered Olvensar's words: "A true monarch is one who knows how to refrain from using his sword in anger or fear." She rested her hand Scalmyùt's hilt, but she did not draw the weapon.

The horseman spoke. "We met once before, human, long ago. This time your belt cannot protect you. You are mine to do with as I wish. You are in my power."

The words, though spoken quietly, nevertheless rang ominously around the clearing. The other horses shuffled a step or two closer, then silence fell. For several seconds there was neither sound nor movement. The horseman and the human looked into each other's eyes, as if each were trying to read the contents of the other's soul. At last the horseman looked away. Then, with a wordless cry, he threw his sword like a dagger into the ground at Catherine's feet.

It buried itself a hand's breadth or more into the dark soil, quivering. Catherine's eyes did not move away from the terrible visage of the Dark Knight. Her emotions were in turmoil: fear, anger and despair vying for supremacy. But still she did not draw Scalmyùt.

The sword stopped quivering. Then, almost imperceptibly, a dark cloud began to form about the blade, as if the ground were on fire where the sword had penetrated it. Swiftly, the cloud spread. It engulfed the sword, and continued to expand. It swept over Catherine, then the horse on which the Dark Knight sat, then the Knight himself. It engulfed the remaining horsemen, then, at last, inches from the hovel's door, it stopped.

Inside, Sherna watched, terrified. A ripple passed through the cloud, as if a slight breeze had sprung up, though no natural breeze could ever have any effect on this cloud. From the edge of the wood a figure in a gray habit appeared briefly, then entered the cloud. A shudder seemed to pass through the unnatural miasma. Then it began to dissipate. A minute later it was if the cloud had never existed.

Sherna opened the door of the hovel and stepped outside. Somewhere a bird was singing. Sunlight streamed down into the clearing. But of the horsemen and the High Queen there was no longer any trace.

XII Audience with a King

Sherna did not know what to do. She spent a futile half hour searching the clearing and the surrounding wood for some trace of Catherine. But apart from a small patch of burned ground where the blade of the Dark Knight's sword had buried itself there was no sign that anything untoward had ever happened in the forest glade.

She called out loudly, first to Catherine, and then merely to attract attention, in the hope that the owner of the hovel would show himself; but in both hopes she was disappointed. As dusk fell, she returned to the building to spend the night there. Inside was the carcass of a deer, inexplicably left in the very center of the larger of the building's two rooms. From it came a nose-wrinkling smell, but she wasn't strong enough to drag the dead animal outside. So she spent the night miserable, alone, and frightened in the the hovel's kitchen, distancing herself as much as possible from the rank odor of the deer's carcass.

Morning came. After one last fruitless search for Catherine, Sherna wearily pulled on her pack, left the clearing, and headed out of Dankenwood towards the Plains of Kradesh.

She crossed into Reglandor early the following morning. The creatures she met on the road eyed her with the same distrust that she had experienced the last time she was in Reglandor. She made a point of greeting them all politely with as much of a smile as she could muster under the circumstances.

And so it was that she dropped into the Dale of Carmadden, in which Pirren Glanwyn lies. She could see the royal flags flying atop the palace from many miles away. The palace's golden sheen reflected the low, wintry sun. It was altogether far grander and more impressive than Dynas Carn Toldwyn. She could not help thinking that Reglandor was far better prepared for war than was her own land.

It was late evening when she approached the great southern gate of Pirren Glanwyn. The gate was already closed for the night, so she joined a small encampment of dwarves and humans who had arrived too late to enter the city.

It was an uncharacteristically mild evening for the time of year, and the group was unusually good-natured and gregarious. They built a tall bonfire to roast the food that the creatures were carrying. Then, afterwards, there was story-telling and singing galore.

About half the travellers were from Reglandor; most of the rest were from Soltarwyn, but some came from as far away as Valguard. Sherna was the only gnome, and the only creature from Palindor. Despite the evident harmlessness of the others, she was cautious, placing her bedroll on the outermost edge of the encampment. She passed an uneasy night in which flickering campfire flames spewed forth dark clouds in her dreams, swallowing her and carrying her to dungeons in distant castles.

The great gate opened with the sunrise and, after a quick breakfast, Sherna gathered her things and entered Pirren Glanwyn.

The capital of Reglandor was quite unlike her own Carn Toldwyn. Pirren Glanwyn, of course, was considerably older, and had been settled long before Palindor even came into existence. In Carn Toldwyn, the streets were relatively wide, and houses far apart. The edges of the town were somewhat blurred, as scattered houses could be found quite some distance into the surrounding countryside. Here things were quite different. Long ago, a wall had been built around the city. This effectively precluded growth beyond a certain size, so that houses here were smaller and closely spaced. The streets were narrower and straighter. The main streets were laid out like a four-spoked wheel, each connecting a main gate to the central hub of the city, which was the palace of the king of Reglandor.

Having entered at the southern gate, Sherna walked northwards along the southmost spoke. The palace, perched on its small hill, dominated the view before her. Pirren Glanwyn was much busier than Carn Toldwyn: in Carn Toldwyn one could barely walk a hundred paces without coming across two creatures who had stopped to pass the time of day with one another; in Pirren Glanwyn, creatures seemed to be hurrying everywhere, as if everyone was late for an appointment.

And the noise: hurrying footsteps; carts being pushed and pulled through the narrow streets; warning shouts as creatures hurriedly turned corners; all these and more echoed off the tall stone buildings that abutted the streets. Just short of the palace, Sherna passed close by an open-air market in which each trader tried desperately to outdo his neighbor in volume, trying to attract passersby to his goods.

When Sherna entered the palace courtyard, the relative quiet was almost palpable. The large, open area gave sound an opportunity to escape, and she was relieved to be free of the feeling that the buildings that lined the streets were about to fall on her. But the courtyard was hardly deserted: even at this early hour, several ranks of soldiers were exercising. She crossed the courtyard and entered the palace, where a small, unhappy-looking elf took her name and asked her business.

This was the tricky part, and Sherna was careful to keep the anxiety she felt off her face as she said boldly: "My name is Sherna, gnome of Carn Toldwyn of Palindor. I am here to see the king on matters of state."

The elf cast his eyes dubiously over her travel-stained clothes. "Is he expecting you, gnome? I see no record here of an appointment."

"No. But he has sent his personal emissary to Carn Toldwyn, and I am here to present the king with news regarding that emissary."

The elf dutifully scribed some words on a sheet of parchment. He handed it to a dwarvish guard, saying, "This is for the king." As the dwarf left, the elf addressed Sherna: "If you would take a seat, I have informed the king of your presence."

Sherna entered a nearby waiting room. Benches lined the wall. Two dwarves were on one bench, eyeing with distrust the three humans who occupied another. Both groups talked amongst themselves in low tones. Sherna uncomfortably occupied a seat between the two groups. As she listened to their conversations, she understood that they were awaiting their turn in court. As far as she could tell, a land dispute had arisen between the dwarves and the humans, and their case was to go before a judge this morning.

Her thoughts were interrupted by the elf entering the room. "Gnome, the king will see you at noon. Until then you are free to leave and to avail yourself of the sights of Pirren Glanwyn."

Sherna thanked the elf and left the waiting room, glad to escape the sullenly opposed parties inside.

She passed the morning wandering around the back streets of the city not far from the palace. Here the streets were even more narrow and the buildings even more tightly packed than along the main thoroughfares. But the streets were also less busy, and she passed relatively few creatures as she wandered the streets and alleyways. The buildings were dirtier and poorer than those she had passed earlier. Several times she saw children, dwarvish and human, playing in the streets, although they should have been in school. It was unheard of in Palindor for a young creature's parents to allow it to take unnecessary time off from school, but such seemed to be a relatively common occurrence, at least in these parts of Pirren Glanwyn.

The immense bell high on the palace tolled half past eleven, and she made her way back through the courtyard — emptier now than it had been earlier — and back into the palace, where the elf still sat at his desk receiving visitors.

He looked up and half-smiled at Sherna. "Ah yes; the gnome from Palindor. If you would wait a moment." He ring a small bell, and a young human dressed in a uniform of green and black appeared. "This is the gnome from Palindor. She has an appointment to see the king at noon."

The newcomer, no more than a child, bowed deferentially to Sherna. "Follow me, please." He turned and led the way past the elf's desk and into the interior of the palace.

Sherna followed him down innumerable corridors. She could not help but contrast this palace with Dynas Carn Toldwyn. There could be no doubting that this building was the center of an ancient, large and warlike empire. Suits of armor vied for places along the wall with paintings depicting battles from Reglandor's past. Huge, sumptuous banners of gold and purple, the triumphal banners presented to now-dead generals, hung between the pictures. Despite herself, Sherna could not help shivering as the immense strength of Reglandor impressed itself upon her.

She began to worry about her mission. What if the king refused to be appeased? What if he decided that the only acceptable justice was the complete subjugation of Palindor? There was no doubt that the peaceful creatures of Palindor would be quickly overwhelmed if Reglandor invaded. She began to feel an uncomfortable tingle of fear in the pit of her stomach.

They halted in front of an ornate elm door. The page pushed it open. "You may enter and wait here. The king's court is through the door on the far side of this antechamber. You will be called when His Majesty is ready for you." With a bow, he pushed the door open for Sherna. She entered, and the human closed the door noiselessly, leaving her alone with her thoughts.

The anteroom was rather small. The walls were decorated with paintings accomplished with considerable skill. Unlike the battle paintings in the corridors, these were images of landscapes, each showing some locality in Reglandor.

She wandered along the walls. Some of the pictures she recognized as places she had visited. Here was the great and mysterious Statue of Reglan, deep in the Reglandor forest; here the mighty Vivverview Falls, whose neverending thunder caused one to shield one's ears when still a thousand paces distant; here the gentle countryside of Mildred Meadows, scene of one of the bloodiest battles in the entire history of the Three Lands.

She halted in front of the next picture, and her stomach sank. She was looking out over the sea from the top of tall, granite cliffs. In the distance she could just make out a shimmering gray whiteness of cloud hanging over islands out of sight below the horizon. The grass in the foreground was a bright, almost iridescent green. She was looking at the view westward from Perendeth.

The far door, a mighty affair of heavy, solid oak, swung open silently, and a short, long-haired human entered the room.

"Good day. My name is Qivir. I am His Majesty's chief minister. And you are?"

Sherna tore herself away from the picture. "Sherna. Gnome of Carn Toldwyn, in Palindor."

"Ah, yes. You have news of His Majesty's emissary and his party. The king will be glad to hear of it: he has been worried. You may leave your pack here. I am sure that I need not remind you to show due deference to our king."

"Indeed not; I shall honor him as if he were king of my own land."

As Sherna removed the sealed parchment from her pack, she heard the human say something under his breath. She was almost certain that what he said was: "But he is, my dear."

Swallowing hard several times, she steeled herself for what was to come, then followed the minister into the next room.

There were only the three of them in the room: Sherna, nervous, fidgeting, bowing low before the king; the chief minister, taking the one remaining seat in the room, below the king's throne; and the king himself.

King Glendour IV wore a crown, a simple affair of intertwined gold filigree with a single square, iridescent green stone set in the center. Robes covered his clothes. The robes were spacious and deep maroon, with gold and silver trimmings that glistened brightly as they reflected the light from tall candles that sat on small ledges protruding from the walls.

The room was windowless and quite small, almost cozy, and the feeling of snug comfortableness was accentuated by the large multicolored tapestries which hung from almost every inch of wall.

The king inclined his head towards his visitor. "You may rise."

The gnome straightened herself. "Sherna, gnome of Carn Toldwyn of Palindor. I greet Your Highness in the name of the Ruling Council of Palindor. I bring you this missive, sealed by the great seal of Palindor. If I may approach the throne?"

The king nodded his permission, and she stepped forward and extended the rolled parchment. The king took it from her without touching her hand, and she returned to her place, careful not to insult the king by turning her back on him.

"I will read this with much interest. But can you tell me first what it says?"

Sherna shook her head. "I am only a messenger, Your Majesty, and the message I bring is in your hands."

"I see."

The king examined the seal, then passed it to Qivir for his minister to examine. Qivir nodded his agreement that the seal appeared genuine. The king ripped the seal and unfurled the parchment.

It was then that the unthinkable happened.

Slowly and deliberately, Qivir stood and turned towards the king, whose concentration was entirely on the parchment. The minister took one step, so that he was standing over the monarch. His cloak swirled around, shielding his actions from Sherna's gaze. All she could see was the sudden look of shock which froze on the king's face.

Qivir's arm made a series of short stabbing motions. He stepped back, and the king, eyes wide in death, fell forward. As the minister turned to face her, Sherna could see the dagger in his hand, blood dripping from the dagger's edge to the floor. With his free hand, Qivir pulled a bell pull from behind a tapestry. He tugged at the cord. No sound was audible, but somewhere surely an alarm was ringing. Sherna looked around desperately for something to use as a weapon against the madman. There was nothing.

Qivir lifted the dagger and buried it high in his own shoulder. A brief fountain of blood erupted, then subsided as a dark stain spread rapidly across his tunic and cloak.

All this was the work of seconds, and Sherna was still transfixed when she heard the sound of running feet. The minister stepped forward, then threw himself at her feet, crying out. She looked down at Qivir. The dagger still protruded uglily from his left shoulder.

The door burst open.

She turned. A young human male stood in the doorway, a wild look on his face and a sword glinting menacingly in his hand. But it was neither of these things that caught Sherna's attention; rather, it was the young man's belt. Even in the single moment allotted to her, she recognized it as almost the twin of the one that Catherine had worn, the only difference being that where the stone in Catherine's belt was white, this one was a dull, brooding, blood red.

At her feet, Qivir gasped, "The gnome. From Palindor. She did it. She killed the king!"

She had no time to protest. The human looked at where the king lay, dead, slumped on the floor in front of the throne, staring blindly at the ceiling. The human drew back his sword. With a roar he fell on Sherna.

XIII Anderskerrin

To the north of Reglandor lies the land of Soltarwyn. Soltarwyn is a land of rolling hills and meadows, in the center of which is the Fire Mountain. Most of the inhabitants of Soltarwyn live in cottages scattered across the land. A short distance south of the Fire Mountain is a cluster of pretty little cottages, two of which were occupied at this time by the dwarf Gondalwyn and his wife Isaderna, and by the fisherelf Anderskerrin and his wife Hervân.

Gondalwyn's story is told in the book *Palindor*. At that time he was a young apprentice to a wizard. After the events related in that book, and after a long period of wandering throughout Palindor, he eventually married and settled in Soltarwyn, accompanied by his young friend, the bookish fisherelf Anderskerrin from the village of Penclaw in northeastern Palindor*.

At this time, Anderskerrin was troubled. For two weeks his sleep had been disturbed by the same dream each night. Unable to interpret the dream, he sought help from his wise old friend, who was one of the few creatures in the Three Lands who had ever spoken with Olvensar face to face. So late one afternoon Anderskerrin made his way through the tall apple trees, the late autumn fruit still weighing the boughs, to Gondalwyn's cottage.

---

* The story of how this happened is related in Anderskerrin's memoirs.

The dwarf was old now, and spent most of his days on his little wooden porch, rocking in a chair that Anderskerrin had made for him, eyeing the Fire Mountain and smoking a pipe. His wife, Isaderna, several decades younger than her husband, still busied herself about the house, determined to keep it as dust-free and comfortable as the homes of any of the busy elves in the neighborhood.

This particular day was overcast and cool. Winter was not not far away, and Gondalwyn had vacated his usual place on the porch in favor of a comfortable chair in front of the fire. As always, the room looked immaculate. Gondalwyn's old battle-axe hung proudly on the wall, gleaming brightly in the flickering light from the fire in the grate*. Gondalwyn was snoozing gently. Anderskerrin was loath to wake his friend, but Isaderna had no such reluctance. She gently poked her husband, and as he harrumphed himself awake she said: "Mind your manners, Gondalwyn. You have a visitor."

Turning to Anderskerrin, she said, "I'll get some tea and fresh buttered scones, and you have your talk with sleepyhead here."

Though Gondalwyn was old, little escaped him and he was the first to speak. "You look tired, my friend."

"I am. My sleep is disturbed every night by the same dream."

"Interesting. Tell me about it."

"It begins with the palace of Reglandor. Then I see creatures fighting, and in the end I wake up. That's all there is, really."

"And how long has this been going on?"

"A couple of weeks now."

"I see. And what do you intend doing about it?"

"I don't know. I'm wondering if it's a sign."

"From Olvensar?"

Anderskerrin nodded. "Yes. I'm wondering if Olvensar is telling me that I need to go to Pirren Glanwyn. But maybe I'm imagining it. I can't tell Hervân that I think we need to go to Pirren Glanwyn on nothing more than a whim. So how can I be sure?"

---

* This battle-axe had originally belonged to the dwarf Tarandron, as related in *Palindor*; the story of how it had passed to Gondalwyn is told in Anderskerrin's memoirs. The axe, Tewlladher by name, was forged by Samuel Ironhand, and was enchanted by the power of kiriàl.

"Well, there's lots of ways, I think. You could ask him to send you a sign. That sometimes works."

"But what sort of sign?"

"Something that is unlikely to happen all by itself. Say... if the Fire Mountain were to spit fire like it did in the Old Days; now that would be quite a sign."

"Could Olvensar do something like that?"

Gondalwyn leaned back in his chair and laughed out loud. His wife entered the room carrying the tea things: a fresh pot of tea, mugs for her husband and his visitor, and a plate full of scones smeared with cream and fresh strawberry jam. She placed the tray on the table beside Gondalwyn's chair.

"And what's so funny, pray?" she asked her husband.

"Oh, this young rascal was just asking me if Olvensar could make the Fire Mountain spit fire."

"Well, I don't know. Could he?"

Gondalwyn shook his head in amusement, then raised his eyes, which were watery with almost-tears. "Oh, Olvensar. They never understand, do they?" Turning to the others, he said, "Olvensar isn't just the High Lord of Palindor, you know. It's true that it's only in Palindor that he is recognized for what he is, but that doesn't mean he has no power elsewhere. Why, if he wanted, he could flatten the very Mountains of Mourn themselves. So of course he could make the Fire Mountain spit if he wanted. Why, he could lift the whole thing in the air if it suited his purpose."

Silence greeted this speech. If it were not for the fact that Gondalwyn had personally met the High Lord in his youth, they would have dismissed his words as mere myth. But coming from the lips of the old dwarf, they had to believe what he said.

"Well, no more of this serious talk," said Isaderna. "The tea and scones will get cold. Now, eat up."

All thoughts of dreams and Fire Mountains were dismissed as they set about demolishing the food and drink. It was in a happier frame of mind (and with a fuller stomach) that the elf made his way back to his cottage an hour later.

That evening after supper (somewhat curtailed because of the late tea), he stood outside looking at the clouds overhead. Quietly, he said. "Olvensar; I don't know what to do. If I'm supposed to go to Reglandor, please give me a sign from the Fire Mountain."

That night, his sleep was deep and uninterrupted.

The following day dawned gray and cloudy. A fine drizzle fell from a clinging mist all day. It was only as darkness came that the clouds began to lift.

"Come look at this!" Hervân shouted from the kitchen where she was making an apple pie. "It's beautiful!"

Anderskerrin hurried into the kitchen. Hervân was staring out the window at the Fire Mountain. Her face reflected a radiant orange-red glow. The sky was aflame, as if the clouds were the embers of a dying fire. After a moment he realized what had happened: the peak of the Fire Mountain was aglow, and the clouds were reflecting its light.

He laid his hands on his wife's shoulders and said, "Come with me into the living room. I have something to tell you."

He had to laugh about it afterwards. It was just so typical of the way in which Olvensar seemed to work. There he was, unsure of his dream, demanding signs, worrying about how his wife would react to the idea that he was to embark on a journey to a strange and warlike land, when all the time she had been having the same dream and wondering how to tell her husband that she thought something was telling her she should travel to Pirren Glanwyn. All this time, all he had had to do was to ask his wife; instead of which, he had demanded signs from the High Lord.

So there was no debate. On the morrow they would set out for Pirren Glanwyn. They went outside, held each other tightly, and together gazed at the glow in the sky.

XIV Sheol

Catherine's heart was beating wildly, and she could taste the fear in her mouth; but she was determined that it would not show on her face. She watched, refusing to turn away, as the Dark Knight approached. The last time they had faced one another, she had defeated him — or, rather, the power of the belt encircling her waist had defeated him — and she was determined that she would not be beaten this time either.

The Dark Knight lifted his sword high. He threw it. The sword shot through the air and buried itself several inches into the ground at Catherine's feet. A dark vapor, blacker than the darkest smoke, began to rise from the spot where the sword had landed. In moments, it enveloped Catherine. She could see nothing save the swirling blackness. The smoke was acrid with the smell of burning sulphur. She coughed on the dark, clinging mist.

The smoke began to dissipate, revealing a garish scene utterly unlike the clearing in which she had been standing.

The smoke was cleared by a hot, humid breeze that carried the smell of brimstone. The sky above was dark, as if it were a starless night; where the sky was not black, it was red: lit by an enormous glowing disk that looked like a terrible parody of the sun. Around her, instead of the trees of Dankenwood, were black boulders that reflected the redness of the sky and the glowing light of puddles of an orange liquid that smoked evilly.

For a moment, she thought she saw a gray figure moving not far away; but then it was gone, hidden behind a boulder. Before her was a Dark Knight astride his horse. Behind him were two other Knights on their horses. As in the clearing in Dankenwood, a fourth horse was riderless, tethered to one of the others. With an unnerving grace, the nearest Knight slid out of his saddle, stooped before Catherine, and retrieved his sword, whose point was buried in the cindery gravel at her feet.

He said, "You have a sword. Why do you not use it?"

It was true. Surely Scalmyùt would be more than a match for the Dark Knight's sword? Her hand moved to Scalmyùt's hilt.

But even as she began to draw the sword, she knew that for some reason this was exactly what the Dark Knight wanted. She pushed the sword back into its scabbard. Scalmyùt's power was for the last time she was in Palindor. Now she knew better: might is a last resort, and only the weak resort to force without exhausting all alternatives. And she was a crowned High Monarch of Palindor. No one could accuse her of being weak. Under her breath, she swore an oath: "In the name of the High Lord Olvensar, I will never draw my sword in anger."

"You are afraid?" The Dark Knight laughed: a rasping, hollow sound that dripped cruelty. He offered her the hilt of his sword. "You are afraid that I and my sword would be more than a match for you? Then take my weapon. Take it and kill me. I tell you now, it is the only chance you will have to see your beloved Palindor ever again."

For a moment, fear gripped Catherine. What if the Knight spoke the truth? But she reminded herself that this was a Dark Knight. Why should she trust anything he said?

He waved his arm in an expansive gesture. "Look around you."

She did so, and the awful horror of the place began to impact itself more fully on her senses. They were standing atop a slight hill. In all directions, the ground fell away into shallow valleys, on the far side of which were hills similar to the one on which they stood. The alternation of hill and valley continued in all directions as far as she could see. In all that vast scene, there were no buildings.

The landscape was dominated by boulders and rocks, interspersed with fiery pools. Here and there were dark, stunted, deformed trees, each one growing in lonely isolation, none much taller than the Knight who stood before her. The air was hot and sticky with a wetness born of some substance other than water, and it burned and caught at the back of her throat.

The Knight's sword was still extended toward her. "I offer you my sword. Here. Take it. Kill me if you dare. I will offer no resistance. I too would like to be free of this place. And to kill me is your only escape. If you do not kill me now, you will remain here for ever."

Catherine's gaze returned to the Knight. Even standing this close, it was impossible to discern his features. Could the Knight be telling the truth, or was this just a trick of some kind?

She shook her head. Killing was no way to escape. She tried to make her voice strong, but it came out squeaky and weak. "No. I will not kill you."

The Knight considered her for a moment, then sheathed his sword. "Then you will come with us. The time will come when you will remember what you have just done, and know that you have none to blame but yourself for what has happened."

He remounted his horse. The riderless horse was brought forward and Catherine climbed into its saddle. The leader of the Knights began to move off down the hillside. Catherine followed, the two other horsemen bringing up the rear.

Just for a moment, out of the corner of her eye, she glimpsed a fleeting gray movement. Then it was gone.

She lost track of time. Her throat became parched and her stomach tightened with emptiness, but after a while these things grew no worse and ceased to bother her overmuch. The glowing red disk moved slowly across the sky, then dipped towards the horizon. Red-brown clouds seemed to form out of nothingness, and preternatural, silent lightning flashed among them, lighting the dark, scarred landscape that, no matter how long they rode, seemed always the same.

The red disk dropped below the horizon and the sky became darker. The storm ended and now the only light came from the orange-red pools. Catherine's horse accidentally stepped in a small pool, and the liquid splashed on to her leg. It stung, although whether from heat or cold she could not tell.

At length the red disk arose on the opposite side of the sky. The sky became a little lighter again. The disk crossed the sky, which darkened again when the disk fell below the horizon. And always there was the gnawing hunger and the parched thirst. It never seemed to get worse, though, remaining merely an unpleasant moment-by-moment reminder of her discomfort.

Very occasionally, she would see movement. Once, she saw something move on the ground in the far distance. But she saw it only for a moment as they crested a hill. Overhead, they were accompanied for many hours by what passed for birds, although they must have been truly gigantic. They wheeled in silence high above the riders for a while. Eventually, they took flight and disappeared into the distance far ahead of the riders.

So passed two full days in the saddle. And in all that time, no one spoke.

Catherine was wondering if the journey would ever end when they crested a rise and the other riders reined their horses to a halt. Her horse stopped, and she looked down into a valley.

The valley floor was filled with a vast lake of the orange-red liquid. The stench that rose from it was almost visible. It caught at her throat, and she spluttered as she tried not to gag. In the middle of the lake was an island, and on the island a castle.

Like almost everything else in this terrible place, the castle was black, and rose from the lake like an immense basaltic carving. From one turret a large flag flew, black with a maroon border. Its fluttering was disconcerting, for at ground level the air was still and heavy. The leader of the Knights urged his horse forward and, without waiting for instructions, the others did likewise.

They meandered down a steep path, pebbles scuttering away under the horses' hooves, until they reached a finger of land that jutted out into the lake. A short causeway linked them to the island on which the castle stood. They began to cross the causeway. Catherine wondered who could be master of this place; who could bear to live in such terrible and awful surroundings?

They reached the main gate, which was blocked by a portcullis that rose ponderously as they approached. She saw no gatekeeper. They passed into a courtyard, and, finally, they halted.

One by one, the Dark Knights dismounted. They did not speak; they merely held the reins of their horses, apparently waiting for someone or something. Catherine slid off her horse, relieved to be out of the saddle. As she touched the ground, a sound came from the immense door of the castle. She turned to look and, involuntarily, she gasped.

The Dark Knights lowered their heads in subservience.

The Master had come.

XV Into Reglandor

Anderskerrin and Hervân climbed out of the valley in which their cottage lay, surrounded by orchards still laden with late-autumn fruit. As they climbed, the Fire Mountain seemed to grow taller behind them, until it stood clear and stark beyond the orchards. The peak of the mountain no longer glowed as it had last night; now there was just the usual plume of smoke rising from the mountain.

"I wonder if we'll ever come back," said Anderskerrin.

"You silly elf. We're just going to Pirren Glanwyn. And Reglandor is not at war with anyone, least of all Soltarwyn. Of course we'll come home again. Now, let's get on, or the first snow will find us on the road instead of snug in Pirren Glanwyn."

With a sigh, Anderskerrin turned away from the Fire Mountain. Hand in hand, husband and wife disappeared over the brow of the hill.

They journeyed for three days without misadventure, making a steady twenty five thousand paces each day. On the afternoon of the third day they reached the River Carbis, which marks the boundary between Soltarwyn and Reglandor. In the old days, this border had been jealously guarded, but now as they approached the bridge that crossed the low waters, there were no signs of guards or soldiers on the Soltarwyn side.

There were plenty of fellow travellers, though. On this particular day, most of the traffic was going in the same direction as Anderskerrin and Hervân, from Soltarwyn into Reglandor.

Most of the travellers were farmers accompanied by strong carthorses pulling carts filled with ripe produce. Soltarwyn is the most fertile of the Three Lands, and the farmers were taking their wares to the vast market at Pirren Glanwyn where they could hope to get the best prices.

The farmers were in a hurry. They knew that the sooner they arrived in Pirren Glanwyn, the better the price they could expect. So carts frequently trundled past the two elves, their wheels making the ground shake, the farmers nodding politely and moving ahead without slowing to exchange more than brief greetings.

Anderskerrin and Hervân crossed the bridge over the Carbis and passed into Reglandor.

Unlike the Soltarwyn side, the south bank of the river was guarded by a pair of warlike dwarves. Never before had the elves seen dwarves dressed for battle — although, truth to tell, these two were poor examples of the species — and they were alarmed at the sight.

The dwarves seemed to be doing nothing more than watching the trickle of creatures flowing into Reglandor. Wordlessly, the elves passed under their gazes. Anderskerrin was more than a little fearful; he could not escape the worrying thought that had these dwarves desired to kill them, there was nothing he could have done to stop them. They passed the guards as quickly as they could, and followed the road around a bend.

They had assumed that the guards had been posted for a special reason, but they talked to the next farmer who overtook them, and he told them that there were always guards on the south side of the bridge. "Better get used to seeing armor," the farmer said. "You're in Reglandor now. There'll be a lot of it." Then he hurried forward, anxious to reach Pirren Glanwyn as soon as possible.

"Gondalwyn told me that Reglandor used to be called the Land of War," Anderskerrin said tp Hervân. "It was the first of the Three Lands, and still believes itself to be superior to the other two."

There were houses hidden amongst the trees, and their construction made it obvious that Reglandor was a warrior's land. The houses were far sturdier than anything in Soltarwyn. Most of them were built of stone, and looked as if they could withstand an attack by a small army.

As dusk began to fall, the elves saw that something was happening on the road ahead. They made their way towards the disturbance and, turning a corner, found themselves on the edge of an encampment. Many of the farmers who had passed them in the previous hour were camped together at a wide point in the road. There were several fires over which meals were being cooked. The smells of fruit and vegetables cooking mingled deliciously. Not far away, half a dozen farmers were singing folk songs.

A farmer lifted a flagon of ale in greeting.

"Is this a camp for the night?" Anderskerrin asked.

"Aye; it be a protection camp," the man replied. His accent betrayed him as an uneducated farmer from northeastern Soltarwyn. "We be in Reglandor now, and north Reglandor be a right proper place for thieves. If any of us'n made camp alone, we'd find our goods and our horse gone be mornin'. Even supposing that us'n throats not be slit."

Hervân and Anderskerrin grabbed one another tightly.

"Oh, be not afeared! They won't attack us while we're in a group like this. That be why we camp together. And the road be too busy during the day, so there be nothing to worry about then. Anyway, you two don't look like you have anything worthy of stealing, so there bain't really anything for 'ee to worry about. Here, come and set your packs down. Then let's us'n go over and join they over there; they look like they be havin' a rollicking good time, even if they cain't hold a tune between 'em."

So the two elves found themselves as guests of the protection encampment. They were given samples of many different kinds of hot soup, each farmer anxious to know how his soup compared to the others'. Anderskerrin and Hervân happily joined in the game. Anderskerrin would say, a serious look on his face, "Oh, I don't think your soup is quite as good as Farmer Milthwaite's. His potatoes seemed especially tasty."

Then his wife would rebut him, poking him in the ribs. "Get on with you, you no-good elf. What do you know about it? I'm the one who spends all her time in the kitchen. And I'm telling

113

you, and good farmer Trent here, that his broccoli makes this soup taste better than anything I've tasted before or ever hope to taste again."

"Broccoli? Aye, well, maybe you're right. Perhaps Farmer Trent could spare some more for me to sample."

"And perhaps I missed the flavor of farmer Milthwaite's potatoes. Do you think I could possibly have another taste?"

And so, with no firm decision made about which farmer's victuals tasted best, Anderskerrin and Hervân retired to their bedrolls, which were drawn out on the soft wayside, pleasantly filled with the good, warming soups of the farmers.

They were woken early the next morning as Farmer Trent, who had been the one who first spoke with them, shook them awake. Anderskerrin groaned lazily.

"Just wanted to waken you up," said Farmer Trent. "We be aleaving now. Want to try to make Pirren Glanwyn by nightfall, but it be a long day's walk, and we'll be lucky to make it by the looks of the weather that be coming in. Anyway, just wanted to be saying goodbye to 'ee."

Anderskerrin looked around. Several of the farmers had already moved out, and those that remained had already reined their horses and would be gone in another minute or two. Farmer Trent's horse was uneasily stomping its feet, already hitched to its cart and anxious to get a start on the long day. The horse's breath formed visible clouds in the chill air.

The two elves said their goodbyes to Farmer Trent. Farmer Milthwaite had already left, but they shouted farewells to the other farmers and, in a very few minutes, there remained just the two of them standing by the side of the road.

They packed up their bedrolls. The day was much colder than yesterday, and low clouds threatened snow. After the enormous supper of last night, neither of them minded missing breakfast. Although neither of them said it, they both had the same hope: to catch up with the farmers and to spend another evening in their company.

But as they adjusted one another's packs for comfort, the first flakes of snow fell.

"Doesn't look good," said Hervân, looking up at the clouds, which were looming lower and becoming grayer with each passing minute.

They set off, but before they had gone a thousand paces the snowfall had become a blizzard.

The snow stuck to the cold ground, and it was no more than a very few minutes before the two elves agreed that they would have to stop to seek shelter from the storm. They had not passed a house yet that morning, so they sought shelter amongst the trees that grew by the side of the road.

There they stayed, watching the storm, waiting for it to pass. The blizzard lasted all morning and part of the afternoon. Then, around the middle of the afternoon, the clouds broke and the sun weakly began to shine. They came out of their hiding place and began to make their way along the wide, white path that lay where the road had been.

The attack came without warning.

One moment they were trudging along lost in their thoughts — Hervân wondering where they would spend the night; Anderskerrin pondering what they would do once they reached Pirren Glanwyn — when, with a sudden bloodcurdling yell, they were set upon by a small band of dwarves.

Half a dozen young dwarves dashed out of the trees and surrounded the elves. One dwarf — the shortest, squattest and most well fed — belligerently waved a short dagger in Hervân's face. "Two elves walking alone? You can't do that sort of thing in Reglandor, you know. Now, my beauties, give us your packs and let's be seeing what we've found."

Hervân looked at her husband. Mutely, he struggled out of his pack and dropped it to the ground. She did likewise.

The leader of the dwarves spoke to two of his band. "You and you; keep an eye on them. They're elves, so they probably won't fight, but they can run faster than a horse" — an exaggeration, but there was no doubt that they could outrun the dwarves — "so if they start to run away, throw a knife after 'em; that'll slow them down."

The leader and three of his band began to sort through the packs. There was nothing of value except food.

"Hardly worth the effort," grumbled one.

"Shaddup!" said the leader, looking fiercely at the one who had spoken.

"Let's just take the packs and be done with it," suggested a third.

The leader's brow furrowed for a moment, then said, "Aye! They ain't from Reglandor anyhow, so we don't care about 'em. Come on then, before we're seen. Let's be going!"

And, in seconds, the band had disappeared into the forest, leaving Anderskerrin and Hervân safe, but without their packs.

The sun went down, and Hervân shivered. It was going to be a long, cold night.

XVI Choosing a King

Michael looked in horror at the scene before him. Slumped on the ground, half on his back, half on his side, lay King Glendour, dead, his sightless eyes staring at the ceiling. Nearby, clutching a shoulder wound, was Qivir, a dark stain spreading across his cloak.

And at Michael's feet, in an enormous pool of blood, was the female gnome from Palindor: the one responsible for the carnage. His sword had sliced into her body as she had turned to face him, and the force of the blow was such that the weapon had cut half way through her sinewy body. The gnome had fallen where she stood, her mouth open, blood sluicing out of her side in a frightening grotesquery. He pulled his sword from her body; blood dripped heavily from its edge into the red pool in which her body lay.

From behind him came the sound of running feet. The king's guard burst into the room. Michael was too dazed to speak as he tried to make sense of what had happened. The chief minister gritted his teeth against the pain and spoke for him.

"It was the gnome... she's from Palindor. She had just given the king a parchment to read when she attacked him. The king was unprepared and died instantly. I tried to stop her, but I was too slow. I did manage to pull the alarm bell, though. She turned her knife on me. Fortunately, the knife stuck in my shoulder and she couldn't pull it out. Then Michael arrived and he killed her." He looked at Michael warmly. "You saved my life again, Michael, and again I thank you."

Michael was still dumbfounded. He heard the minister's words, but could not respond. One of the king's guard spoke. "We need to get a nurse to look after that wound, chief minister; and we'll need a detachment to clean up this mess. You, go see to it!" He barked the order at a young dwarf whose face bore an expression almost as horror-filled as Michael's. The dwarf made no move to leave. "Yes, you! Go! Now!" the guard repeated his order, and his hand moved threateningly toward an ugly dagger that was stuffed in his belt.

The young dwarf came to his senses. "Yes, sir! Right away, sir!" He left the room at a run.

It was several hours before a semblance of order was restored. A nurse had carefully pried the knife from Qivir's shoulder and now his arm was in a sling, a poultice of herbs pressed against the wound. He paced his chamber, deep in thought. Michael looked on, amazed and gratified that the minister was able to consider the problems raised by the king's death even while in such great pain himself.

The minister was speaking to himself under his breath as he paced. Michael caught only brief snatches of phrases: "...no heir...," "...Palindor...," "...a lesson...." Suddenly, as if he had come to a decision, the minister stopped pacing. He felt underneath his cloak and withdrew a parchment. Thrusting it at Michael, he said: "Here, read this. The gnome gave it to the king just before she killed him."

Michael took the parchment and read it.

To His Majesty, Glendour, Fourth of that Name, King of the Land of Reglandor.

From the Ruling Council of Palindor, in session in Carn Told-wyn:

Greetings!

It is our unhappy task to inform Your Majesty that your envoy and his party have been attacked while passing through the Forest of Palindor. None survived the attack. Those responsible for this cowardly deed are unknown to us, and we fear that it is unlikely that they will be caught and justly punished.

We extend to you our heartfelt sympathies at this unfortunate circumstance; we would be happy to entertain Your Majesty in Carn Toldwyn to discuss this matter at your earliest convenience.

Signed and sealed by the Ruling Council of Palindor, this thirteenth day of Metheven.

Qivir looked at Michael. "What do you make of it?"

Michael shrugged. "I don't know."

"Well, I'll tell you what I think." Qivir took the parchment from Michael's hand and replaced it in the folds of his cloak. "It's a pack of lies! This whole business is utterly transparent. The king had sent his emissary and a small party to meet with the Ruling Council of Palindor, which sits in a pitiful excuse for a town called Carn Toldwyn, away over on the other side of the so-called Third Land. To get there is many days' journey, much of it through thick forest. Somewhere along that journey, maybe even after they reached their destination, the Ruling Council had them all killed. That gave them the excuse to choose a warrior to come in disguise and meet with our king: a warrior who would kill the king as soon as the moment was right.

"Oh, they were very clever; they chose a female gnome instead of a male dwarf or human, of whom we would have been more wary. She had a simple, small dagger such as any creature might carry for protection. Since we didn't know that our emissary had been killed, there was no reason for us to be on our guard. No, it was all planned very carefully."

"But why? What is Reglandor to these people?"

"Who can say? Once, long ago, there was no Land of Palindor, merely a vast wasteland of forest in what was then the western part of Reglandor. There was an uprising, led by a young human, Toldwyn by name. He and a band of followers wrested western

Reglandor from the rightful king — although, truth to tell, I suspect he felt that it was no great loss — and they called the new land 'Palindor.'

"There have been battles since that time, of course, but the borders have remained more or less intact, and it is many generations since the last conflict. Recent kings have concluded that Palindor would be more trouble to retrieve than it is worth. Perhaps they made a mistake. It seems clear that the Ruling Council of Palindor desires war, whatever the reason for this desire might be."

Michael had followed these words carefully, and he pondered them for some time before speaking again. Then he asked: "You spoke of a Ruling Council. Is there no king in Palindor?"

"No. For many years they had monarchs, but the last queen, Cerebeth by name, died several hundred years ago, after living to be a thousand years old. I, of course, was not alive at the time, and there are conflicting stories about what happened at the time of her death. But most historians agree that there was a struggle for power and the result was that they developed a very strange system of government.

"They crowned a human who had had some part in the struggle for succession, and called her a High Queen, whatever that might mean. But they left the day-to-day running of the land in the hands of a council of five ministers. The High Queen lasted only about a year before she mysteriously disappeared, obviously killed by one of the members of the council. No successor was crowned in her place, and since that time the so-called Ruling Council has controlled Palindor."

"Well, it seems clear that this Ruling Council is responsible for the death of our emissary and of the king himself. They must be confronted and killed." Michael's words were spoken in a voice of absolute conviction: there was no doubt in his mind whatsoever.

The minister considered this suggestion for some time. "Well..., what you say has merit, warrior Michael. But it would not be an easy task. In the first place, we no longer have a king to lead us into battle. King Glendour died unmarried and childless, and there is no obvious successor. And without a king to lead an army, the course of action you suggest would not be easy."

Now Michael was excited. "But why do we need an army? You said that the original council had five ministers. Is that still true? Are there still only five members of the Ruling Council?"

"Yes."

"Then it's simple. We don't need an army; we need only a few good, hand-picked warriors. We travel quietly to... what did you call it? Carn Toldwyn?" The minister nodded. "And when we get there we simply find the members of the Ruling Council and kill them. After that we either return silently to Reglandor or we proclaim that Palindor is once more part of Reglandor. With their leadership defeated, there would be no fight left. After all, from everything I hear, the creatures in Palindor are not true warriors."

The minister resumed his pacing and considered this plan for several minutes. Finally, he stopped, turned and said: "You know, warrior Michael, that might work. If we leave now and travel stealthily, we can be in Carn Toldwyn before they know that their plan to kill the king has succeeded."

Excitedly, Michael interrupted. "Look, it's only a few hours since the king was killed. If we seal the city now — let people in so they can bring in food, but let no one out — then the news of the king's death won't get out. That way we can guarantee total surprise."

The minister responded gleefully, "Brilliant! Brilliant! Yes! Let's do it! Stay here, and I will order the city sealed." He hurried out of the room, his cloak almost flying behind him, no sign of the pain in his shoulder.

Michael was pleased with himself. He turned the plan over in his mind and could see no flaws. The only danger was that the news of the king's death had already reached an accomplice of the treacherous gnome and that the news had already passed beyond the city walls. It was a chance they would have to take. But it seemed unlikely: Qivir had wisely ordered that the news be confined to the castle, because without a designated heir, chaos might break out in the city.

The more Michael thought about it it, the more perfect the plan seemed. Reglandor would show these ignorant savages from Palindor that they could not simply kill people for the sake of it.

He imagined himself yielding his sword, fighting bravely, exacting revenge for King Glendour's death.

His musings were interrupted by Qivir's return.

"It is done," the minister said. "The city is sealed. Creatures may come in, but none may leave without permission from either you or me. Now, come. There is one thing further we must take care of."

Michael followed Qivir out the chamber. They walked down a series of corridors, and soon Michael found himself in a part of the castle where the walls seemed darker and thicker; no trappings muffled the sound of their footsteps here, and they created strange, eerie echoes.

The minister stopped in front of a small wooden door at the end of a passage. He rapped on the door. After a few moments, the door opened slowly. There was a greenish light in the room beyond, rendering the figure who had opened the door a featureless silhouette. The silhouette beckoned them to enter. Michael followed Qivir into the room, and the creature inside closed the door behind them.

It was a large room. There were no windows, but a strange, green light came from a series of globes standing on shelves, lighting the room in an eerie manner.

As his eyes adjusted to the dim light, Michael found himself looking into the eyes of a stooped, wizened old man. His face was wrinkled deeply, yet his eyes were oddly youthful, darting back and forth watchfully. Michael was not at all sure that he could trust those eyes.

There was a smell in the room: a pungent blend of herbs, cooked meat and fish. The room was untidy, with tools and utensils strewn haphazardly around the floor and lying on the chairs and tables. Near the center of the room, a pot was simmering above a small fire of blue flames.

Qivir performed the introductions.

"Warrior Michael, this is Naomin, the necromancer. He has helped the king and me many times in the past. Naomin, this is the king's warrior Michael. He saved my life from the gnome who killed the king. Do not be misled by his youthful appearance; he has the makings of a great warrior, perhaps the greatest Reglandor has ever seen."

Michael blushed as the necromancer nodded a greeting. Naomin betrayed no surprise at Qivir's mention of the king's death, which puzzled Michael: surely no one would have taken the trouble to seek out the old man to tell him the news? But Qivir continued, "Michael has a plan for Reglandor to revenge King Glendour's death. Michael, please explain your plan."

What followed was an odd, one-sided conversation that unsettled Michael. As he explained the plan, the necromancer stood as still as stone. There were no interjections of "I see," no questions, no noddings of the head. Several times Michael found himself stumbling and stammering, but eventually he had laid the plan bare.

Qivir said. "So, Naomin, we have come for your advice and prognostication. It would be foolhardy indeed to embark on such a venture without your approval."

Still the necromancer said nothing. Michael began to wonder if he had somehow lost the power of speech.

At length the necromancer shuffled forward. He leaned across a table and picked up a pinch of some herb, then dropped it into the pot in the center of the room. Taking a jar from a shelf he poured a small quantity of a glutinous, dirty ocher substance into the pot. Finally, he retrieved what looked like the petal of a rose from a table in a distant corner of the room. He added it to the pot, then grasped a large wooden spoon and began to stir the mixture.

From the necromancer's throat now came a kind of quiet distant hum. It was neither pleasant nor unpleasant. Not musical, it simply *was*, hanging in the room as if it had a physical presence.

As Naomin stirred the pot, the hum changed. It got quieter, then louder, then quieter again. Unaccountably, the sound made Michael feel grossly uncomfortable, as if it came not from the necromancer's throat but from some dark and distant land where pain and terror thrived. Michael swallowed hard, several times. His heart was beating rapidly. He wanted to vomit.

He was almost on the point of running from the room when the sound died away into silence. Michael was panting, sweat on his brow.

The necromancer spoke.

He turned towards Michael, looked him fleetingly in the eye —
and in that moment, Michael wished that the ground would open
up and swallow him; never had he seen such a powerful gaze — and
then Naomin lowered his gaze to the floor. "My liege; my king. I
am yours to command."

For a moment Qivir stared with wide eyes at Naomin. Then he
looked at Michael. Moving to the necromancer's side, he said, "You
mean... you mean... he's to be our king?"

For reply, the necromancer indicated the pot. Qivir looked into
it, and his face blanched.

He turned and bowed towards Michael. "My king. You are to
be crowned. The pot tells no lies."

Michael took a step forward. From where he had been standing,
he had been unable to see into the pot. Now he looked into it
— but he saw only an ugly, gray mixture swirling gently around
and around, odd patches of tiny, strangely red bubbles spinning in
eddies on the surface. "I see nothing."

Qivir said, "Then it is not for you to see. But the pot cannot lie.
You are to be crowned king."

Michael peered into the mixture, straining to see what the others
saw. He tried to make the bubbles join together to form some sort
of picture, but he gave up. The bubbles joined and split so rapidly
in their spinning dance that no picture could hold together. He
relaxed then looked away. But in that fraction of a second, just as
he turned his head, an image registered itself in his mind.

He looked back towards the pot. Instead of looking at the
bubbles on the liquid's surface, he now looked beyond them. He
tried to relax his gaze, looking past the bubbles into the liquid,
and then beyond even the slowly gyrating grayness into the depths
of something that both was and was not. And a picture formed,
brilliant and so real that it made the room in which he was standing
seem like an insubstantial dream.

It was an image of himself, dressed magnificently in purple and
gold, standing high above a huge crowd. On his head was a crown.

As Michael stared, the image faded, to be replaced by another,
equally powerful.

This was a picture, not of himself, but of a woman. Somehow, he knew that she represented the enemy, Palindor. She was considerably older than he, and she bore herself proudly, like a queen. As he watched, the image dissolved again and reformed as a picture of the woman's face and upper body. She had long, dark hair, and a strangely pretty face that, with a vague sense of unease, he felt certain he had seen before. But it was the eyes that held him.

The eyes looked at him from the depths of the cauldron, and they burned with a fire that held his gaze tightly. The only word he could use to describe those eyes afterwards was "awesome." There was no fear in those eyes; neither was there love nor hate; there was just raw, blinding power.

He wanted to look away, but was powerless to do so.

Then the image changed once more. He saw the woman again, but now there was a second figure. He recognized himself, standing over the woman, who was sprawled on the ground. She was speaking to him — he could see her lips moving, but could not hear the words — and he stood over her, listening to her, his sword unsheathed and ready to swipe down on to her body.

Nothing moved for a long time; then, with a terrifying suddenness, his sword flashed down into the woman's chest. Briefly, a fountain of blood erupted, then the woman's face turned sideways, so that he could no longer see it. In the vision, Michael stood triumphantly over her, his sword buried deep in her torso.

He felt a momentary revulsion, then a strange new power seemed to course through his body. The image dissolved into nothingness. He looked away from the pot.

Qivir said. "Accept our allegiances, Your Majesty. Then we must crown you."

"What? Oh...." Michael was momentarily confused, his mind still on the vision in the pot. Recovering himself, in a firm voice he said, "I accept your allegiances with thanks. I shall be crowned, and you, Qivir, will be my chief minister. You, Naomin, will be my necromancer. It seems that I am to be king, and the pot has shown me that we will travel to Palindor and there we will meet a strange woman whom I shall slay."

The necromancer and the minister looked at one another. Qivir said, "A strange woman, you say. I saw no woman. Tell me: what did she look like?"

Michael tried to describe her; he found it difficult to remember anything except her eyes. He could not shake the uneasy feeling that he recognized the woman from some place far away — a dream perhaps? "It was the eyes; they held me fast with raw power."

"It is the one they crowned High Queen," Qivir said. "Some of the stories speak of her look of fire and determination. How she can still be alive I do not know. But if the pot declares that you will meet her and slay her, then it will be so. The pot cannot lie. Now, come! We must announce your accession, and then we must be on our way. There is no time to lose if we are to reach Carn Toldwyn while the council still suspects nothing."

With a final backward glance at the pot, Michael allowed himself to be led from the room.

XVII Inside the Castle

The pain of the past two days' ride was forgotten as a wave of shock swept over Catherine. Coming down the steps of the castle was a massive black creature, one that she had last seen vanishing in a black cloud high atop Machrenmoor*.

Malthazzar descended the steps hurriedly. Behind him came two creatures, each a kind of shiny gray and almost as tall as Catherine. The creatures had small wings: not large enough that they could fly, but by flapping the wings continually, they came down the steps in a series of jumps, touching every third or fourth step and executing slow, airborne arcs in between. As Malthazzar stopped and drew himself to his full height before Catherine, the two attendants fluttered behind the Lord of Evil.

Malthazzar spoke, his voice a deep rasp. "So, Catherine. We meet again, but now you have no power over me. Instead, it is I who hold power over you. Take her to the Great Hall." He lifted a gigantic arm, so dark that she could not tell if she was seeing part of Malthazzar himself or merely a black cloak.

The two fluttering creatures came closer to her and made as if to take her hands. She recoiled from them.

"No. I'll come. You don't have to grab me."

---

* In *Palindor*.

She began to climb the steps, and the creatures emitted wisping laughs, amused at her reluctance to be touched. One hurried before her and one came behind. For a moment she hesitated at the top of the steps, then the one behind her came close, as if to push her inside, and she hurried through the castle's massive door.

As soon as she was inside, Malthazzar turned furiously to the leader of the Dark Knights. "You fool! Even now you do not know what you have done, do you?"

The Knight shook his head blankly.

"I'll tell you, you idiot. You were followed here. One of his minions came through the cloud with you, and now he is loose somewhere in my land. He must be caught before he does any damage. Go back the way you came and find him. And when you do find him, be careful; don't try to deal with him yourselves. Send me a messenger and I will come deal with him. His power is too great for the likes of you." He turned and climbed the steps furiously.

Until she entered the castle, Catherine had seen few living things in this strange land, but now she was amazed to discover that the castle, which had given every appearance of being deserted, was busy with creatures. None of them were like any she had seen before: most were like the two that had escorted her inside: dark, shiny beings that moved in jumpy bursts of wing-fluttering motion. But there were other creatures as well: ratlike animals with piercing dark red eyes that seemed to look at her greedily as she passed, and small dwarflike creatures in dark armor with a design consisting of a sideways cross in red on their breastplates. Twice she thought she saw out of the corner of her eye creatures dressed in a golden white shimmering cloth, but as she turned her head to look more closely, the glistering color disappeared and was replaced by dirty brown clothing.

She was led into a large hall lit by torches in sconces along the walls. A massive table nearly filled it; on the table were piles of unappetizing, dark food. Apart from Catherine and her escort, the room was empty. She examined the food, her stomach reminding her that she was hungry. All the food was dark and unrecognizable. Even its odor was unpleasant. But even so, she was hungry enough to wonder if perhaps she could force some of it down.

Before she bring herself to try the disgusting food, though, Malthazzar entered the hall. Her guards hopped into the background as Malthazzar strode forward. He towered over her for a moment, then took a seat at the head of the table.

"No doubt you are hungry after your journey. You may eat whatever you desire. Drink as much as you need. My castle is your castle."

Catherine was sure she was being mocked, but she was past caring. She grabbed a piece of some sort of meaty substance from a plate and began to gnaw at it. The taste was burnt and bitter, but at least it was food.

She filled a goblet from a large jug nearby. The liquid glistened in the light from the torches. It was a deep red color, like fine aged wine. She sniffed it before drinking. There was no odor. When she drank, she discovered that it had exactly the same unpleasant taste as the meat. Even so, at least it slaked her thirst.

Finishing the meat, she took a bowl of vegetables and began to wolf them down. Their taste was indistinguishable from that of the meat and the liquid.

Eventually, she had eaten her fill. The meal left a bitter taste in her mouth, and she wished that there was some fresh water to cleanse her mouth, but one look at Malthazzar, brooding at the end of the table, convinced her that she would be foolish to ask for any.

"You have finished?"

She jumped. She had thought that Malthazzar was deep in thought. "Yes; and thank you."

"Ah, it is so refreshing to be in the presence of someone with manners. You have no idea how lonely it is here sometimes, seeing so few creatures of culture. Still, now you are here, that will no longer be a problem. Come with me. I want to show you something."

There was a commotion at the entrance of the hall as Malthazzar rose. The door opened and a gray creature with tall, pointed ears and large, red eyes entered the room. The creature cast a momentary glance at Catherine, then bowed low toward Malthazzar.

"What is the meaning of this interruption?" growled the Lord of Evil.

The gray creature straightened. "I came to report, Master. He is to be crowned, and then he will lead a party to exact revenge.

He believes and trusts me completely; he is like potter's clay in my hands. Very soon now, the land will be yours."

"Excellent! This is good news indeed. You will be well reward-ed for your work, my general. Now, if you'll excuse me, I have something to show my visitor."

The creature bowed once more, staightening as Malthazzar swept past. As Catherine passed, the creature's red eyes fixed on her, and she felt a revulsion and a fear as great as any that Malthazzar had ever engendered. She hurried out of the room behind Malthazzar, her two winged guards bringing up the rear.

The ill-matched foursome walked the length of a corridor, then climbed a wide, twisting staircase. The steps seemed to wind on forever. Catherine was quite out of breath when they reached the top of the steps. Still trailing Malthazzar, she passed through a wide door and found herself standing atop one of the castle towers.

"This is my home; this is my land," said Malthazzar with a sweep of his hand. "And I give you free rein. You may go where you wish, do what you will."

Catherine gazed out at the landscape. The forlorn empty dead-ness of it was as uninviting when seen from the castle rooftop as it had been when she had been crossing it on horseback. The only color to relieve the blackness of the ground and the reddish orange of the pools that puddled the land was in the distance, where a range of mountains stood, capped in white. She felt an immediate attraction to the mountains: the cool whiteness of the distant snow was a welcome respite from the harshness of the rest of the landscape.

As she looked at the distant peaks, wondering how long it would take to reach them, she noticed that, even though it was only minutes since she had eaten her fill and slaked her thirst, her hunger and thirst were returning. Torn between the pangs and the distant mountains, it was difficult to concentrate on what Malthazzar was saying.

"Ah! You have noticed the mountains. As of course you should, for they represent your only hope of escape from this land. You see the tallest mountain, the one in the middle? At the very top of that mountain there is a cave. If you enter that cave, you will find yourself in a labyrinth. There is only one other entrance to the tunnels, and it lies not in this land, but in Palindor. Once you have entered my kingdom, there is no way out save the Pit or the labyrinth. But I would not dwell on it if I were you, because no creature has ever found its way to safety through the tunnels. Far better that you stay with me and enjoy my hospitality."

Catherine looked once more at the grim, stark landscape surrounding the castle. Involuntarily, she shuddered.

"The Pit? What is that?"

Malthazzar laughed. At least, she assumed that it was a laugh, for he bared his teeth and assaulted her ears with a load roaring sound.

Calming himself, he said, "The time will come when you will beg me to cast you into the Pit. But surely you would not so soon deprive me of the delight of your company? The Pit is for later, when your despair is complete and you seek an end at any cost.

"But let us not talk of such things. For now, I give you the freedom of my land."

Looking at the distant mountains, she asked, "What is this place called?" Her mind was barely on the question, though, for her mind was already made up: she would travel to the top of the mountains and thereby escape this wretched place.

"Its name? I thought you knew. This is my kingdom. This is Sheol."

———————————

After showing her his land, Malthazzar dismissed Catherine. Despite her increasing hunger and thirst, she left the castle without stopping in the hall. Her hunger was more urgent than ever; but she realized that even though she had gone two days without food while on horseback, she had not felt so hungry then as she did now, less than an hour after eating Malthazzar's food. She decided that in future she would eat and drink only when the pangs became unbearable.

She crossed the moat, then walked around the castle until she was facing the mountains. On the castle roof she had half convinced herself that the mountains were no more than a few hours away. But now she realized that they were much farther, and it would take several days to reach them.

The red disk of the sun was falling quickly toward the horizon. She was tired, and she wondered if sleep in Sheol was as pernicious as the food. She tried to put her tiredness from her mind.

She looked at the castle brooding ominously high above. Nothing moved on its battlements. Reddish lights flickered through some of the slit windows, but no shadows passed in front of the flames. The castle looked lifeless.

She was about to turn away and begin her journey in earnest when a thought struck her. She walked a few steps over the blackened ground to the lake's edge. Then, very carefully, she dipped the end of her little finger into the red-orange liquid.

It was warm rather than hot, yet stung oddly. She sniffed the air above the lake and could detect the merest trace of sulphur in the air. Her nostrils must have become accustomed to the stink that she knew hung heavily in the air.

Her loss of sensitivity to the malodorous air was suddenly frightening. If she could become used to that, might she not become used to other things?

With a grim determination, she turned her back on the castle and began the long journey to the distant mountains.

XVIII To Pirren Glanwyn

That night was the worst that Anderskerrin and Hervân had ever spent.

The two elves huddled together in the shelter of a tree all night. The snow stopped for a while soon after sunset, and they thought about trying to catch up with the farmers; but then the snow started again and they decided there was nothing for it but stay in the forest for the night. Glum, cold and exhausted, they curled up on a narrow patch of snow-free ground under the branches of a tree. They slept.

Toward midnight, the snow stopped and the clouds dispersed. Under the clear sky, the temperature began to drop. First Hervân, then her husband, woke, shivering with the cold. There didn't seem to be any point in trying to go back to sleep, so for a while they tramped through the snow along the track. But the snow was wet and cold, and deep enough that it soon seeped over the tops of their boots, numbing their feet and causing them to stumble. Retreating to the shelter of the forest, they took off their boots and tried to dry their feet. They held on to one another to try to get warm, and prayed for the night to end.

Eventually, the sky in the east began to brighten. After a seemingly endless dawn, the sun rose weakly through the trees. The elves — tired, hungry, dispirited and cold — hobbled out from under the tree. They swept away as much of the snow as possible beside the track and lay down in the sunlight. They fell asleep.

When they woke, it was midmorning. Most of the snow had melted, and they were lying in muddy puddles. They stretched their limbs and tried, with little success, to remove some of the filth that now adorned their faces and clothes.

"Shhh!" hissed Hervân. "What's that sound?"

They tipped their heads, trying to make sense of what they were hearing. Neither of them had heard anything like it before. It was the sound of a tune — but not sung, or even played on an instrument. It was a cheerful song, although neither of them recognized it. Accompanying it was a rhythmic crunching of footsteps. Before they could gather their wits and hide, around the corner came a human carrying a small pack.

At least, both of them thought at first that the creature was human, but when he stopped and eyed them with a quizzical expression, they became less sure. He was awfully *short* for a human. But he was not a dwarf — not stocky enough, although his beard was rather dwarf-like — neither was he an elf — too tall — nor an imp, nor a goblin, nor a sprite, nor a pisky, for all the obvious reasons. So he must be a human, even though he was no taller than a human child.

Whatever he was, there was no escaping him now. He trudged forward and halted before them. His eyes twinkled, but his merriment seemed tinged with sadness. Without warning, he made a low bow. It would have been graceful, except that his pack nearly caused him to lose his balance: he prevented himself from falling in the mud only by flailing his arms indecorously.

He introduced himself. "Treadlong, Traveller and Storyteller, at your service."

It was not exactly the formal greeting usually used between creatures, but it sufficed. Anderskerrin introduced the two of them: "Anderskerrin, elf of Fire Mountain Meadow in Soltarwyn, and my good wife, Hervân, at your service."

"Pleased to meet you," added Hervân, politely.

"Well, and now that the expected introductory requirements have been fully accomplished, might this traveller be permitted to ask his new-found and rather muddy acquaintances if perchance they might be in need of assistance? It's all very well and good, no doubt, for the elf Anderskerrin (who, I must say, speaks with an accent as much of Palindor as of Soltarwyn) and his good wife Hervân (a particularly beautiful name, if I may be permitted to make that venture) to offer this traveller their services, but at the present juncture, it seems to the traveller that perhaps they are more needful of his services (such as they are) than he is of theirs."

This extraordinary speech — made all the more strange by the lilting sing-song tones in which it was delivered — rendered the elves speechless for several seconds. Eventually, Anderskerrin responded.

"What? Oh, yes. Well, you see, we were attacked late last night and all our provisions and money were stolen. We were on our way to Pirren Glanwyn. It can't be far away now."

The traveller nodded wisely. "Ah yes. Pirren Glanwyn. Called Pirren Glanwyn the Fair by some. Pirren Glanwyn the Dangerous is what I call it. But few ask the opinion of this poor traveller, even though there are but few places in the Three Lands that Treadlong has not visited, and many are the things he has seen. So, now tell me, my good elf" — at this point he lowered his arm and pulled Anderskerrin to his feet; together they then assisted Hervân — "which of the pastoral houses of the salubrious Fire Mountain Meadow do you call home?"

This seemed a rather peculiar question. But then, the human — if that was indeed what he was; neither of the elves was yet quite sure on that point — seemed a rather strange creature all around. Hervân answered as she busied herself trying to wipe the mud from her face and clothes, efforts which unfortunately were having the effect mainly of spreading the dirt over even those parts which had heretofore been relatively clean.

"I grew up there, good traveller, and now we live in the cottage known as the blue cottage. It's not really blue; it's white like most of the others. But we painted the trim blue when we first were married and it seemed to suit the cottage so well that we left it that way."

The traveller nodded as if he was thoroughly familiar with the cottage in question. "Ah yes. The beautiful cottage near the south end of the meadow; not far from where the dwarf from Palindor lives with his wife. Now, what was his name? Oh, yes. Gondalwyn. That's it, isn't it?"

The elves could not hide their amazement. "Yes, that's right, but how did you know?"

"Oh, I visited there a few years ago. Let's see, when was it now? Eight years ago, come next spring. I passed through your most salubrious of meadows on my way to the Fire Mountain. The visit before that was before the dwarf arrived."

"I came over from Palindor with Gondalwyn," Anderskerrin volunteered, although it seemed irrelevant.

"Ah. Most interesting. This good traveller thanks you for that information, Anderskerrin of Fire Mountain Meadow, previously of Palindor. Penclaw in fact, if my ear does not misinform me as to the origin of your charming accent. And now, I think we have stood here indulging in conversation for quite long enough. You are hungry, no doubt. And it is even more certain that you are in need of a stream, for in all my years of travelling, I believe I have never seen quite such a disreputable sight as you two. So, which is it to be first: food or water?"

The elves exchanged glances. "Food, if you please," they said in unison.

With a twinkle in his eye and a smile on his face, the traveller opened his pack. Inside were apples and pears, several farls of good honeybread, a canteen of water, and a large, dark fruitcake. He spread the food on the ground and the two elves, joined by the traveller, set to.

The good food and the warming sun combined to make the elves feel more comfortable. By the time that they had eaten their fill, they were also feeling considerably more cheerful. As they packed the uneaten food in the traveller's pack, Treadlong said to them: "You are right. Pirren Glanwyn is not far. Mayhap we shall reach it by nightfall. But first, we need to clean you up. Even the guards at Pirren Glanwyn, never ones noted for fastidiousness, would refuse you entrance. Come with me; there's a stream not far away." And he set off through the woods.

It was clear that he knew exactly where he was going, even though there was no discernible path through the trees. He led them for nearly half an hour — obviously, his idea of "not far away" was rather different from their own — before they heard running water. Another couple of minutes and they were standing on the edge of a small stream of clear, bubbling water.

The elves washed gladly in the stream, so that very soon they were clean again, and only a couple of especially stubborn soiled patches were evident on their clothing.

"There; at least you look presentable now." Treadlong looked up at the sky. "Now, we must hurry. We'll go through the woods instead of along the track. It will be drier and easier than slogging through the mud. Come with me." And he set off once more through the woods.

They walked for most of the rest of the day, resting only briefly to make further inroads into Treadlong's food supply.

The sun was beginning to fall towards the Mountains of Mourn in the distance as the three companions stepped out of the forest. They were on a hill; below, grass-covered slopes led down to the capital of Reglandor. Away to their right, several hundred paces distant, was the track along which they had been travelling until they had left it in search of the stream. Struggling with his cart, exactly at the boundary between the forest and the grasslands, was Trent the Farmer. The cart was bogged down in the mud of the track, and, as they watched, the wheels of the cart became more and more mired. Trent's workhorse struggled vainly against the grip of the mud and finally gave up in disgust.

The three approached the farmer. Trent was redfaced and dispirited by his fruitless efforts. He stared disconsolately at the stuck wheels. He looked up and gave a nod of recognition as the elves drew near.

They introduced Treadlong, who looked at the cart thoughtfully while the farmer explained that this was the third time that day that his cart had got stuck. "Just my luck for it to 'appen again right here. Another ten paces and I'd be on the grass, but now I be bogged down worse than ever. I'll be stuck here till another cart comes along with a 'orse to 'elp pull it out of the way, and that won't be till the morrow now. The other farmers be all ahead of me and it be getting late; there bain't be anyone else coming along here tonight."

"Oh, I think we can get you out of here," volunteered Treadlong.

Trent eyed him dubiously. "Well, I'm not saying as I'm not appreciative of your 'elp, but she's stuck firmer than what she looks. With Dobbin and me pulling and pushing for all we's worth, we cain't budge the cart. It's the weight of the produce, you see. It makes the wheels sink deeper. It's not that I ain't grateful an' all, but I be afeared that yourself and these two kind elves wouldn't be of much 'elp."

"Oh, I wasn't thinking of simply adding our weight to yours. You're perfectly right; that would simply get the cart even more firmly stuck. No, I was thinking that if we were to put something firm under the wheels, it would give them something to spread the weight, and then we could pull the cart out."

The elves and the farmer looked puzzled; none of them grasped the traveller's meaning.

Treadlong moved to the cart and lifted the canvas that protected the wares underneath. He indicated a plank that separated two different kinds of apples in the cart.

"This plank, and the canvas; do you mind if they get dirty?"

"Well, I suppose not. The canvas be just to protect the food. And as long as it don't come on to rain or snow afore we reach Pirren Glanwyn, then it's no matter what 'appens to it. And that plank be just an old piece of wood. You can 'ave that and welcome."

"Well then, good farmer, if you would help me with it...."

The traveller and the farmer together removed the plank from the cart. Under Treadlong's guidance, they placed the plank crosswise under the cart, just in front of its wheels, then spread the canvas on top of the plank. "Now, if you would be so good as to turn your horse towards the grass and to instruct it to pull, and if we all push as hard as we can, we'll see what happens," said Treadlong.

The farmer spoke a few words in Dobbin's ear, then gave the animal a sharp smack on its rump. The horse began to strain, trying to pull the heavy cart out of the mire. The farmer hurried around to the rear of the cart, then added his weight to that of Treadlong, Anderskerrin and Hervân, who were already pushing.

For several seconds nothing happened, then one of the wheels turned just enough that it caught at the cloth-covered plank. The cart hurtled forward as the wheels gained purchase. Treadlong, who knew exactly what was going to happen, let go of the cart quickly.

The others, completely surprised, fell forward on to the now-muddy canvas.

Dobbin slowed to a stop, the cart now safely behind him on the grass. The three who had fallen got to their feet and dusted themselves off.

"Well I never. I ain't never seen anything like that afore. Quite a trick, that be; I'll 'ave to remember it," said the farmer.

Treadlong looked momentarily bashful, then suggested that they get a move on, otherwise the gates would be closed for the night. "They close at sunset, which is not far off now. We must hurry if we aren't going to be forced to spend the night in the open."

The farmer and the traveller bundled the filthy canvas into a ball and placed it on the cart along with the plank. Then, at a rapid walk, they made their way down the grassy slope towards the city.

The sun had set when they reached the gate. But to their surprise, the gate, although firmly guarded by a healthy detachment of half a dozen warlike dwarves in full battle armor, stood open.

Treadlong approached the guards.

"You are here for the big event tomorrow?" asked one of the armored dwarves, a particularly mean-looking creature with a sneer on his face and in his voice.

"The big event. Yes, that's right," Treadlong replied, although he had no idea what the dwarf was talking about.

"You're lucky. Normally the gates would be closed by now, but tonight you are permitted to enter the city. But you must understand that the new king has made a proclamation that all those inside the city must stay inside until it's all over."

Treadlong nodded. "A small condition to which my friends and I readily agree."

The dwarves stood to one side, opening a path through which the four passed, the cart trundling behind them. The dwarves closed ranks immediately the party had passed.

Even though only a few steps separated the inside of the city from the outside, it was like walking into another world. Outside, there had been quiet and calm; inside, creatures scurried in all directions.

"'Ave 'ee anywhere to stay the night?" the farmer asked, raising his voice to be heard above the hubbub. The others shook their heads. "Then you must stay with me. Come."

Farmer Trent took the lead, walking along the streets with a practiced step, until they found themselves in a courtyard in which stood half a dozen carts similar to his, their bulging canvases covering food waiting to be sold the next day. A human boy stepped forward, and the farmer tossed him a coin. "Take good care of the cart, and if I get a good price 'morrer, I'll remember 'ee and pay 'ee more." The youngster grabbed the spinning coin and grinned. "Thank you, master farmer. You can be sure that your goods are safe with me."

"You touch anything and I'll tan your hide, mind."

"Of course, sir. You can trust me."

"Hmmm...," the farmer said under his breath as he turned away.

He led the others into the large hostelry that adjoined the courtyard. They entered a massive room, filled with tables and chairs occupied by farmers who were speaking loudly and eating from steaming plates of food and drinking from tankards of beer or mugs of posset or bishop.

A young human female (and a rather attractive one, as humans go) with rosy cheeks, golden hair and a broad, cheery smile was waiting on the tables. Trent waved his hand to attract her attention. She finished serving a wrinkled red-cheeked old farmer then came across the crowded room to the four newcomers.

Trent greeted her warmly. "Megan, me ol' wench! I'd like rooms for meself and my three friends, if it not be too much trouble for your mother."

Megan curtseyed. "I think we have only a couple of rooms left, master Trent."

"Then we'll take 'em and double up. Do 'urry. Go tell your mother afore she be lettin' someone else 'ave 'em."

Megan gave another curtsy, then disappeared amongst the throng, making her way towards a nearby door.

"Come us on. I'll treat us to food and drink while we be waiting for our rooms," said the farmer. Treadlong tried to refuse, but the bighearted farmer would have none of it. "If it weren't for 'ee, I'd 'a been stuck till mornin'. No, it be the least I can do for 'ee."

140

They found an empty table in the far corner of the room and placed their orders with a spry young elf: beef broth for the farmer, vegetable stew for the elves and dumplings and gravy for Treadlong.

While they were waiting for the food, the crowd parted for a middle-aged human woman, who approached their table. Trent stood and embraced her in a powerful hug. The woman was large (which is to say, verging on fat) and had a massive, smiling red face. She wore an apron, and her arms were covered with a dusting of flour. Releasing the farmer, she said, "Trent, you old good-for-nothing! I should have known you wouldn't miss such a time as this. There'll be good prices tomorrow. You only just made it in time; you got the last two rooms in the house. Now, who're your friends?"

Trent introduced the traveller and the elves. Treadlong bowed politely to the mistress of the house and asked: "Good woman, it seems that by the most fortunate of circumstances we have stumbled on a happy occasion. The dwarves at the city gate made mention of some event tomorrow? And a new king was also mentioned?"

The woman looked around for a chair. Finding none free, she unceremoniously leaned over a nearby table and said: "If you'll excuse me?" A farmer stood politely to bow to his hostess, who promptly whisked away the chair on which he had been seated and plopped it down at Trent's table. She lowered her bulk on to it.

"Ah, that's better," she sighed. "All this standing does a body no good at all. Anyway, you mean to say you're here but you don't know about the coronation?" Her expression was partly bemused, but mostly a large, warm grin.

The four shook their heads. "Then you must be the only ones in the entire city who don't know the news," she said.

She lowered her voice — a completely unnecessary measure as the room was loud with conversation and, in any case, as she had already indicated, what she was about to say was already known to everyone else in earshot.

"King Glendour the Fourth was killed just three days ago, leaving no heir. He was quite a young man, you see. His death was unexpected, so it's hardly surprising that he hadn't named an heir. Anyway, the king's personal necromancer boiled up one of his potions and in it he saw who was to be the new king. It's a

141

new warrior in town. Nobody seems to know much about him, except that he saved the king's life just a few days ago by killing the warrior Laird, who was supposed to be unbeatable and who attacked the king in broad daylight.

"This new warrior, Michael is his name, stepped forward and killed Laird, just like that! Michael seems to have the support of Qivir, the king's chief minister, and, as I say, the necromancer has declared that it's his destiny to be king. So there's to be a coronation tomorrow. The city is full, and you'll be able to get a good price for your produce, mister Trent." She gave the farmer a broad wink and a sly nudge in the ribs.

Megan returned, carrying the food, and her mother stood to leave. Treadlong asked her, just as she was turning to go. "You say the old king was killed? How did that happen?"

Her cheery face became angry for a moment, and the redness of her cheeks deepened. "A gnome. Some slimy, heathen female gnome from Palindor wheedled her way into a private session with the king and his minister. She drew a knife on the king and killed him. She would have killed the minister too — as it was, he was only injured in the shoulder — but fortunately this warrior Michael was nearby and rushed in and saved the minister."

She looked away and spat with disgust; the saliva landed in a farmer's soup, but no one noticed. "Nasty creatures, those Palindorics. None of 'em worth a year-old fig." With that, she turned, drew herself up, and waited for a path to open before her. It did so, she passed through it, and was gone.

Megan was looking at Anderskerrin. The elf looked sick. "Are you all right, sir?"

Anderskerrin's eyes hadn't moved from the place where Megan's mother had been standing. Palindor, she had said. How could anyone from Palindor have done such a thing? It was impossible. No wonder his face was as pale as yesterday's snow.

XIX The Mountain

The sky became a few shades lighter as the red disk rose and arced its way overhead; then, as it dropped below the horizon again, the sky retreated into darkness once more. Sometimes, clouds filled the sky and great flashes of lightning flickered silently across the hemisphere above Catherine's head, or gigantic jagged columns of light would flash into momentary existence between clouds and ground. Then thunder would roll, resonant and grand, around the hills and valleys of the black landscape. But never did it rain. The heat remained oppressive, the humidity strength-sapping. But through it all, Catherine continued making her way towards the distant mountains.

She was beginning to understand some of the ways of Sheol. She was ravenously hungry and her throat was aching and parched. But even had she been able to find food and drink to assuage her pangs, she would not have partaken of them. She was certain that her guess at the castle had been right: to eat and drink would bring only temporary relief, and when the hunger and thirst returned, they would be worse than ever.

She wished she had not eaten or drunk in the castle: it had only made things worse for her; but there was no way that she could have known that at the time. Instead of regretting her actions, she tried to concentrate on being thankful that she had not eaten or drunk more than she had, otherwise her pain now would surely have been unbearable. And, as she had guessed earlier, although she was sore and tired and perpetually wanted to sleep, the aching fatigue, once it settled on her, became no worse.

So Catherine plodded on, trying to keep track of time, but unsure now whether it was four days or five since she had left the castle. For the first two days, she had wondered if this land was playing another foul trick on her: the mountains seemed just as distant as when she had set out from the castle. Perhaps they would simply recede from her as she walked, for ever. But for the last day or so, this fear had left her: she was in no doubt now that the mountains were getting closer.

For most of the time, she had been walking alone through the barren, monotonous landscape that she was beginning to hate with a passion. Only occasionally was there something out of the ordinary to break the monotony. Birds sometimes wheeled high above her, too far away to identify; twice she had passed close by stunted trees in which birds roosted, asleep. They were larger than the most massive eagles, their black beaks clearly capable of ripping flesh apart as if it were paper. She shuddered and hurried quietly on her way.

Once, watching a bird high above, she saw it suddenly drop like a deadweight. Through the air it plunged. Counting seconds, she reached eight before the bird plummeted out of sight behind a boulder-topped hillock. Moments later it roared up into view a thousand paces distant, wings wide, some small black creature held in its talons. It began to flap its wings lazily and soon the bird and its prey were lost in the distance.

Several times she almost saw small ground-hugging creatures — perhaps like the one that the bird had caught — but each time she was frustrated: she would see a sudden quick movement on the ground near a rock out of the corner of her eye; but by the time she turned her head it was too late and the animal was gone. She stopped a few times to investigate, searching around the rock behind which she thought the animal was hiding — even, in one case where the rock was small, rolling it across the ground a short distance — but never again did she see the animal whose movement had attracted her attention.

Slowly, the mountains came nearer. At last she was close enough to see that the lower slopes were stark, bare, boulder-strewn rocky inclines. High above, she could see the snow. Now that she was close, she could see that the snow was not pure white; rather it had a kind of dull pinkish tinge. But even so, the sight was a welcome relief from the brooding darkness by which she had been surrounded until now.

She found herself on the edge of a shallow valley, on the far side of which the largest mountain rose. Squinting, she tried to make out something on the valley floor: after a few moments, she was almost certain there was a small cottage in the center of the valley.

Catherine's heart beat with excitement; she had not realized how lonely she had been these past few days. Hurriedly, she began to scramble down the slope into the valley, sending pebbles and small rocks scuttering down the slope ahead of her. The sound echoed around the wide bowl of the valley.

She approached the cottage cautiously. There was no sign of life. She began to wonder if perhaps her excitement had been for nothing: perhaps the building was deserted. Like everything else she had seen (except the snow), the cottage was dark and brooding. The thatch that covered its roof was old, almost black with age. The cottage walls were built from the same black rock as the boulders that littered the landscape. As she approached the door, she wondered what she would find inside.

The door opened before she reached it. An old woman stepped out and looked at her threateningly.

Under other circumstances, the woman's face might have appeared friendly. It was reddish and deeply lined and topped with a mass of gray hair: the kind of face that ought by rights to be affixed to a kindly great aunt or grandmother. But there was nothing grandmotherly about the way that the woman looked at Catherine.

She was short, no more than five feet tall, but she drew herself up to every inch of those five feet and tried to look haughtily down her nose at Catherine (which was difficult as she was at least six inches shorter than Catherine). She spoke in a cracked voice in which Catherine detected both anxiety and belligerence.

"Who are you? How dare you approach my castle without permission?"

Catherine was puzzled. Words like "hovel" and "hut" might be a reasonable description of the building, but never "castle." Catherine looked more closely at the woman as she considered how to respond. The woman's clothing was filthy and in tatters. She spoke again. "Come on, you stupid creature. Answer me or I'll have you thrown into the dungeons."

As Catherine looked steadily at the woman, she noticed a most peculiar thing. Small creatures with wings, tiny relatives of the strange creatures in Malthazzar's castle, seemed to surround the woman in a veritable cloud. There must have been at least half a dozen of them. And as she watched, one of them suddenly dived into the woman's body. A few seconds later, it (or a different one) popped out and flew around her head several times, before diving back inside once more.

The woman stepped forward until she was no more than an arm's length from Catherine. "Are you deaf? or simply stupid? I am Cerebeth, queen of all this great land." The old woman swept her hand around in a gesture that included the desolate valley. "And now, for the last time: tell me who you are and what you want in my great country."

Still Catherine hesitated, unable to decide how to answer this crazed old woman. Finally, she said, "I am Catherine, High Queen of Palindor...."

She got no further. At this pronouncement, two things happened.

First, the small black creatures fluttering around the woman, some of which were passing dangerously close to Catherine herself, stopped, regarded Catherine, and then dived into the strange woman's body. Then, a moment later, the woman stopped her ears with her hands and screamed at Catherine. "No! no! You are a witch and a usurper, come to take my palace away from me. Begone from here. You have no power over me, you witch. You are sent by the evil one who claims my land. Return to your master and tell him from me that he will never succeed in deceiving me. I am the rightful queen in this land, and he shall never take that away from me."

The woman turned and stormed into the cottage, slamming the door behind her.

Catherine waited for several minutes, to see if the woman would reappear, but there were no further signs of life. Eventually, with one final, quizzical glance and a shake of her head, she moved past the cottage and started up the hill on the far side of the valley.

She climbed steadily. Soon, she had left the cottage far behind. She became ever more tired as she climbed. The featureless landscape that had surrounded her all this time became a narrow path between dark rock, on one side a low wall and on the other the mass of the mountain.

Patches of the pinkish snow began to be visible, first on the rocks above her, and then here and there beside the path, and finally all around. She touched a patch. Surprised, she hurriedly withdrew her hand. It was warm! She had been wondering how snow could survive here because the temperature on the mountain was not noticeably different from what it had been down on the plains. Now she had her answer. The rose-colored substance, whatever it was, was *not* snow.

She looked back across the great plains she had crossed. Even from this great height, they seemed featureless. There were no cities, no forests, no mountains other than the range that she was now climbing. All she could see was black terrain interspersed with orange-red puddles, pools and lakes. In the far distance, she could just make out Malthazzar's castle.

Something caught her eye, not far away, near the base of the mountain. Something was moving on the ground below. She watched for some time and realized that there was not one, but several somethings moving around down there, but they were too far away to see clearly. They moved more quickly than any two-footed creature could have done, but in a haphazard pattern, as if they were searching for something. They were moving toward the valley in which the strange old woman lived. With an uneasy feeling, Catherine turned and continued up the mountainside.

The low wall of rock on her left began to get taller, so that it wasn't long before it was towering over Catherine, and she felt like she was walking along the bottom of a sloping canyon whose walls gave the impression that they might fall in on her at any moment.

Night fell. The snow emitted a feeble pinkish glow, so that her shadow moved eerily around as she passed patches of the weirdly glowing substance. She became more and more tired, but forced herself to continue climbing. The top of the mountain couldn't be far above her now.

Then she turned a corner and froze with astonishment and fear. Her automatic reaction to halt saved her.

A terrifying creature, fully three times as tall as Catherine, with bulging arms as large as her trunk and enormous wings each as large as a small house was crouching a hundred or more paces distant. As soon as she rounded the corner, the beast sprang, its wings beating the air madly. It covered the distance between them in a single bound.

Landing no more than ten paces away, it leaned towards her, its mouth showing two sets of teeth: an outer yellow set, an inner red one. The creature's slobber splashed in great drops to the ground. It raised one huge arm and struck at her. The creature missed, its reach too short by no more than a foot. A great bellow came from the creature's mouth and its hot, foetid breath swept over Catherine like a warm, noxious gale. She cowered, hiding her face behind her arm, waiting for death to strike.

Once, twice, three times, she heard the creature bellow. Three times she felt and heard a swish of air as the creature's arm swept past. Three times she expected instant death.

But death did not come. Slowly, fearfully, she lowered her arm and raised her head. The creature was still standing where it had landed, ten paces distant. It seemed to be leaning towards her at a most unlikely angle. One look at its hate-filled eyes was enough to convince Catherine that it wanted to kill her. But it did not seem able to do so. It stood, thrashing at the air in front of Catherine's face, all the time leaning forward crazily.

Only slowly did Catherine realize that a thick chain was attached to a collar around the great creature's neck. The creature was chained to a point some way up the canyon, and it was now at the full extent of the chain. It eyed her murderously and made several more attempts to reach her. Then, quite suddenly, its expression changed. Instead of pure hatred and greed, it looked sad and forlorn. Wearily, as if it had done this a thousand times before, the creature turned away and with great lumbering steps began to trudge back to where it had been standing when it had originally sprung.

Warily, Catherine began to walk after it. She had taken three steps when, in a single motion that seemed much too quick for one so large, the creature turned and bounded towards her. Catherine fell back in shock. The creature landed and its arm stretched out to its full extent; lethal-looking claws ripped through the air and thudded into the ground no more than a hand's breadth from Catherine's foot. Again and again the creature clawed at her, as Catherine slowly crawled away until she was well beyond the monster's reach. As she got to her feet, she realized that she was shaking with fear.

She sat down against the canyon wall and watched the creature warily. It retreated a few paces, then returned her gaze malevolently. It sat on its haunches and folded its wings. It opened its mouth and said in a voice that caused the ground to tremble and reverberated off the canyon walls: "You shall not pass!"

Catherine lowered her head into her arms and cried.

XX Coronation

The crowning of a monarch was something that occurred only once or twice in the lifetime of most of the human inhabitants of Pirren Glanwyn. Most of the dwarves, of course, would see many such events during their long lives, but still it was a cause for celebration and festivity, and even dwarves are not immune to such attractions.

Anderskerrin, Hervân, Treadlong and Trent slept well on the soft beds in the homely establishment at which Trent had found them rooms. Even so, they woke early, their rest disturbed by the bustling sounds of preparations for the coronation rising from the courtyard below. After a hurried breakfast, Trent said his goodbyes to the others. For him this would be a busy and profitable day, and, if he were to make the most of it, he needed to be away early so that he could find an advantageous spot for selling his wares later in the day.

His companions breakfasted more leisurely. After finishing their meal, Treadlong took it upon himself to show Anderskerrin and Hervân the sights of the city.

The streets were already lined with creatures dressed in their best attire, waving flags and swords, chanting songs glorifying Reglandor's past, waiting for the procession that would wend through the city before the crowning took place on the palace steps. On every street corner, a farmer or barrower was setting up his wares, and most were already doing a steady trade. Even at this early hour, the sweet aroma of fresh bread, honey, flowers, cooked meats and cakes filled the streets.

After an hour or so of wandering the streets more or less at random, the three found themselves near a great square at the base of the palace's entrance. Here the crowd was at its thickest, for from this square the coronation itself could be watched. Uncomfortably squashed between a large family of dwarves and an unruly group of what looked like adolescent giants, the three were pressed this way and that as they awaited the beginning of the procession's march through the city.

A bell high inside the palace began to toll. The plangent sound of the massive bell rolled around the city, so that each strike of the clapper could be heard several times, first loudly, then more and more softly as the sound echoed, gradually dying away. A full thirty seconds passed between each sonorous knell. The crowd became quiet.

"A salute to the dead king," whispered Treadlong to his companions. They, along with the thousands around them, bowed their heads in reverence to the memory of the fallen king.

They lost count of the number of times that the bell tolled. But eventually the last echo died away into nothingness. The crowd began to fidget. There was a movement on the palace steps. An armed guard of dwarves, swords drawn and held vertically in front of them, appeared at the top of the steps. The guard parted, creating a wide pathway. A horse appeared, a charger bedecked in finery; a tall, handsome human sat comfortably astride the enormous animal.

The horse stepped down the flight of stone steps towards the square. A cheer went up from the crowd. "The herald!"

The charger stopped halfway down the steps. Once more the crowd fell silent. The human astride the charger spoke in a loud voice that could be heard clearly all over the square: "Glendour, King of Reglandor, Lord of Valguard, is dead."

A load moaning and wailing went up from the crowd. The flags that had been fluttering atop the palace dipped out of sight. The charger continued its descent to the level of the square. The armed dwarves hurried forward down the steps and cleared a path through the crowd for the great horse and its rider. The herald began a steady chant, still easily audible over the murmuring of the crowd: "Glendour, King of Reglandor, Lord of Valguard, is dead." Those nearest him wailed more loudly.

As the herald passed through the crowd and paused near the far edge of the square, those nearer the steps fell silent. A second guard, this time of humans, appeared. Red plumes hung from their helmets. Like the dwarves, they held their swords unsheathed vertically in front of them, near their faces. They marched down the steps. "The king's guard of humans," one of the younger dwarves nearby said. "Next will come the new king, and then the king's guard of dwarves."

Two horses appeared. The first was a grand, white charger, more impressive even than the herald's. As the crowd caught sight of the horse and its diminutive rider dressed in purple and gold, they let out a cheer.

"The new king," Treadlong said. The elves were surprised (as indeed were many in the crowd) when they saw the new king for the first time. The rider was a remarkably young human. He sat astride the mare uncomfortably and gave every indication that he was in imminent danger of falling off.

The boy-king held the reins tightly as the horse made its way down the steps. Instead of acknowledging the waves and cheers of the crowd, he seemed to be concentrating entirely on staying seated. Behind him came a smaller, grayer horse, on which sat another human, not much larger than the new king. Unlike the king, this man was dressed in a sumptuous robe of gold and red ("no purple, only the king may wear purple," said Treadlong). He seemed as comfortable on his horse as the king was uncomfortable on his. He waved to the crowd, which was cheering him just as much as it was the king.

Treadlong frowned. "He's new."

A dwarf, one of the family against which the three were pressed, overheard the remark. He turned to Treadlong. "That's Qivir, the king's chief minister. He hasn't been chief minister long, but the old king placed great store in his advice." The dwarf turned back to the spectacle and added his voice to the throng with renewed vigor as the first of the king's guard of dwarves appeared, dressed just like their human counterparts, except with golden plumes flying from their helmets.

The procession moved out the square: the dwarves moving forward to clear a path; the herald shouting his message of death; the human guard for the yet-uncrowned king; the boy; the minister; the dwarf guard bringing up the rear.

The crowd pressed together behind the procession, following it. The gathering in the square thinned, and the elves and Treadlong took advantage of the space to move forward, closer to the palace steps. The sounds of costermongers hawking their wares could now be heard above the crowd. Around the edge of the square, they were doing a brisk business. At the rear of the square, underneath a protected walkway, Trent was busy selling fruit. Treadlong waved, but the farmer was too busy to notice.

They waited in the square for the rest of the morning. Towards noon, the crowd began to thicken once more, until creatures were pressed together even more tightly than they had been earlier. There was a commotion and the crowd was parted by the returning dwarves at the head of the procession. The path passed close by the elves and the traveller, so that they could have reached out and touched the dwarves had they desired. As before, the herald came, still chanting his message of death (although now with rather less vigor). The humans, then the uncrowned king and his minister, passed, then the dwarves brought up the rear. The crowd surged, closing the gap behind the procession.

The royal guards climbed the steps and stood around the figures of the minister and the boy. The boy dismounted at the top of the steps, obviously glad to be on his own two legs at last, while the minister slid easily and gracefully off his mount. The horses were led away and were lost to view.

The crowd quieted, expectantly awaiting the coming event. As the hush settled, a page appeared, carrying a cushion of the deepest purple and edged with cloth that glittered golden in the late-morning sun. He took his place next to the chief minister, who stepped forward to address the crowd.

Qivir spoke loudly, repeating the herald's words: "Glendour, King of Reglandor, Lord of Valguard, is dead." A brief, final wail went up from the assembly. The bell tolled one last time.

The echoes of the bell reverberated around the town. Silence fell. The chief minister turned towards the page and took an object from the purple cushion. He held it high in the air, for all to see. The wintry sun reflected brightly from the crown: gold, green, blue. The boy-king came forward and knelt before the minister, his back to the crowd.

"Michael, I crown you King of Reglandor, Lord of Valguard, and King of Palindor. Serve your lands well. Lead them in time of war. Unite them in time of peace." The minister lowered the crown on to the boy's head.

The boy arose and turned towards his subjects. The minister shouted the words: "Long live King Michael." The shout was taken up by the crowd. From all around, voices united, echoing the refrain over and over again: "Long live King Michael! Long live King Michael! Long live King Michael!" A peal of bells began, replacing the mournful tolling with celebration.

In all the crowd it seemed that only Anderskerrin had noticed. His wife turned to him and asked: "Why so glum? What's the matter?"

"Didn't you hear what the minister said? He crowned the boy King of Palindor."

Hervân was dumbstruck as she realized the ramifications of her husband's words. Anderskerrin continued, "As soon as this is over, we have to go to Carn Toldwyn to warn the Ruling Council. There is treachery afoot here. They must be armed and ready for whatever this new king is planning."

Treadlong said quietly, "You are right, my percipient friend, but we cannot depart this place yet. The crowd is too thick. But as soon as it begins to disperse, we must make our way to a gate. Palindor must be warned."

Michael was flushed with success. He was the king. *He was the king!* He turned toward his minister and asked, speaking loudly to be heard over the tumult of the crowd below. "Are we ready?"

Qivir bowed. "We stand ready, Sire."

"Then let's get started. Call them."

154

The minister made a gesture, and from the palace keep strode five warriors: three humans and two dwarves. All were dressed in light armor, and all were armed.

"Come! We depart!" their new king ordered.

Michael turned and led the minister and the warriors down the palace steps, the dwarvish guard clearing a path for them.

"Come on, let's follow them!" said Anderskerrin.

He grabbed his wife's hand and dragged her through the crowd, trying to follow the king's retinue. After a couple of minutes it became obvious where they were heading. "They're making for the southern gate," said Treadlong, struggling to keep up with the elves.

"Of course. That's the quickest way to Palindor," said Anderskerrin. Breathlessly, he continued to push his way through the crowd that thronged the streets.

They were about two hundred paces from the southern gate when the king reached it. The guards at the gate stepped to one side to let the king's party through. As soon as the last of the five warriors had passed, the guards closed the gate and resumed their positions in front of it. The elves and the traveller hurried to the gate.

"Please let us pass," said Anderskerrin.

The chief guard, a dwarf, stood his ground, his sword glinting ominously in the sun. "By order of the king, none may pass. No one is permitted to leave the city."

"But that was before the coronation," argued the elf. "He has been crowned now. We are free to leave."

The dwarf shook his head. "The king has ordered that none may pass until he returns."

"Where has he gone?" asked Treadlong in a very reasonable tone of voice, trying to defuse the situation.

"I cannot say," replied the dwarf unhelpfully.

The three looked at each another, their fears written on their faces. Anderskerrin stepped forward, to remonstrate further with the guard. The dwarf raised his sword until its point was resting on the elf's clothing, and a second guard stepped forward, his sword also unsheathed.

The first guard said, "My orders are to imprison any creature that insists on passage, and if any creature should somehow pass through the gate, then he is to be killed without benefit of trial." The look on his face made it clear that he intended to obey his orders.

Hervân pulled at her husband's sleeve and Anderskerrin fell back. Several passersby who had watched the confrontation with interest began to disperse. Within moments, the three stood alone in the small area in front of the gate.

"Come," said Treadlong. "We must retire to consider what this means and what we are going to do about it."

"What it means and what we're going to do about it? Isn't it obvious? That new king is going to Palindor with a squad of warriors to destroy the Ruling Council. We must get... ow!"

Anderskerrin's tirade was ended by a sharp, painful kick on the shin administered by his wife. She whispered "Shhh... do you want everyone to know? Treadlong is right. We must go somewhere quiet and plan a way out of here."

Rubbing his shin, Anderskerrin was half led, half pulled away from the gate. The three companions returned to the hostelry. Trent was there, along with twenty or more merchants, celebrating the day's profits. Trent raised a glass of ale as the elves and the traveller entered the building. "Come, join us and celebrate!" he called. The traveller shook his head, whereupon the farmer made his way around the tables and quietly drew the three to one side.

His face, which had looked pleased, suddenly looked grim now that others could no longer see it.

"'ave you tried to leave the city?" he asked.

Anderskerrin nodded.

"Then you know we be trapped?"

The elf nodded again.

"Something mighty strange be afoot."

Treadlong spoke quietly. "We think the king is leading an attack on the Ruling Council of Palindor. Consider: Pirren Glanwyn has been sealed since Glendour's death. No one in Palindor even knows of the king's death, much less that it was caused by a Palindoric gnome. They'll be completely unprepared when Michael and his warriors arrive in Carn Toldwyn."

"Aye. Well, I suppose it be none of my business. If a Palindoric creature were stupid enough to come 'ere and kill their king, I suppose the new king be in 'is rights to go looking for a fight."

A thought struck Anderskerrin. "This gnome who is supposed to have killed the old king? Who is he and what happened to him? I wonder if there's some way we could see him? I'd love to find out what's really going on here."

The farmer shook his head. "You won't be able to do that, me young elf. Anyway, it were a female gnome, not a male. And she be dead. The new king killed 'er as she were tryin' to kill the chief minister."

"You mean a female gnome is responsible for all this? What was her name? Does anyone know?"

"Well, I 'ave 'eard she were called Sherna. She carried some sort of letter from the Ruling Council of Palindor; that were 'ow she got in to see the king. He thought she were an emissary of some kind."

Anderskerrin had turned white. "Sherna? That cannot be...."

"Well, 'tis what I 'ave 'eard. Sherna, that were 'er name."

"Then there can be no debate. We *must* get out of here. Sherna was the daughter of Drefynt, the last of the Holy Gnomes of Palindor, and the sister of Benglubber, a member of the Ruling Council. She was a traveller, not a warrior. She would no more kill a king than would our friend Treadlong here."

Treadlong was looking mystified. He nodded his head slowly. "Aye, Anderskerrin speaks the truth. I have met this gnome Sherna. She would not kill a king. There is more here than meets my eyes. While I am by nature an observer, the time, it seems, has come for action. We must find a way out of this walled prison for at least one of us, so that the Ruling Council may be warned. Come. Let us walk the city wall and see if there is not some point that is undefended."

With a large gulp, the farmer emptied his glass of ale, then banged it down on the table. "Right. Let's be going, then." The four of them pushed their way through the celebrating merchants, their faces drawn into hard lines.

They walked the boundary of the city twice, their spirits falling with each step. The defense of the wall was strongest at the gates, at each of which a squad of six armed dwarves stood guard. The gates were bolted shut, and the dwarves stood in front of the heavy doors, many with swords unsheathed and ready for immediate action. On the city wall above each gate, a gatekeeper looked outwards, beyond the wall. If a traveller from outside the walls desired entrance to the city, the gate was unbolted to permit him to enter, then the doors were closed and bolted as soon as he had passed through into the prison city.

Between the gates, along the inside of the wall that stood higher than the tallest human, a dwarf was posted every hundred paces. Each dwarf was in sight of at least his two closest colleagues, so that at the slightest sign of trouble he could call for help. All the guards were alert and looked willing to use their weapons without a qualm.

Treadlong approached some of the guards on the eastern side of the city, always with the same result. As soon as he came within ten paces, the guard would unsheathe his sword. At five paces Treadlong was told to stop. If he moved closer, he was warned that if he came any farther, he would be detained in a cell until the king returned to deal with him.

It took them the entire afternoon and into the early evening to circumnavigate the city walls twice. When the four gathered once more in the hostelry, they were tired and dispirited. By now, the merchants staying at the inn had discovered that they were to be kept in the city until the king returned. They grumbled amongst themselves, but not too loudly since two of their number had already been taken to the dungeons.

Over their meal, the four talked quietly in one corner of the dining room.

"Whatever we do, we must do it soon. The king already has half a day's lead on us. Fortunately, the king's entourage was travelling on foot, otherwise we'd never catch them."

"They want to reach Carn Toldwyn without warning," said Treadlong. "Horses would give them away."

Anderskerrin said, "If we leave it much longer we won't be able to reach Carn Toldwyn before them even if they are on foot. An elf can travel through forest much more quickly and silently than a human or a dwarf, but it's not a forest I know and it's easy to lose one's way in a strange forest."

Hervân suggested, "How about if we try to break out in the middle of the night? The guards will be sleepy then, and they won't be able to see one another so well once night falls."

"Full moon tonight," said Treadlong, glumly. "And the guards were changed twice this afternoon to keep them fresh. I expect they'll be changed every two or three hours throughout the night. It may be the best we can do, of course, and we should keep it in mind if we can't think of something better."

It was Trent who made the suggestion that they eventually adopted. "Y'know, if we could just attract the attention of those guards, the wall ain't so 'igh that it couldn't be scaled. The elves are nimble enough that they could probably get over it without too much trouble."

"But we'd have to distract at least two guards," said Hervân. "Every point in the wall is visible to at least two of them."

"Aye. I can't think 'ow to do that without looking suspicious," agreed the farmer.

Treadlong gazed into his broth, thinking. After a few moments he said, "I think you might have something there, Trent. When we've finished eating let's look at those walls one more time."

XXI Out of the City

None of them save the farmer slept well that night. Treadlong, who had refined Farmer Trent's idea, was weighed by a sense of responsibility for the plan that they had adopted, and kept going over it in his mind, looking for flaws. Anderskerrin and Hervân were worried that they would not be quick enough or quiet enough to put the plan into action. The three were bleary-eyed as they greeted the cheerful farmer at breakfast the next morning.

If the plan was successful, it would be the last good meal that the elves would eat for some time, but even so they were not hungry. They forced down the fresh cream and buttered pancakes without enthusiasm, becoming more and more nervous as time went on. "I wish we could just get this over with," muttered Anderskerrin.

"I understand, my friend," said Treadlong, "but we must wait until midmorning, when there will be crowds around."

Anderskerrin nodded, and went back to playing morosely with his pancakes.

––––––––––

The sound of the palace bell tolling eleven was the signal for them to start.

The last of the eleven strokes died away. Treadlong looked around. Everything seemed as ready as it would ever be. The nearest guard was twenty paces away, looking idly around, not expecting trouble. The wall behind him was not tall, perhaps twice the guard's height. One other guard was visible, about eighty paces to Treadlong's right. Anderskerrin and Hervân were leaning against a building midway between the two guards, chatting quietly to themselves. Treadlong was relieved: they had overcome their nervousness and no one would suspect that they were anything other than a pair of harmless elves discussing some triviality.

Treadlong took two paces forward into the open area in front of the wall. The closest guard eyed him nervously for a moment. Treadlong ignored him, licked his lips, pursed them, and began to blow. A pure, liquid tone flowed forth, causing all in earshot to stop their business and turn towards the source of the strange sound. The tone changed and, almost like magic, a tune issued from Treadlong's lips. It was a trick that none of the nearby creatures had seen before, and quite a crowd had gathered by the time he had finished the tune.

As the last note died away, Treadlong called out: "Hear ye! Hear ye! Treadlong, Traveller and Storyteller, will now amaze you with tales of far away places! Come hear of the Fire Mountain of Soltarwyn! Hear of the ancient glories of the Barrows of Perendeth. Hear the tale of the Land Of Giants in the east where the sun rises each morning! Come one; come all!" He continued in this manner for some time. When he was satisfied with the size of the crowd, he took off his hat and laid it on the ground before him, to catch the pennies that were traditionally given at the end of a storyteller's tales.

The guard near the wall moved a couple of steps closer, so that he was just a few paces from the rear of the crowd.

In a clear voice, Treadlong began: "The first of my tales, all amazing, all true, concerns the great and magnificent Fire Mountain of Soltarwyn. Has any of you esteemed creatures ever seen this most amazing spectacle?" Fifty heads shook in unison. "Well, gather around, and I will tell you about this most awesome, this most unbelievable and aptly named of mountains. But what you are about to hear is not some tale given to me by some other storyteller. For I am Treadlong the Traveller, and I tell you truly, that this tale is no mere story fabricated for your amusement. For it happened to me...."

An expectant sigh went up from the crowd, and Treadlong began the story.

The bell tolled the quarter hour: the second signal. Treadlong was well into his second story, an ancient tale of the founding of the Holy Barrows at Perendeth. His cap was more than half full of coins from the first tale, and the crowd had grown even larger as he began a tale both well known and universally loved.

As the bell chimed, he permitted himself a brief, inaudible sigh of relief. He had timed it perfectly. He was just reaching the part where the phantoms materialized to tell the old gnome how to escape the woods. He lowered his voice dramatically. The crowd pressed forward. The guard, unable to hear clearly, edged closer.

Treadlong continued.

Trent heard the toll of the quarter hour. Slowly, as Treadlong had shown him, he counted to sixty on his fingers. Then he walked forward casually. There were few passersby, but enough for the plan to work. He moved slowly, keeping his eyes away from the dwarvish guard who was a hundred paces away, then fifty, then twenty.

The farmer took an apple from his pocket and began to munch it with obvious relish. Still he kept his eyes firmly away from the dwarf. In the distance, he could see a large crowd gathered around Treadlong. Everything looked perfect. A young dwarf mother was walking towards him, dragging a child by the hand. The child was whining: "...but I wanted to hear the end of the story, Mama...." The farmer slowed his pace, judging distances.

The woman was talking to the child, and neither the child nor its mother was paying much attention to where they were going. Trent stepped half a pace to one side and the child knocked against his arm. The apple jumped out of his hand and rolled across the ground until it stopped, no more than five paces from the guard. It was too much to hope for, of course, that the guard would stoop to retrieve the apple, but that would not be necessary.

"Now look what you've done. Say sorry to the human, Mirnâh," the woman berated her child.

Trent glanced at the guard; the dwarf was watching the scene playing out before him with unconcealed amusement.

162

Fifty paces away, Anderskerrin nodded. "Now!"

Anderskerrin and Hervân dashed across the short distance from the building against which they had been lounging to the wall. As Anderskerrin reached the wall, he bent down. A moment later, his wife bounded lightly on to his back and jumped nimbly to the top of the wall. She lay flat and extended her hand. Anderskerrin flung a pack over the wall, then jumped high, reaching for his wife's hand. A moment later, they jumped down on to the grass on the far side. The whole thing had taken less than ten seconds.

The two elves breathed deeply as they regained their breaths. Anderskerrin recovered the pack and both of them pressed themselves against the wall to avoid being seen by one of the guards atop the wall near each gate, posted there to watch for creatures approaching the city.

He took two farls of honey bread from the pack. "Now we wait for darkness," said Anderskerrin.

They munched the sweet honey bread and drank sparingly of the water in their canteens. The wintry sun shone weakly, but the stones of the wall were warm. They whiled away the afternoon in fits of dozing.

The sun set, and night fell. The moon arose. They stretched, and Anderskerrin pulled on the pack. Cautiously, he checked for any sign of gatekeepers atop the walls. They had gone for the night.

"All clear," said Anderskerrin. "Let's be on our way."

Now, if only they could reach Carn Toldwyn in time.

XXII *Fayorn*

Catherine became aware that someone was standing nearby, watching her.

She wiped her arm across her eyes, drying her tears. A dozen paces away stood a short figure in a gray habit, the hood completely hiding the figure's face in its shadows.

The figure took a step closer.

A loud bellow came from the huge black creature that had attacked her. It lunged again, straining at its chain. The newcomer moved closer, ignoring the creature. The creature bellowed twice more, then retreated a few steps, where it sat on its haunches and watched them malevolently.

The newcomer halted beside Catherine.

"Why do you not use your sword, Catherine?"

She got to her feet. "How do you know my name, sage?"

The sage did not answer. It seemed to be waiting, and at last Catherine broke the silence by answering the question that the sage had posed.

"My sword would be no use against that creature..." Her answer died away. She was thinking something more, but she did not voice her thought.

She unsheathed Scalmyùt. The sword glistened in an ugly manner in the oppressive light of Sheol. She looked at the monstrous creature that barred her path. It moved two steps closer. Its tongue lolled out of its cavernous mouth, almost as if it hoped that Catherine would try to attack.

She finished her thought. "...and anyway, I don't feel like attacking the creature. There's too much darkness and a feeling of death about this place. I don't want to add to that. I'm tired of fighting things by destroying them. All I want to do is to get past the creature and return to Palindor. I don't want to harm it."

"It wants to harm you."

"Doesn't matter. Killing isn't the answer."

"My Lord will be pleased to hear you say that, Catherine. Come, let us walk together. The creature will not harm us. Have no fear; there will be no need to use your sword." He held out his hand, and Catherine took it. The sage's touch was dry and lifeless. His hand was ancient and wrinkled. She wondered how old this sage was.

"How did you know my name?" she said again.

"We met long ago. You were much younger then, of course; but then, as now, you wore the belt of the first High Monarch."

Catherine searched her memory, but could not remember meeting a sage when she was last in Palindor. "When did we meet?"

"You probably don't remember. It was in a part of Palindor that used to be known as Dankenwood. That was my domain."

Catherine's mouth dropped open. "But Dankenwood was Fayorn's...."

"At your service, Your Majesty." The sage bowed.

"But Fayorn was nothing like you. You're the wrong shape! He was dumpy and fat and...."

"...ugly? Yes, that was the way I appeared then. But you are surely wise enough not to judge by appearances. Come, let us walk. We can discuss these matters some other time."

The sage, still holding Catherine's hand, took a step toward the monstrous creature. With her free hand, Catherine gripped Scalmyùt more tightly, holding it in front of them.

Together, they walked towards the black monster.

The creature did not move, but its eyes glowed evilly red. They walked past the invisible line on the ground beyond which the creature could not reach. Now there seemed to be nothing to prevent it pouncing on them and crushing them. But the creature did not move. Still the sage led them closer. The monstrous creature waited until they were no more than five human paces away, then it drew itself to its full height, and arched its evil head down towards them.

The twin rows of teeth parted, as if it were ready to remove Catherine's head with a single bite. She screamed and drew back her sword, ready to strike. She was on the point of slashing at the creature when she realized that the sage had let go of her hand. She hesitated.

Fayorn spoke quietly. "Do not use it. To use your sword is death. The creature cannot harm us."

Her sword arm still drawn back, Catherine breathed deeply. Her heart was beating wildly. Saliva from the creature's mouth dropped inches from her face. But the creature did not strike. Slowly, she pulled the sword back. Fayorn grasped her hand again. "Whatever happens, don't use the sword. It's what the creature wants." Catherine felt the sage pull her firmly forward. With one last look up at the gaping mouth, she turned away. Together they passed by the creature.

It watched them take several steps, then fell in behind them, taking one step for every three of theirs. In this manner, they passed the point where the chain around the monster's neck was anchored to the ground.

They kept going. After a short while, the thud of the creature's footsteps ceased. Catherine turned and saw that the creature was straining against its chain. They had safely passed it by! The creature opened its mouth and bellowed, then retreated, head hanging, back to the point where its chain was attached to the ground.

Catherine let out a long breath and sheathed Scalmyùt.

"Thank you," she said to the sage. Fayorn inclined his head silently. Their hands parted as they continued forward.

The path began to rise more steeply. They kept going. Half an hour later they found themselves at the very top of the mountain, in a flattish clearing, covered with a thin layer of the pinkish snow. There were plenty of boulders scattered around, but there was no sign of the entrance to the labyrinth that Malthazzar had talked about.

She searched for some time while Fayorn stood in the center, silent and apparently unconcerned. Eventually she gave up and said to the sage. "I can't find it."

"What exactly are you looking for?"

"A cave, or some kind of tunnel. Malthazzar said that there was a labyrinth whose entrance was around here somewhere. The labyrinth is the way back to Palindor."

"And you believed me, you fool!"

Catherine's head whipped around in shock.

Standing at the entrance to the clearing was the enormous creature they had passed earlier, one end of its chain in its hand. As she looked in horror, the chain melted away and the creature slowly shrank and changed shape, until it was a form that she knew only too well.

Malthazzar strode forward. He pointed angrily at Fayorn. "You! If it weren't for you, she would have used the sword on me, and I would have cast her forever into the Pit. You will never leave this place alive."

Fayorn did not move.

Malthazzar turned to Catherine. "And as for you... you're pitiful. You came all the way to the top of this mountain because you believed me!" Malthazzar roared with laughter. "Oh, how they'll love to hear this tale told and retold in the Great Hall! Catherine, the great High Queen, the minion of Olvensar, trusted Malthazzar's word so much that she climbed Mount Perilorn itself!"

The laugh became a gale of merriment, which only gradually subsided.

"Is there no way out of this place then?" Catherine's voice was more than halfway to tears.

Regaining his composure, Malthazzar said, "A way out? A way out of Sheol? No, my child, there is no way out of here. Unless, of course, you regard the Pit as a way out. Tell her, silent one. You know I speak the truth."

Fayorn looked at Malthazzar. Slowly, his hand went up to his hood. He grasped it firmly, then drew it back.

Malthazzar took a step backward. Catherine's eyes flickered between the two of them. Fayorn's face, now exposed, was full of a peace and a power that she had seen on only one face before: that of the High Lord Olvensar.

It was *not* Olvensar's face, though. Fayorn's visage was drier, less comforting, more weary than the High Lord's; but the eyes were the same: so peaceful, yet so powerful.

While Catherine was comforted by Fayorn's look, Malthazzar seemed to suffer the opposite reaction: there was a look of naked fear on his face. He took another step backward. Then he screamed at the sage. "You! I could sense that Olvensar had sent one of his Mighty Ones. But I had no idea it was you. How dare you walk in my kingdom? There is no place here for you! Begone."

"We will leave Sheol, Malthazzar. But be warned: we shall meet again, you and I. Now it is you that must be gone, for while we are here, this ground is no longer part of your dominion." The sage raised his hands. "In the name of the High Lord Olvensar, I command you: begone from this place."

A single, terrifying shaft of darkness rent the air, like a bolt of dark lightning. The ground shook and a thunderclap stunned Catherine with its loudness. When she recovered, Malthazzar was gone, and a pall of miasmic smoke hung over the place where he had been standing.

A warm breeze sprang up, and dispersed the smoke. Where Malthazzar had been standing there was now a most peculiar sight. Two wooden doorframes stood side by side, with no obvious means of support. Through the doorways, Catherine — she cried out for joy! — could see colors.

The left doorway showed a slate gray sky hanging above ground that was green and purple with close-cropped heather. In the distance, she could see a town. Suddenly, she recognized the scene: she was looking at Carn Toldwyn, seen from Machrenmoor.

But the brightest colors came from the second doorway. She stepped forward and halted a couple of paces in front of it. On the other side of the doorway was a glade in a wood. A cerulean pool reflected the light from a bright, yellow sun. The colors seemed to stream out of the doorway to light up the forlorn mountaintop on which she and Fayorn were standing.

As she looked, a shadow crossed the grass on the other side of the doorway, and into the frame walked an old man dressed in shabby clothes. As soon as she saw his face, she realized that she had been wrong, and the sage's face was merely a pale reflection of the original. She took a step towards Olvensar, intending to walk through the doorway. But he smiled and lifted a hand to stop her. "Catherine, you did well, my child. But tell me, why did you not release the creature from its chains?"

Catherine was taken aback. "I never thought of it. And I was so afraid."

"But it could not have harmed you. You were with Fayorn; and even if Fayorn had been worlds away, did I not tell you that I would be with you?"

Catherine nodded unhappily. "I'm sorry. I was so stupid. I forgot all about what you'd said. If only I'd realized how scared the creature was of Scalmyùt..."

Olvensar's face crinkled in laughter. In response to Catherine's puzzled expression, he explained: "The creature wasn't scared of the sword. He was bound by our agreement: he couldn't harm you unless you first harmed him. So he desperately wanted you to attack him with the sword. But you wouldn't. It was Fayorn's advice that protected you, not the sword. Never put your trust in things, Catherine; such trust is always misplaced."

Catherine hung her head in shame. "I see now; I got it all wrong."

Olvensar's hand reached out through the doorway; he put his hand under her chin, lifted her head, and looked into her eyes. "But you have learned a most important lesson." He released her. "Now, Fayorn; come here."

Fayorn walked forward. Catherine moved to one side, to let him stand in front of the doorway. She was surprised to see that he looked guilty and uncomfortable.

"How do you feel, my child?" said the High Lord.

"Humble. Sorry."

"And tired?"

"Oh yes, Lord Olvensar. So very, very tired."

"Then it is time for you to be with me. Catherine still has a job to do. She must return to Palindor, but your job in the world of mortals is over. You have done well. Come now, let us walk and talk together in the cool of the evening."

He stretched out and grasped the sage's hand. The sage walked through the doorway.

As he did so, a strange thing happened. For several seconds, it seemed to Catherine that there were *two* sages. One remained, motionless, standing on the Sheol side of the doorway. The other, as it passed through the doorway, seemed to glow brightly; the gray habit was replaced with one of gold that glistered brilliantly as it reflected the sun on the other side of the doorway. The face of the sage on the Sheol side looked old and careworn; but the one in the garden looked young, bright and full of hope.

The sage in the garden looked around in amazement; he looked down at the new habit he was wearing, then back through the doorway at his other half. A brief cloud crossed his face, as if remembering a dark nightmare from which he had just awoken. He shrugged vaguely and looked into Olvensar's face. A smile replaced the frown, as if the nightmare were forgotten.

The sage standing next to Catherine seemed to dissolve into wisps of smoke. As she watched, the doorway into the garden too began to dissolve. In moments, Catherine was standing alone on top of the mountain, a single doorway showing the way back to Palindor.

She took a deep breath and stepped through.

XXIII Across the Border

Michael was proud of himself.

He had successfully turned Pirren Glanwyn into an enormous prison. His guards would make sure that no one escaped from the city. Even better, Qivir had done a superb job of arranging things outside the walls even as the coronation was progressing.

Michael and his party had left the city on foot, to mislead anyone who spotted them and subsequently escaped. They soon took a turning off the path and entered a small wood. Inside the copse, tied up and waiting for them, were seven warhorses outfitted with weapons, their saddlebags full of food. They mounted the horses, went back to the road, and continued on their way. Within two hours of being crowned king, Michael — much happier to be riding over level ground than trying to negotiate steps on horseback — was leading his party at a canter towards Palindor.

They reached the River Chân as the sun was setting. The warhorses were lathering from the alternating pace of gallop and canter that Michael had set. Coming in sight of the border, he could see, on the nearest bank of the Chân, several small groups of figures laying fires for the night. His party approached the closest group.

Michael slid out of the saddle. A tall human, a quiver on his back and a longbow in his hand, detached himself from the rest of his group and bowed before the king.

171

"How go things, Haller?" asked Michael.

"Everything is exactly as planned, Your Majesty. The fires will be lit within the hour. After that we will post our first watch. From now on, no creature that tries to cross into Palindor will survive." He lifted his bow and gave it a friendly pat. "In terrain like this, my archers cannot miss."

"Excellent! We will stay with you and rest for an hour or two. Then we shall continue on our way."

Michael motioned the others to dismount. They unpacked food from the saddlebags and cooked it over the fire while the horses nibbled at the late-season grass. Michael looked at the full moon as it rose on the eastern horizon. It seemed to be smiling at him. *Good*, he thought. *This is going perfectly. The Ruling Council will never know what hit them.*

Some of the dwarves and humans travelling with Michael engaged in target practice, battle axes against arrows; others nodded off to sleep. Michael and Qivir discussed their plans.

The moon was halfway towards the zenith when Michael kicked awake those who slept. They mounted their horses, settled themselves in their saddles, and crossed the wooden bridge into Palindor. The horses' hooves echoed hollowly as they clopped over the bridge, then, as they began to climb the slope of the low hill on the western side of the Chân, relative silence descended once again.

They climbed the hill and paused briefly as they looked down on the land they had entered to subdue. One of the dwarves drew in his breath and asked: "What's that over there? In the sky?" He pointed to the west where, far away, hung a single brilliant star.

"Who cares? Now, come on! We have no time to waste," said Michael. He kicked the flanks of his horse, which moved forward at a trot, then a canter, then a full gallop. The seven warhorses descended the low-lying hill and thundered on to the Plains of Kradesh.

They rode wordlessly for four hours, staying close to the boundary between the forest and the plain. Then Qivir drew alongside Michael and said, "I think it is time, Your Majesty."

Michael looked up at the sky. The moon was now ahead of them, and the night was more than halfway over. Michael signalled for the party to halt.

He whispered urgently, "Now, remember: we must be careful. We are in enemy country, and we know what they'll do to us if we're discovered."

Everyone dismounted. The moon glinted off their light armor, which made quiet crunching sounds as they moved about. The bags were pulled from the horses and hefted on to backs. Soon everyone in the party save the king and his minister was loaded with a pack.

Michael turned his horse to face Reglandor, spoke quietly in its ear, and slapped its rump. It whinnied, walked a few steps, then broke into a canter. The other horses followed.

They watched the animals heading back the way they had come. By morning, the horses would be back in Reglandor and no one would know that a party of seven, intent on killing, had been deposited inside Palindor.

Michael led them into the wood. The trees were well separated and the going was easy, even though they stayed away from paths. For four more hours they travelled as the moonlit night drew to a close. As the sky behind them began to lighten, they looked for a hiding place to spend the day. They found a small dingle: a narrow, steep-sided valley through which a stream noisily passed. At the bottom of the valley, next to the stream, they were invisible to anyone outside the dingle. There they ate a breakfast of honey bread and water; a sentry was posted to keep watch, then the rest of the party curled up on the grass and slept.

XXIV Ordeal by Water

The two elves settled into an easy, loping gait. Anderskerrin's pack was small and light, holding just enough food to last them until they were inside Palindor's forests, where food should be plentiful. Hervân carried nothing.

Elves, small though they are, can travel much more quickly than humans when they put their minds to it, and these two were determined and in a hurry. The thousands of paces went by quickly. They stopped for a while around midnight, to refresh themselves at a stream, then set out again. They reached the wide, open valley of the grasslands near the border just as the first light of dawn touched the sky behind them. A chain of fires was lit on the plain below, following the path of the River Chân.

Hervân asked, "What do you make of those fires?"

"I don't know. But we must be careful."

They loped onward, wary now. Distances on the grasslands were deceptive. The elves had expected to reach the nearest of the fires in only a few minutes, but it was over an hour before they began to approach it, and the sun was by now well risen.

They slowed to a walk. "The fires seem to be at all of the bridges," said Hervân.

"Yes. I wonder if it's the custom?"

"I don't think so. I've never heard of it. And it looks like there are people around them."

"Guards of some kind?"

"It certainly looks that way. Let's hope they're just for show."

Anderskerrin nodded in doubtful agreement.

An archer scrambled to his feet, detaching himself from the other half dozen humans who were roasting a small animal over the fire for breakfast. He retrieved his bow and nocked an arrow. Tensioning the bowstring, he lowered the weapon so that the arrow was pointing safely towards the ground. Striding forward, he intercepted the two approaching elves.

"Good morning," said Anderskerrin cheerfully.

"Good morning," nodded the archer. "I'm afraid the border has been closed, by order of the new king."

The elves exchanged glances. "He has been this way then?" asked Hervân.

"Yes, he...." The archer recognized his mistake and stopped himself. "That's unimportant. The point is, the border is sealed until further notice."

Anderskerrin said, "But Palindor is my home. I was born there, and my wife and I have journeyed from Soltarwyn, where we now live, so that I might show her my land. Surely, your king meant only that the border was closed to his subjects. My wife and I hail from near the Fire Mountain in Soltarwyn; you can tell as much by our speech. Your king cannot have meant that such as we were to be denied crossing."

The archer looked unsure of himself. "Wait here," he said. "I'll consult our leader."

He walked over to the fire, bent down, and spoke hurriedly with another human. This human got to his feet, picked up a bow, removed an arrow from his quiver, set it to the string, then walked across to the two elves, waiting nervously.

"What seems to be the problem?" he asked in an officious tone.

Anderskerrin repeated his story, and the archer said, "I am ordered by King Michael not to permit any to pass. Further, if any creature attempts to pass, my men and I will shoot that creature dead before it has taken five steps across the bridge." His eyes narrowed. "Do I make myself clear?"

It was obviously pointless to argue. "Yes, sir. Forgive me; I did not intend to challenge the authority of either you or your king."

The archer turned to the human who had first spoken to the elves. "And you, Slachar; is that clear enough for you? It would be quite easy for there to be an accident with my bow, you know. No one here would dare testify against me."

Slachar gulped. "Yes, yes, quite clear. Sorry to have bothered you, sir."

"Now go back to your post. And you" — he turned to the elves — "there's no point in just hanging around. You aren't going to get across the border. All the bridges are guarded. And you needn't think you can cross the river at night, because we have patrols going up and down the river from dusk to dawn. Now, begone with you."

He turned away dismissively and stomped back to the fire. Slachar looked at the elves, then shrugged as if to say: I'm awfully sorry, but I did try.

The elves turned away and began to retrace their steps. After they had gone a few hundred paces, they stopped to discuss the situation.

"Was he telling the truth, do you think?" asked Hervân.

"About all the bridges being guarded? I think so. Remember the other fires we saw burning? I can't remember how many bridges there are along the Chân, just a handful, I think. It wouldn't take many men to guard them all."

"What can we do then? The river is much too wide to cross without a bridge."

Thinking aloud, Anderskerrin said, "Further upstream, where it's narrower, it's probably much fiercer. The slopes and rocks of the mountains will see to that."

"So what are we going to do? We can't just give up."

"Well, if it were just me, I think I could get across once the sun goes down. But I'm not sure how we're going to get you across."

"How would you cross? I'm as strong as you are."

"I know, but it's got nothing to do with strength. I was brought up as a fisherelf, remember. So, although I don't much like the thought of it, I could probably swim across the river..." He needed to say no more. A horrified look had crossed his wife's face. The thought of being immersed in water terrifies elves almost as much as the idea of being trapped in a cave or tunnel. Hervân was not going to cross the river that way.

As they continued discussing what they might do, the elves began to walk slowly northward, parallel to the river. They walked for most of the remainder of the day, in which time they passed two more bridges. Here too archers were camped. Anderskerrin approached them and told them the same story he had told their companions downstream, but to equally little effect. Morosely, the two elves continued on.

As the day stretched on, Hervân reluctantly began to concede that the only way across the river was going to be to try to cross it at night in the hope that they would not be spotted. Sweat broke out on her brow at the thought of all that water and how easy it would be to drown. She wondered if perhaps it was really necessary that both of them cross into Palindor; after all, surely one elf was enough to warn the Ruling Council?

As they walked and talked and thought, the land began to rise as they approached the base of the forest that covers the lower slopes of the Mountains of Mourn. As the sun was setting, they entered the trees. For the first time that day, they stopped to eat, under a large fir tree.

After they had eaten, Anderskerrin led Hervân to the bank of the river. As he had expected, the river was much narrower than it was lower down on the grasslands. There didn't seem to be any rocks in it, but the water sluiced with worrying speed through its narrow channel. He eyed it nervously.

The sun went down. The moon would rise in another hour or so, and he dearly wanted to be on the far side of the river by the time that the moon was up. "Stay here," he said, and went back downstream, to the edge of the forest, where he could look across the grasslands they had crossed earlier. The light of bonfires stretched along the now-invisible river, and doubtless patrols were passing between the fires. He hurried back to his wife.

"All right. Here's the plan. We don't have much time. I'm going to go alone. But this river is too fast for me to swim across. So I'll break off a sturdy tree branch and use it for support. That way all I need do is kick across the river. But I've got to hurry; they said there would be guards patrolling the river and I'm sure it won't be long before a patrol gets here. Keep a lookout; I'm going to try to find a good solid branch."

He climbed into a nearby evergreen, and began to walk out along one of its lower branches. The bough began to bend. He jumped up and down. The branch bent and swayed, but gave no sign of breaking. Hervân hurried forward to help him. She jumped up and grasped the branch then bounced up and down in time with Anderskerrin's jumping. Suddenly, and with a loud crack, the branch broke off at the trunk.

Anderskerrin tumbled to the ground. He looked dazed for a moment, then shook himself and stood up. He ripped the remaining bark and cambium away from where the branch was still attached loosely to the trunk, then set about removing the twigs that grew along the limb.

Even though he hurried, the light of the moon was beginning to filter through the trees by the time that the limb had been stripped of the twigs. He looked up at the sky anxiously, then towards the grasslands. Surely it could not be long before a patrol passed by.

The branch was heavier than he had expected. He could drag it along the ground, but that made too much noise, so Hervân lifted the other end and together they carried it to the water's edge. Hervân dropped her end into the water. She nearly screamed when the water splashed up on to her. She took two steps away from the bank: she felt giddy just standing so close to so much water.

It all happened so quickly, much more quickly than the time it takes to tell. Anderskerrin was looking at the branch and the water, steeling himself to say goodbye to his wife and jump into the terrifying, swirling liquid; Hervân was standing back from the bank, her eyes shifting between her husband and the water into which he was about to throw himself. There was a sudden noise nearby: a big, heavy creature — obviously a human — was coming through the forest towards them. Anderskerrin looked anxiously towards the sound. He could see nothing, but the sounds were unmistakable. Another few moments and they would be discovered. There was no time for thought: grasping his end of the branch, he jumped into the river.

He had expected that the swirling current would pull him quickly downstream, but it did not. The riverbed near the bank was extraordinarily muddy. It was also much shallower than he had expected. Instead of being carried downstream with the branch, both he and the branch were instantly stuck in the mud.

He tried desperately to free himself. The mud sucked at his legs. He yanked the branch, but it was as stuck as he was. He grappled with the branch, at the same time trying to free himself from the sticky mud. He was too busy to pay any attention to what was happening on the bank.

Hervân had heard the sound of the approaching guard; she too, had waited fearfully for the human to appear. She watched, terrified, as Anderskerrin jumped into the water. The loud splash as he jumped into the water was followed almost immediately by the sound of heavy human feet pounding the earth. There was not just one human bearing down on the elves: there were two!

She took a step closer to the river, but she could not bring herself to jump in. The archers appeared, just a few steps away. They halted and each pulled an arrow from his quiver. One faced Hervân, and one turned towards Anderskerrin, still grappling with the branch.

A fraction of a second apart, they loosed their arrows. The one aimed at Anderskerrin missed, for at that moment the branch finally came free, and Anderskerrin fell forward, grasping the branch tightly as the arrow splashed into the water behind him.

The other arrow hit Hervân.

Involuntarily, she stepped backward as the arrow buried itself in her shoulder. She began a shout of pain. It finished as a scream of terror as she lost her footing and fell backwards into the river.

The archers paused for a second to take stock of the situation, and it was that momentary delay that allowed the elves to escape. While the humans stood on the bank, trying to decide what to do, the current dragged Anderskerrin's branch into the center of the river. Anderskerrin grasped Hervân with one hand as she spluttered to the surface. Still holding the branch with his other hand, he kicked furiously to propel them into the fastest-moving water.

The archers rushed to the river edge and pulled another pair of arrows from their quivers, but the elves were already several paces downstream. The dim shadows made it impossible even for warrior archers to aim at the moving targets with any accuracy. Two arrows splashed harmlessly into the water near the elves. The archers nocked more arrows and loosed again. One arrow struck Anderskerrin a glancing blow, the other buried itself in the log. The elves turned a corner and were swept out of sight.

Now the real battle began, for Anderskerrin's arms were tiring. He strained to hold on to both the log and to his wife, who was screaming at the top of her voice in his ear. She was on her back, and he had his arm around her neck, supporting her so there was no chance of her drowning as long as he could keep his strength.

"You're all right," he shouted. "Stop screaming. It'll bring the archers." But it was no good: she was too terrified to pay any attention.

Then the ice cold of the water finally hit him.

The river was fed from the slopes of the high mountains to the north and its temperature was barely above freezing. Anderskerrin realized that they had escaped one danger only to find themselves in a greater one. If he could not reach shore quickly, they would either freeze because of the cold water or drown from simple tiredness.

And how his arms ached.

Anderskerrin kicked as hard as he could, but his strength was as nothing against the force of the current. Now that the branch had found the center of the river, the waters kept it there. Kicking with all his might, all the elf could do was make the branch turn in circles as it was swept downstream.

The edge of the forest loomed. Another minute and they would be in the open. There was nothing for it: he couldn't fight any more, so he simply let go of the branch. The branch was swept instantly away, out of reach.

Kicking fiercely, and still holding on to Hervân with one arm, he swung his free arm in the quick circles he remembered from his swimming lessons as a young fisherelf. It seemed much harder to keep his head above water than he remembered. Then he recalled his father saying, "You must only swim in the sea, never in rivers or lakes. Swimming in water that is not of the sea is too difficult for elves." He wished he had remembered those words earlier, but now it was too late. His life, and that of his wife (who was still screaming in his ear) depended on his being able to reach the bank.

He kicked furiously. Slowly the shore came closer. By now, he was too confused to know which shore he was heading for, but he was also too tired — and too scared — to care. At last the current weakened as he approached the shore; he swam five more strokes, and, panting with exertion, he lowered his feet, which sank into the soft mud of the riverbed.

Hervân was still screaming. Now he had a free hand, and he started to shake her. "It's all right. We're safe."

His hand brushed against something, and he realized that in the darkness he had not noticed that an arrow was sticking into her shoulder.

He tried to remain calm. "You're all right! You're all right! Come on now, let's get you up on shore and then we'll take a closer look at you." But even this was not going to be easy. The bank stood above them — not far, but far enough that it was going to take two good, strong arms just to pull himself out of the water.

But at least Hervân had stopped screaming.

"Stand up," he encouraged his wife. "It's not deep."

As she lowered her feet, he heard a crashing sound from the far shore. It was the archers, coming after them. A momentary wave of relief passed over him: at least they were on the right side of the river. How pointless all this would have been had they been still on the Reglandor side.

"I'm going to let you go. Don't worry. You're perfectly safe. I'm going to climb up on to the bank. Then I'll pull you up." He kept his explanations simple. His wife, her mind numbed both by her experience in the water and by the wound to her shoulder, was beyond understanding anything more than the simplest phrases.

Even so, she shouted: "No! Don't leave me." She threw her arms around him; he saw her wince with pain from her injured shoulder.

"Count to ten. I'll be back by then. With me now: one... two...."

She began to count with him.

Anderskerrin lifted her arms gently away from him. Grimacing and grunting with the effort, he reached up and pulled. He put every ounce of his remaining strength into the effort. He would never have had enough strength for a second attempt. But a second attempt wasn't needed. He rolled over, panting, on the bank. He remained there, unable to move, for a few seconds.

The archers were on the shore opposite, speaking to one another.

Forcing himself to move, he stretched his hands down towards Hervân. "Grab my hands. I'll pull you up." Her hands closed about his. Levering himself on to his knees, he gave one long, last pull.

On the far bank, the archers had reached an agreement. One turned away to run back to the nearest bridge, where he would lead reinforcements across the river into Palindor. The other nocked an arrow, sighted along it at the screaming elf being pulled out of the water, and let fly.

In other circumstances the shock of the second arrow's impact would have killed Hervân. But by now she was in so much pain as Anderskerrin pulled at her injured shoulder that the impact of the second arrow in her thigh was barely noticeable. She had been screaming in agony before the arrow hit; she simply kept screaming after it struck.

Anderskerrin saw the arrow hit her leg, but there was nothing he could do about it. He felt her shudder, and heard the added urgency in her screams, but he was already doing all he could.

She slithered up out of the water and on to the riverbank. She lay face down, and the arrow in her shoulder tore into her flesh. He turned her on to her side, then dragged her into the shadowy protection of the trees. An arrow buried itself into the ground by his left foot; then another struck a tree; then, at last, he was hidden behind a screen of trees and they were, for the moment at least, protected from attack.

He collapsed beside Hervân.

XXV Rescued

Murdoch the archer was horrified.

King Michael had it made it quite clear what the penalty would be were any creatures to cross the border into Palindor: all the archers responsible for that section of the border would be imprisoned for ten years. Worse, if any single archer was held especially responsible, then that archer would be summarily executed.

He and his colleague Plynvir had no choice: they had to enlist the others in their group to capture the elves, and quickly. Plynvir agreed to stay at the place where the elves had escaped, while Murdoch went to get the others.

Murdoch crashed through the trees, not caring about the noise. In no more than half a minute, he burst out of the forest and on to the steep, grass-covered incline that led to the grasslands below. Dotted along the river were the fires of the archers' camps. Jogging at a steady pace, he headed for the closest one.

It took about half an hour. He called out as he approached; by the time that he drew up, panting, beside the fire, half a dozen archers were standing, their weapons at the ready, waiting for him to explain what had brought him running from his duties.

After a few moments to catch his breath, he explained the situation. The leader of the group, Klanrich, said, "It'll mean your head if we don't catch those elves, Murdoch. And the rest of us

183

won't see the light of day for ten years. Come on, everyone: we have some elves to catch."

Leaving a single man behind to guard the bridge, Klanrich led them at a fast jog into Palindor and northward along the west bank of the river.

Anderskerrin was exhausted. Dragging Hervân to the safety of the forest had sapped the last of his strength. All he wanted to do was lie down and rest. But one look at his wife convinced him that she was in desperate need of help. Two arrows stuck out of her body: one in her right shoulder; the other in her right thigh. But at least she was, for the moment, alive.

Hervân groaned as she lay on her left side under the trees. Anderskerrin shook her and said in an urgent whisper, "Hervân, Hervân, can you hear me? Try not to make so much noise."

But she continued groaning. Around the two arrowheads, dark stains covered her green clothing. She had lost much blood and was doubtless in the grip of mindnumbing pain. But what to do? what to do?

He rocked the arrow in her shoulder gently, trying to remove it. Her cries became louder. His eyes began to tear at the thought of the pain he was causing his wife. But at last the arrow came free

The dark patch of blood on her tunic expanded as blood seeped from the open wound. His hands were covered with a sticky substance that shone blackly in the silvery moonlight, but which he knew would have been bright red in daylight.

The arrow in Hervân's thigh was too deep for him to try removing it. Besides, she was already losing too much blood. He held his wife's head in his arms, cradling it and rocking to and fro. Hervân's cries became weaker. Within two minutes, they ceased, and she was asleep.

At first he was grateful for the quiet that now descended; but then he began to worry about how easily Hervân had fallen asleep despite her pain: surely that was hardly a good sign. Should he wake her again?

He decided to let her sleep. Ripping two patches off his own tunic, he pressed them to her wounds, to stop the bleeding. He held her tightly. Was it his imagination or was her breathing becoming shallower?

Desperate, he looked up at the sky and prayed: "Olvensar, High Lord, please, please, do something. You sent us on this journey. Now help us to finish the job you've given us." It was hardly the most eloquent of prayers, but, like all true prayers, it was from the heart.

The words, spoken in no more than a whisper, were barely out of his mouth when he became aware of the sound of voices coming from somewhere not far away. He turned his head, trying to tell where the sound was coming from.

At first, he thought that the voices must belong to archers, searching for them in the forest on this side of the river. But then he realized that these were women's voices — old and cracked, to be sure, but women's voices nonetheless. They were arguing about something, but they were still too far away for him to make out the words.

They came closer, and the words became clearer.

"They're around here somewhere, I tell you."

"I don't care. Every time we get involved in things like this it leads to trouble. Why can't we leave things alone?"

"Oh, you silly old thing. You don't fool me. If you really felt like that, you needn't have come."

"'Course I needed to come. You'd've got lost without me. Anyway, I thought the whole point of this was that it was me they needed."

"Oh, do be quiet; stop arguing and help me find them. They're not far away. Oh, this would never have happened when I was younger; I'd have taken us straight to them."

Into view ambled two ancient and decrepit crones looking around them vaguely as if they had misplaced something valuable. He drew back into the shadows, hoping they would pass by. But it was no good: one of them looked directly at him and said: "Look, there they are. Well, one of them, anyway."

"Told you they were around here somewhere," the other said, a smirk of triumph in her voice. They began to walk directly towards Anderskerrin.

He had never seen their like before. The moonlight did not help, of course; things that would be perfectly distinct and common in daylight took on an air of strangeness and mystery in the light of the moon. But even trying to make allowances, the couple that now halted before him presented a strange sight.

They were dressed in clothes that were ragged to the point of holes, but they seemed to wear them comfortably, as if they were quite happy to be so shabbily dressed. One of them carried a linen bag of some kind; the other was empty handed. He tried to judge their age, but the moonlight played tricks with his eyesight: one moment they looked indescribably wrinkled and ancient, the next they looked like women who were merely old and dressed in rags.

"Well, don't just stand there gaping, young elf. Are you feeble-minded?" asked the one with the cloth bag.

The other interrupted. "Shhh, dear. He's tired and scared, that's all. Although why anyone should be scared of the two of us is beyond me."

"He's half-witted. He can't speak. I told you no good would come of this. Why didn't you tell me we would be dealing with an elf with an addled brain? You didn't see *that* did you, Miss Know-it-all?"

The other one ignored this jibe and instead addressed herself directly to Anderskerrin. "Good elf, I apologize on behalf of my sister. She doesn't like leaving our home. Between you and me, I think she's getting rather too set in her ways." She said this last in a conspiratorial tone quite loud enough for her sister to hear.

Anderskerrin's mind was completely befuddled by these two women. But now they seemed to be waiting for him to say something.

"Er, Anderskerrin, elf of F-Fire M-Mountain Meadow, originally of P-Penclaw in Palindor," he stammered.

"All well and good, elf. But there's nothing wrong with you that a good rest won't take care of. Where's the other one?"

"Er, what?"

"The other one, fool," said the one with the cloth bag. "See, I told you he was half-witted," she offered as an aside to her sister.

Anderskerrin stepped to one side, and Hervân was revealed in all her misery. He opened his mouth to speak, but he was brushed aside so suddenly that he was almost knocked over as the crone with the bag hurried forward. She knelt by Hervân's head and opened the cloth wrapper.

He tried to explain to the other woman, who remained standing while she looked on. "That's my wife. Her name's Hervân. We were shot at by archers on the other side of the river. She's been hit" — this last was spectacularly unnecessary, as the moon glinted brightly off the shaft of the arrow still buried in her leg — "and now I'm afraid they'll be sending out a search party for us. She's lost a lot of blood," he said to the woman who was kneeling over his wife.

In seconds, several phials and small bottles appeared from the cloth bag and the old woman placed them on the ground beside her. She opened a small phial and rubbed the contents with her fingers. Then she took hold of the arrow impacted in the elf's leg.

"It's too deep; it won't come out without drawing too much blood," Anderskerrin said, trying to be helpful.

The woman said something under her breath. She spoke too quietly to be certain, but he was *almost* sure that what she said was: "Idiot! What does he know?"

Then, transfixed, he watched as the woman gently withdrew the arrow. She looked at the tip, which glistened evilly. She touched it with her other hand, then licked her finger. "Sharp, but not poisoned. That's something, I suppose."

Casting the arrow to one side, she ripped Hervân's clothing near the two wounds, stared aghast for a moment at the mass of congealed blood, then selected another bottle from the store beside her.

Anderskerrin's attention was distracted by the other woman. "She's very good, you know. People used to come from all over the Three Lands to consult with me or to be treated by my sister. Of course, that was a long time ago. But still, I think she probably knows what she's doing. And, let's face it, dear, right now she's all the help you're going to get."

"What? Oh, er, yes," said Anderskerrin feebly.

"My name's Iadron. And that's Harsforn," the old woman said. "We're sisters, you know."

"Oh, er, quite." The names meant nothing to the elf, although Iadron had made it sound like he was supposed to recognize them.

"Now, my dear, you'll be needing shelter, won't you," Iadron continued. "Those archers will come looking for you before long. I don't suppose you'd be strong enough to carry your wife a couple of thousand paces, would you?"

The elf did not answer. He was completely bemused by the rapid changes in the conversation. Iadron supplied her own answer. "No, you certainly don't look strong enough."

"All finished." Her sister interrupted.

Anderskerrin turned around and his mouth dropped open in amazement. Surely his eyes had to be deceiving him? He knelt at his wife's shoulder. She was still asleep, but now the rise and fall of her chest was steady and strong. Her clothing was still pulled back to reveal her wounds. Of the two deep, blood-caked wounds, the only trace that remained was a vicious, red scar on her leg. But the wound itself was already completely healed; and of her shoulder wound he could see no trace at all.

"Sorry about the scar. If I had thought to bring the right ointment, I could have got rid of that too, but this was the best I could do without it."

"Enough of that," Iadron interrupted her sister in turn. "Did you bring the powdered horn like I asked?"

"Of course I did, and you know it. You made sure I packed it at least half a dozen times."

"Well, come on and give it to the poor thing. He'll need it if we're going to get back before those nasty archers come looking for us."

"It's not us they'll be looking for. It's them."

"Don't be pedantic. Just give him the powder."

"Hmmpphh," said Harsforn, but she rummaged around in the bag and withdrew a small twist of paper. Untwisting the paper, she revealed a large pinch of a bright yellow dust and handed the paper to Anderskerrin. "Here, dear, get this down you. All in one go, if you don't mind."

He accepted the powder absentmindedly as the truth gradually dawned. "But... you're a healer! How can I ever thank you? Will she be all right?"

"Oh, just swallow the stuff will you? There's time enough to waste hobnobbing later, for those that like that kind of thing." She looked meaningfully at her sister.

Anderskerrin tipped the paper, pouring its contents into his mouth. He emptied the paper with a single swallow. The powder caught at the back of his throat and he coughed. Neither of the women offered to help him as he spluttered. Harsforn gathered her medicines, placed them into her little bag, then lifted herself uneasily (her sister offered no help) to her feet.

When the coughs had subsided, Iadron said to Anderskerrin. "Now, elf, pick her up and follow us." The sisters turned and, without waiting, began to walk away.

The elf bent down and pushed his arms under his wife. He knew that the task they had set him was impossible, but they had given him no chance to argue. He lifted. To his amazement, his wife weighed no more than a feather! He could lift her easily! With his wife cradled in his arms, he followed the two old women into the forest.

Murdoch fell behind the other archers as they jogged up the slope towards the forest. Klanrich and the other archers halted impatiently at the edge of the forest, and Murdoch called ahead, "Just follow the river! An archer from Talbot's company is waiting at the place opposite where the elves escaped. They can't have gone far; at least one of them is wounded. Go on! I'll catch you up."

Klanrich led the troop into the forest. They had followed the river a hundred paces when they heard a shout.

"Sir! You're nearly there."

Looking across the quick-flowing water, Klanrich could see an archer standing on the far bank fifty paces upstream. "They went into the forest directly opposite me. I got one of them as she climbed the bank. A good shot into the thigh. She can't have got far with a wound like that. She might even be dead by now."

Klanrich called back: "Thank you, mister archer. Stay there, if you please."

He turned to his own men. "Let's spread out. You, go north; you head northwest; I'll go west; you go southwest. Remember, go carefully. Look behind every tree. You heard what the archer said: they probably haven't got far. If you find one of them, call out. Otherwise try to be as quiet as possible. And if you have to shoot, shoot to wound, not to kill. I want to know why two elves were so desperate to get into Palindor."

The others nodded and dispersed, just as Murdoch caught up with them.

"You, Murdoch, come with me," Klanrich ordered.

Moving as quietly as possible, he led Murdoch away from the river and into the shadows of the trees.

Klanrich and Murdoch soon found the spot where Anderskerrin had dragged Hervân, no more than fifty paces from the riverbank. The two archers knelt to read the signs.

"One of them lay here for some time," Klanrich said. "Wounded," he added.

"Here are two arrows," Murdoch said. "This one was only a glancing hit, you can see that from the mark on the haft. But look at this one, there's something strange about it. Have you ever felt anything like this before?"

Klanrich took the arrow and ran his fingers along the shaft near the point.

"No. It's strange. I'd say, from this mark here, that this arrow has been buried in flesh, but there's no sign of flesh or blood on the wood, or even trapped under the tip. And it's covered with this greasy substance." He lifted the tip to his nose and smelt it. "And it smells, well, almost like flowers of some sort. Have you ever smelt anything like it?"

"I thought I smelled something strange." Murdoch held the arrow under his nose and sniffed. He shook his head. "I don't know. It's sort of like roses, but with a peculiar, bitter base. It must be some sort of elvish substance."

"Anyway, one thing's obvious. One of them was badly wounded. You can see that from the marks here on the grass. It's blood, no doubt of that. They rested here for a while, which means they haven't been on the move for very long. And with the wounds that these arrows must have inflicted, they won't be travelling very quickly."

"Look, over here, sir! There's been more than just the two of them."

Klanrich hurried over to where Murdoch was standing and examined the tracks on the forest floor. "Two more creatures. Humans possibly. Too heavy for elves, that's for sure."

"And not heavy enough for dwarves."

"Small, though. Women?"

"Women," Murdoch nodded in agreement.

"It looks like they all went this way." They followed the tracks a short distance, then came to a place where the ground was damp and the tracks clearer.

"No doubt about it: two humans, probably women. And this third track."

"Yes. That's a strange one. I'd say it was elvish, except that the weight is all wrong."

In unison, they realized what they were looking at. "One of them's carrying the other."

"Well, in that case we'll soon catch them. An elf carrying another elf is going to move pretty slowly. It's not as if they were dwarves."

"Come on then, they can't be far ahead."

And the two archers set off, following the trail of the women and the laden elf.

There was no sound of humans trailing them yet, but Anderskerrin was in no doubt that by now the archers must be trying to find them. He and the two strange old women had been travelling northward for several minutes. The lower slopes of the Mountains of Mourn were nearby to the west. Even though they were travelling quite quickly (by human standards, anyway), he was in little doubt that they would soon be overtaken by the desperate archers.

Then, suddenly, the two old women stopped. They had halted beside a kind of crack in the mountain. The crack was almost invisible behind a curtain of green creepers and vines.

"Follow us," said Iadron.

Harsforn stepped through the curtain and disappeared from view. Iadron followed.

Anderskerrin adjusted the weight of his wife, then followed after the two women. On the other side of the curtain, he found himself at one end of a long, narrow path. On one side of the path was the mountain; on the other was a narrow wall of rock that was so high that from the other side one could easily mistake it (as he had) for the mountain itself. The narrow path twisted to the south, hidden behind a wall masquerading as a mountain. Neither of the women had waited for him: he saw Iadron turning a corner ahead of him. He followed.

The path went perhaps a hundred paces, then turned sharply to the right. Within another fifty paces, the path opened out into a grassy valley, roughly circular, perhaps a thousand paces across, and completely surrounded by mountainous cliffs. The two women were still hurrying ahead of him, around the edge of the valley. In the shadowed shelter of the mountains, the grass was covered with an integument of frost.

At the far end of the valley, the women stopped outside a small cave.

"They won't find you here," Iadron said. "Wait here and I'll get a blanket for your wife."

Iadron disappeared inside the cave. She returned a few moments later, carrying a thick blanket. She placed it on the ground and Anderskerrin gently laid his wife on it. As he straightened, Iadron bent down and folded part of the blanket carefully over Hervân. "It would be warmer inside, but I expect that the poor dear is frightened of caves."

"Yes," agreed Anderskerrin. "Although she was also frightened of water, but still she jumped into the river when it was necessary."

"Well, there's nothing to be frightened of here, and I dare say she'll be warm enough. All she needs is a couple of days' rest, then she'll be as good as new."

"Better," interrupted Harsforn. "But I'm getting cold. I'm going inside." So saying, she disappeared into the darkness of the cave.

In the starlight, Iadron looked at Anderskerrin with interest. "I expect you wish to remain with your wife?"

The elf nodded. "Yes. I'll keep her warm, and if she wakes then she won't be so frightened if I'm with her."

"Oh, she won't wake yet for two days at least. And she'll be warm enough here against the mountains, wrapped up in the blanket. It gets cold in the valley, but it's not too bad here against the rock. And we have much to talk about. I would be more comfortable inside the cave. And if I am not very much mistaken, you have no fear of such places."

Anderskerrin looked first at his wife, then at the old woman, then, finally, at the cave. Once, he would have been terrified of entering such a place, but no more; he had traversed too many miles of tunnel on the long journey across the mountains with Gondalwyn after leaving Penclaw*. Caves and tunnels held no fear for him now. But even so, he was reluctant to leave his wife.

The old woman continued. "Come. We have a warm fire and good food inside. I promise you that your wife will fare well. You can move her closer to the entrance if you prefer."

Anderskerrin bent down to lift his wife. Placing his arms under her, he tried to lift her, but discovered that she now was too heavy to carry.

"Ah, the powder has worn off. Well, it is to be expected. She no longer has the skills of her youth."

"I heard that," came from the cave. "What about you, eh? We rescued the things but what are we to do with them now, eh? Tell me that." Harsforn sounded smug.

"Hmmpphh! Look, elf, you can probably drag her to the cave entrance if you try hard enough. Anyway, I'm going inside."

Iadron turned and went into the cave, leaving Anderskerrin alone with his sleeping wife. He grabbed a corner of the blanket and pulled, dragging the blanket with its burden the half-dozen steps to the cave entrance; then he pulled them another two steps, so that Hervân was just barely inside the cave.

He maneuvered his wife so that her head was close to the entrance, so that when she woke she would not think herself entrapped in a cave. Satisfied that he had done all he could, Anderskerrin straightened and took stock of his surroundings.

The cave was obviously the home of the strange old women. Although it was impossible to tell so from its small mouth, inside

---

* A story told in Anderskerrin's memoirs.

the mountain the cave opened out to be large and roomy. The air was filled with the sweet scent of fresh flowers, although the source of the scent was a mystery. Candles glowed around the edge of the floor, lighting the center of the cave from all directions. To one side, two bedrolls were laid out on straw; there was an area in which there were many small piles of leaves (perhaps the source of the flowery scent?) to which Harsforn was now attending; towards the rear of the cave, a low fire was burning. Iadron was bending over the fire and placing a pot on a trivet over it.

He approached Iadron. He felt a slight draft, and saw that the thin smoke from the fire was quickly whisked up and away through a crack in the ceiling of the cave. The pot on the fire held some kind of vegetable stew, and its scent quickly mingled with, and then overcame, the smell of flowers.

After a few minutes, Iadron ladled three helpings of steaming stew into bowls, and passed the bowls around. Realizing how hungry he was, Anderskerrin was about to start eating the aromatic mixture when Iadron said, "Now we will ask a blessing of Olvensar."

Guiltily, Anderskerrin stopped and hung his head: he had not said a blessing over his food since he had been a child elf, and now he felt unaccountably guilty about the omission.

Iadron continued, "High Lord, we thank you for the gifts that you have bestowed on us. We especially thank you that this day you have led us to one of your creatures in distress and have been the instruments of her saving. We ask that you bring peace to Palindor in your own way and in your own time, and that when peace comes, all creatures will be the wiser.

"We ask that you bless those who seek to kill these two good elves, that they will come to know you. We seek your blessing on this food, that it will serve to strengthen us. Finally we ask your wisdom in helping this good elf to know what he should do next. We bless you and we ask your blessing on this good food which you, through your bounty, have provided for our use. Bless the High Lord Olvensar."

"Bless the High Lord Olvensar," the elf and Harsforn echoed.

They started to eat, and for several minutes no one spoke.

The archers were finding it difficult to follow the trail. The moonlit night had clouded over and now snow was threatening. By morning all trace of the path taken by the elves would be gone, and unless they were caught quickly there was a real chance that they might escape after all. Murdoch was nervous as he scoured the dark ground for clues. If they did not catch the fugitives, he might lose his head.

In the darkness, they blundered past the green curtain that hid the path to Iadron and Harsforn's cave. Klanrich shouted at Murdoch: "It's all your fault they got away. The king will have your head for this."

Murdoch did not need to be told that this was indeed a distinct possibility. He decided that attack was the best form of defense. "What do you mean? You're supposed to be in charge here. You're responsible for what happened. If you had distributed the patrols properly we would have seen them earlier and they would never have got away."

Arguing noisily, they moved deeper into the wood.

White flecks began to fall. Five minutes later, Klanrich, shook his head. "It's useless. They've escaped. We'd better get back to the encampment. This looks like it will be quite a blizzard."

They began to retrace their steps, calling out for their colleagues. A few minutes later, the archers broke out of the forest and began to make their way down the grassy incline toward their camp, invisible now through the swirling flurries.

All their mouths were set grimly, and no one spoke.

XXVI Across the Findell

Things had not been going well for Michael and his entourage.

The first evening after crossing into Palindor passed without incident, and the party moved away from their small encampment in the dingle early the next morning. Moving as quietly as possible through the Palindor forest, Qivir acted as their guide, for he seemed to know the geography of the land better than anyone else.

The party headed northwards, along the western edge of the Mountains of Mourn. Qivir told the others there was a bridge over the Findell some distance to the north; once they crossed the river, they should be able to reach Carn Toldwyn after another five days' travelling through the forest.

But it is not possible, no matter how hard they try, for a group of seven creatures to move noiselessly through a forest. Not half a day passed before Qivir moved to Michael's side and said quietly, "We have been observed and are being followed. A Hunter, I think. Just one."

"You keep leading the others. I'll deal with him," said Michael.

Michael let the others move ahead of him. As the dwarf Torbyn, who was at the rear of the party, was about to pass by, Michael said to him, "Qivir says we're being followed by a Hunter. Let the others go ahead. We'll hide and ambush him."

So saying, he turned away from the path they were following and hid behind a bush. The dwarf hid on the other side of the path. The rest of the party moved out of sight.

They did not have long to wait. A minute later, a tall, black-haired human male wearing a green tunic emblazoned with a small white cross padded softly along the track. A longbow and a quiver were slung across the Hunter's back, and his hand rested on a scabbarded broadsword. As soon as he was past, Michael and Torbyn jumped from their hiding places. The Hunter turned, startled by the sound.

Michael drew his sword and Torbyn began to swing his battle axe as the Hunter, looking from one to the other, drew his own sword.

"Who are you?" the Hunter demanded. "You are not of Palindor. Why are you skulking through our forest?"

"Drop your sword," Michael ordered.

The Hunter made no movement to obey. His eyes locked on Michael's, then he took a step backward. Michael realized that if the Hunter tried to flee, he would probably escape unless Torbyn chanced to hit him with a lucky throw of his axe.

Michael called out loudly, "We've got him." Then he added, speaking to the Hunter, "Drop your sword. You're surrounded. Our friends will be here in a moment"

The Hunter looked around. Then he cocked his head. Not far away, he could hear creatures heading towards them.

He feinted to the left then turned and darted to the right. In a flash, a glinting metal object flew through the air after him. Torbyn's battle axe thudded into a tree, causing it to shudder with the force of the impact.

There was a flash of green clothing and the Hunter had disappeared into the forest.

The other warriors burst upon Michael and Torbyn.

"A Palindoric Hunter; he went that way!" Michael pointed. "Split up; he might try to double back and we don't want to lose him. If the sun reaches its highest point and we haven't found him, meet back here."

They separated and searched for nigh on an hour without finding him.

197

Dispirited, Michael turned away from the undergrowth he had been searching and began to make his way back to the agreed meeting place. Without warning, an arm came from behind and wrapped itself around his throat. Someone pushed his knees forward, and he fell to the ground, helpless. Looking up, he saw the Hunter standing over him, broadsword in hand.

"Now, child. It seemed to me that you were in charge. What exactly are you up to? Come on now, be honest. There's nothing to be scared of; I'm a Hunter, not a murderer... unh!"

The Hunter opened his mouth in an exploding breath. He turned unsteadily, and Michael saw a dagger buried in his back, dripping blood. Torbyn stepped out of the forest.

"No one threatens our king, human."

The Hunter staggered toward Torbyn, then fell to his knees. The dwarf moved forward, releasing his battle axe from his belt. He looked at Michael, who was still spreadeagled on the ground. "With your permission, Your Majesty?"

Michael nodded, unsure exactly what permission he was granting.

The dwarf drew back his axe and with a mighty swipe severed the Hunter's head cleanly from his body. For a long moment that burned itself into Michael's brain, he stared at the headless human, kneeling in front of Torbyn, a fountain of blood where his head should be. Then the human keeled over on to the ground.

Michael was momentarily sickened. The Hunter had never meant to kill him, of that he was sure. The sight of the sudden, ghastly death made him realize that this was just the beginning: there would likely be many more deaths before his job in Palindor was complete.

But this was no time for weakness. He cast his revulsion aside and got to his feet. "Come," he said, "the others will be waiting for us. We've wasted long enough. Time is not on our side. We must hurry to make up for lost time."

They regrouped, and headed northward at a fast pace. Qivir led, with Michael following, then the others. Torbyn brought up the rear.

The dwarf began to fall behind. Something was bothering him, but he could not put his finger on what exactly. There was something about the morning's events that was *wrong*; some sort of warning was ringing in part of his brain, but he could not quite puzzle exactly what it was. He realized that he had fallen behind, and hurried to rejoin the others, pushing the problem from his mind.

They walked late into the evening before Qivir declared a halt for the day. The king and his warriors were exhausted; only Qivir seemed fresh. They pulled out rations and ate them under the cold, starry sky in the shelter of the evergreens. After eating, they slept, with Qivir taking the first watch.

As he waited for sleep to overtake him, Torbyn returned to the problem that had been gnawing at him. He went over the events carefully: a Hunter had been following them; the Hunter had ambushed them; he had escaped; they had had to split up to go looking for him; the Hunter had found King Michael and forced him to the ground; Torbyn had attacked and killed the Hunter before he could harm the king.

Everything seemed in order, so what was troubling him? He began to go through it all again from the beginning, but sleep overtook him.

Next day, they continued northward, the mountains to their right and the river to their left. Few creatures lived in these parts, and there was little chance of them being discovered except, as had happened yesterday, by a passing Hunter. Today their luck held, and the morning passed without any sign that they had been observed.

It was as they halted for lunch that the puzzle that had been niggling at Torbyn since yesterday finally came into focus. Today, as yesterday, Qivir had been leading the band, since he seemed to know the country better than anyone else. Yet, Torbyn suddenly realized, it had been Qivir, at the head of the group, who had first sensed the Hunter's presence. The Hunter had been following at least a couple of minutes behind the soldiers. How, then, could Qivir have known he was there? Torbyn, at the rear of the group, had never heard the Hunter, so how could Qivir have done so?

"Just a few more minutes," said Qivir, interrupting Torbyn's thoughts. "The bridge across the Findell is just ahead. We must proceed with caution now; there are likely to be creatures on the paths near the bridge, and we must not be seen."

They ate lunch in silence, all thinking about the danger ahead. As soon as they had finished, they continued on their way, moving as quietly as possible.

They halted a few minutes later, at a place where they could look out from the forest at the bridge. The bridge was built over a pinch in the river, where the two banks came within about twenty paces of one another. The river was low at this time of year, but even so, fording it was impossible, and the water flowed swiftly under the dirt-covered wooden boards.

A wide path led from the bridge on both sides of the river; on the far side, the path disappeared into the trees that grew up the slopes of the easternmost of the Redfyre Hills.

Qivir gathered the others around him. "We'll cross the bridge one at a time. As soon as you're on the other side, leave the track. There's a small clearing not far away to the right of the path. We'll meet there."

"I'll go first," said Michael, in a tone that brooked no argument.

"Torbyn, you next," said Qivir, "then I'll go." He pointed to each member of the party in turn, setting out the order in which they would cross the bridge, then he said to Michael, "Whenever you're ready, Your Majesty. It looks clear."

Taking a final look around, Michael stepped out of the forest and on to the path that led to the bridge. His hand on the hilt of his sword, he crossed and began to climb the hill on the far side. Fifty paces past the bridge, he stepped off the path and into the forest. As Qivir had said, there was a small clearing where he could look back through the trees at the bridge. Safe, he watched as Torbyn stepped out of the forest on the eastern bank, walked easily across the bridge and, within thirty seconds, was at Michael's side. Qivir followed.

Thorrain the dwarf was next. Thorrain watched as Qivir crossed the bridge and disappeared into the forest on the far side, just as the king and Torbyn had done. Thorrain stepped out of the forest. He had taken no more than half a dozen steps when a sound caused him to freeze in his tracks.

It was the sound of singing. Thorrain halted and turned his head, trying to locate the source of the sound. It was coming closer. A movement on the far side of the bridge caught his eye. A young elvish girl, little more than a child, was skipping down the hill towards the river, a small pack on her back and a smile clearly visible on her face.

She took several more hops and steps before she spotted Thorrain watching her. She stopped, a look of puzzled curiosity on her face. Thorrain, wearing light battle armor, realized that it was too late to turn back: she had seen him. He started walking towards the bridge. The elf child took two uncertain steps, then stopped at the far end of the bridge.

Thorrain continued walking towards her. A look of uncertainty crossed the child's face. She took two steps backwards, hesitated a moment, then turned and began to run back the way that she had came.

Thorrain began to run after her.

Qivir stepped out of the forest in front of the girl, blocking her escape.

She halted and looked back and forth at the human in front of her and the dwarf behind her, both clad in Reglandor armor. A look of terror crossed the girl's face, and she opened her mouth to scream.

A dagger thrown by Qivir thudded into her chest, and instead of a loud scream all that escaped her throat was a strangled cry. She tried to catch her breath; then, gasping, she slipped to the ground.

She croaked twice, trying to get enough breath to shout. Qivir approached, and her eyes opened wide in terror. He pulled the knife from her chest. Then he slashed the blade across her throat.

Watching from behind the trees, Michael gasped.

"Do we put her body in the river try to hide it in the forest?" Thorrain asked Qivir as he reached the elf child's body.

"In the forest. Quickly. Her family may be nearby. Torbyn, come here and help Thorrain while I clear up the mess."

While Torbyn and Thorrain carried the girl's body and head into the forest, Qivir waved the others to cross the bridge while he scuffed the path, hiding the bloody evidence of what had happened only moments before.

Shaking, Michael came out of the trees. He knew that their expedition would involve deaths. But an innocent young creature like this? Surely something here was not right?

His warriors evidently did not share his distaste. They were soldiers of Reglandor, trained to kill; killing was their job, and they did it without compunction.

Only one other person in the party had any concerns about what had just happened — and that was not about the killing itself. Torbyn had watched at Michael's side as Qivir had stepped out to trap the elf child. Only a moment later, Qivir had thrown his dagger — but in that moment, Torbyn had been watching the minister instead of the little girl. And it had seemed to him that for the merest fraction of a second, Qivir had flashed out of existence, and in his place had stood a shadowy gray creature with a long nose, pointed ears, sharp teeth and blood red eyes.

Before the image could register fully on Torbyn's brain, it was gone. But he now realized that a look of sheer terror had been on the child's face *even before Qivir had produced his dagger*.

Whatever Qivir had momentarily become, the elf child had seen it too.

XXVII A Narrow Escape

Anderskerrin slept well. Twice he opened his eyes and was momentarily frightened by the flickering light of candles reflecting off the walls of the cave. But each time, after the initial shock, he remembered where he was, and, with a glance towards his wife to make sure that she was still sleeping soundly near the entrance of the cave, he adjusted his position on the bed of leaves that Iadron had provided for him, and soon he was asleep once more.

When he awoke next morning, the sun lit the world outside and his nostrils were filled with the smell of a delicious stew. Harsforn was gently stirring the large black pot that hung low over the fire. He looked around for Iadron, but could see her nowhere.

Somewhat afraid of Harsforn, he refrained from asking her about her sister. Instead, he stretched, then walked to the mouth of the cave to check on his wife. Hervân still slept, her torso rising and falling rhythmically in slumber. He bent down and gave her a kiss on the cheek. There was no response. Stepping outside, he took his first good look at their surroundings.

The sun shone behind his left shoulder, lighting the scene before him. The cave was located in the side of one of the lesser Mountains of Mourn. Below was a grassy valley, perhaps a thousand paces across and surrounded by the hills and mountains. The sun reflected with a painful brilliance off a light snowfall that had covered the grass in the night. The valley was dotted with clumps of low shrub. He could see numerous birds, some high above, others pecking vigorously at the snow-covered grass, digging for morning worms. There was no sign of Iadron.

Anderskerrin retreated back into the cave. The smell of the stew sharpened his hunger. He approached Harsforn.

As he did so, there was a movement deep in the darkness of the cave. A moment later, Iadron appeared out of the depths of the cave beyond the fire. Accompanying her was a creature the like of which he had never seen before: a large, golden-haired dormouse-like animal whose tread on the rock was so quiet that he emerged from the darkness in complete silence.

Iadron spoke. "Ah, you are awake. Good! Come, you must help me bring your wife farther into the cave." She strode towards the mouth of the cave. Anderskerrin followed dumbly. The seer gave no explanation until they had dragged Hervân's blanket into the cave, near the fire.

Anderskerrin said, "She'll be terrified if she wakes up. Most elves are frightened of caves."

"Shhhh!" Iadron hissed urgently, finger on her lips.

Gesturing for the elf to follow, she led the way back to the mouth of the cave. She pointed to the opposite side of the valley, and Anderskerrin sucked in his breath. Climbing down into the grassy valley from a gap in the cliff walls were two archers.

Anderskerrin listened intently. The archers were talking to one another. He could just make out the words, carrying across the valley in the still morning air.

"Sure as my name's Murdoch, they must have come this way."

"Aye. We must have missed the path in the dark last night, but I can't see them anywhere now."

"No. But I don't see any way out, either. They might still be nearby."

By now, the archers had descended on to the snow-covered grass and were looking up at the slopes that surrounded them as they walked slowly across the valley toward the cave. Anderskerrin ducked back inside.

A moment later Iadron joined him. "They saw us, and they're heading this way. Come with me. They'll be here directly."

They hurried back to the fire, where the dormouse creature sat on its haunches, watching the healer out of dark, unreadable eyes. Harsforn and the creature turned towards Iadron as she said, "We've been spotted by a couple of the archers. We've got to do something."

"We could go into the tunnels," Harsforn suggested, the first words Anderskerrin had heard her say that morning.

The golden creature stood up, then hurried past, heading toward the mouth of the cave with an almost incredible noiselessness. Anderskerrin watched as the creature stopped at the mouth of the cave, stayed there for a few seconds, then ran back inside.

"Put the fire out," the creature said, and Iadron instantly moved to obey. The creature ran around the walls, more quickly than even Anderskerrin himself would have been able to, blowing out candles. The cave was plunged into darkness, and Anderskerrin, against his will, began to feel a rising tide of panic. He felt a brush of fur against his skin; it must have been the golden-haired creature, but even so he could not completely stifle a scream.

"Close your eyes, elf, and do not open them until I tell you to."

Anderskerrin obeyed the creature's instruction and, with his eyes tightly closed, he leaned against the rock wall of the cave, taking low, deep breaths. He began to feel a bit better.

He felt another brush of the creature's fur, but this time he managed not to make a sound.

Then he hard the archers, frighteningly close. "Here it is! I told you I saw a cave."

"Hang on a minute. You don't want me to go in there, do you? I hate dark places."

"G'on; what's wrong with you? It's just a cave. What can be in there? An elf, or possibly two, and a couple of women. We're both armed. I tell you, there's nothing to be afraid of."

"I don't care. You ain't getting me in there."

"Oh, all right then. You stay here and guard the entrance while I go in and fetch 'em out."

Anderskerrin could stand it no more. He opened his eyes. A silhouetted shape moved in front of the entrance. There were footsteps as the archer made his way into the cave.

"Something smells good in here. Been cooking your breakfast have you?" The voice came closer. The archer was less than ten paces away now.

Suddenly there was movement nearby. Iadron stepped forward in the darkness and called out: "Halt!"

The effect on the archer was immediate. He took two hurried steps backward.

"Who are you?" he called uncertainly into the darkness.

"My name is Iadron. I am a seer, and this is my home. You will not find those whom you seek here, archer Klanrich."

The archer was visibly shaken at the use of his name, and took another step backward. "A seer? You can't be. You're all dead."

"I would not be so quick to believe the stories if I were you, Klanrich of Pirren Glanwyn, Son of Klentor, son of Kranth. I have lived in Palindor for years beyond measure; what know you of the ways of this land, archer? You are a stranger here; aye, and an unwelcome one at that. Begone now, lest I conjure a dablik to eat you for breakfast. I say again, you will not find those you seek here."

The archer took yet another step back. "How do you know who I am? And how do you know who I'm looking for?"

"You are Klanrich, an archer in the army of Michael, newly-crowned king of Reglandor. You seek two elves. But they will escape you; you will never find them. Now begone, I lose my patience." As she spoke, Iadron moved towards the archer, her voice aged but steady and unmistakably threatening. The golden-haired creature moved to her side, so that the light from outside fell on the two of them. The creature bared its teeth.

The archer's nerve failed him. He turned and ran outside.

"Come on! Let's get out of here. There's a seer in there, and I'm not going to tangle with her. She conjured up some kind of creature to eat me."

"A seer? but they're...."

"...dead? Yes, I know. Now go in there and tell *her* that. Come on, the elves aren't here. She told me that herself, and seers never lie. That's enough for me. Now, let's go."

The voices were already getting fainter. Within seconds they were gone. Anderskerrin let out an audible sigh of relief. It was several more seconds before anyone spoke. Anderskerrin himself broke the silence. He said, in a tone of voice that was almost accusatory, "The archer's right. Seers aren't supposed to lie. But you told him we weren't here."

"No, I didn't," rejoined Iadron. "I told him that he wouldn't find you, which is quite a different matter." There was a note of triumph in her voice. "No need to thank me, of course."

Anderskerrin swallowed guiltily and rushed to thank Iadron and the golden-haired creature.

The creature merely said, "I think we can relight the candles and the fire now. And then let's get something to eat; I'm hungry and we have a long journey ahead of us."

They rekindled the fire. From that the candles were re-lit, and, within ten minutes, the two sisters, the elf and the strange golden-haired creature were sipping bowls of hot stew.

The golden-haired creature was introduced as "the dablik," not a name Anderskerrin had heard before, except when Iadron had used it when trying to scare the archer. "He lives in the tunnels that run underground throughout Palindor," Iadron said. "He'll get you where you need to go faster than anyone else could."

Iadron then insisted that Anderskerrin tell his story to the dablik, from the beginning, while they ate.

Harsforn was the first to finish eating. She disappeared for several moments into the flickering shadows on one side of the cave, returning with an unstoppered phial in her hand. Carefully, she knelt down beside the still-sleeping form of Hervân, then decanted the green contents of the phial into the space between Hervân's lips. Hervân stirred slightly in her sleep, turned on to her side, breathed deeply a couple of times, then resumed her steady breathing.

"She'll be as good as new this time tomorrow," Harsforn said.

"When will she wake?" Anderskerrin asked.

"I just told you, don't you ever listen?" Harsforn snapped.

Iadron leaned across and said quietly to the elf: "My sister means that your wife will waken at breakfast time tomorrow. By that time, of course, you'll be long gone."

"I will?" Anderskerrin asked, startled.

"Of course. Why do you think I summoned the dablik? You have a message that must reach the Ruling Council in Carn Toldwyn.

If King Michael reaches them before you do, they'll be caught unawares. They could all be killed."

"Well, yes, I suppose that's true. But couldn't the dablik go? Or one of you?"

Iadron smiled. "Oh no! That wouldn't do; that wouldn't do at all, would it?" This last question was addressed to the dablik.

The dablik's whiskers quivered. "No; the elf is the one who saw what happened in Pirren Glanwyn. And in any case, Olvensar gave this task to him, not to me. The High Lord would not be happy if I took the task for myself. He's a bit funny that way."

These words sent a shiver up Anderskerrin's spine. He had lived so long in Soltarwyn that he rarely thought of Olvensar any longer. And never had he heard any creature — even Gondalwyn — speak with such assurance — and such familiarity — about the High Lord's wishes. He wondered who exactly the dablik was, and what his relationship was to the High Lord.

But Iadron gave him no time to consider these questions. "And as for me or my sister going all the way to Carn Toldwyn, I don't think you realize how old we are. No, I've had enough excitement this morning to last me a century or more. Besides, we are both much too old to go gallivanting around Palindor, especially in tunnels." There was a "Hmmpphh" from her sister, as if she, for one, did not consider herself too old for such doings. But Harsforn said nothing more, presumably not wanting to run the risk that she might actually be called on to make the journey.

Iadron continued, "Anyway, like the dablik says, it's as plain as grass from what you've told us that Olvensar has given you a job to do. Why else do you think you were led away from your home? Why else do you think you escaped Pirren Glanwyn without getting caught? No, my dear elf, there's nothing for it: it's Carn Toldwyn and the Ruling Council for you."

"But what about Hervân? I can't just leave her here."

"That's exactly what you can do. She'll come to no harm. The archers won't be back. Anyway, I don't know what to think of you, wanting someone in her condition to be traipsing around all over the Three Lands. No, she'll be much safer here."

"What do you mean: 'in her condition'? Your sister said that she'll be as good as new when she wakes."

"What? Oh! Don't you know? Don't tell me you hadn't realized. She's carrying an elfling, you silly thing. Oh, men!" She said the last with such a tone of disgust that Anderskerrin almost believed that she meant it.

He looked down at Hervân, sleeping soundly in the light from the fire. An elfling! He had never suspected, not even for a moment. He wondered if Hervân herself knew. But anyway, that changed everything. Now there was no question but that the seer was right. Hervân must stay here, protected from danger, and he would accompany the dablik to Carn Toldwyn. He bent down and kissed his wife.

The dablik cleared its throat. "If we're going, we'd better be on our way."

"Oh, yes, I suppose so." Looking down at his wife, a quite unexpected wave of love and tenderness came over Anderskerrin. The dablik moved to stand beside him.

"But before we go, I expect you'd like us to pray over your wife."

Anderskerrin blushed. Prayer was not at all what he had been thinking of: he had been thinking simply how wonderful and how peaceful his wife looked in her sleep.

"Olvensar" — Anderskerrin bowed his head quickly as the strange creature began to pray — "we know that you will be with us as we hurry to do your will. We ask that you also guard and protect Iadron and Harsforn" — Anderskerrin expected a "Hmmpphh" at this, but none came — "and this good elf Hervân and the elfling she carries, and that Anderskerrin may be reunited quickly with those he loves. We thank you for our escape from the danger of the archers, and ask that you will lend us your strength as we try to do your will. Bless the Lord Olvensar."

The echo of the blessing sounded around the cave. The dablik moved toward the rear of the cave, and Anderskerrin picked up his pack and followed after him. "Goodbye and thank you for everything," he said to the old women.

"Goodbye," said Iadron. "May Olvensar be with you."

"Goodbye. Don't let that animal lead you astray," said Harsforn, and Anderskerrin suddenly realized that, underneath her gruff exterior, she cared both for the dablik and for himself.

"Come," said the dablik. He padded noiselessly towards the darkness. The last glints of flamelight shone from his fur, and suddenly he was gone.

Anderskerrin hurried after him, turned a corner, and began the underground journey to Carn Toldwyn.

XXVIII Shadow Revealed

Anderskerrin soon lost track of time. As he left the cave of the seer and the healer behind, he found himself travelling along a tunnel whose walls glowed dimly, so that he could see the dablik hurrying ahead of him. It was fortunate that he could see the creature for, try as he might, he could not hear him. Even his own almost-silent elvish footfalls sounded heavy in the silence of the tunnel; but of the dablik's footsteps there was no hint.

For some time, the tunnel led them steadily downward. Although Anderskerrin had a good sense of direction, the tunnel twisted and turned so that within a thousand paces he had completely lost track of which way they were going.

At first this did not trouble him overmuch, as he was willing to trust to the dablik's obviously superior sense of direction. But after a while other tunnels began to join the one along which they were travelling, and he began to worry about what would happen if he were somehow to be separated from the dablik. If he were to lose sight of the dablik, he could easily be lost forever.

The tunnels levelled off. They continued in this way for perhaps two hours: the dablik confidently and noiselessly leading the increasingly anxious elf. Eventually, the dablik halted in a small chamber. He turned to Anderskerrin and spoke for the first time since they had left the cave.

"We should stop now for a meal. We've been making good time. If we keep this up, we could be in Carn Toldwyn in about four days."

Anderskerrin was aghast. Had he stopped to think about it, he would have realized that the Reglandor border was usually reckoned to be a week's travel on foot from Carn Toldwyn. Travelling underground was obviously much faster than journeying on the surface, but even so the journey was bound to be long and tedious. He opened his pack and looked at its contents: certainly not enough to last the two creatures more than a couple of days.

The dablik saw his look of dismay. "I know. It's longer than you expected, and we don't have enough food. You needn't worry about food for me; I generally eat fresh food from the surface: berries and leaves and suchlike. And the stew we ate earlier will suffice for quite some time. Most of the time we'll be travelling near the surface, where we'll both be able to find food.

"But I've been giving our route some thought. If you don't mind being left alone for a few hours, I'm thinking that I'd like to scout out the forest to the south of us. That's the route King Michael and his party have been taking. Perhaps tonight while you're asleep I could go to the surface and see what progress they're making. I'd be happier if I knew how fast they are travelling."

"What about sleep? Won't you need to sleep?"

"Me? Oh, yes, every now and then. But probably not for a day or so yet. Now do hurry up and eat so we can be on our way again."

Another thought struck the elf: "Your name; no one told me your name."

"Yes they did: I'm the dablik," the creature answered, as if that were sufficient. "Now, eat something; we've a long way to go before we rest again."

It had been a difficult day for the king's party. The morning had passed well enough, but ever since the incident at the bridge, a pall had descended on them.

They had marched wordlessly forward, up the first of the Redfyre Hills, then down its slopes and into a strange, dark wood. Green shoots on the trees did little to alleviate the dispiriting blackness of the forest around them. Torbyn, already unnerved by the apparition of Qivir at the bridge, felt the air grow heavy and oppressive as they entered the dark place. He overheard one of the others mutter as they entered the wood: "Dankenwood. No good will come of this." He wanted to ask more, but his question would have shattered the silence of the place, so he trudged on with the others, his questions unasked.

In the afternoon, just to complete the misery, the sky clouded, and cold, white flecks began to fall, pushed by a sharp, biting wind that threaded through the trees, carrying its frozen, wet burden. They were travelling west, precisely the direction whence the wind came, and Michael veered towards the north to give the party some relief from the freezing blasts of snow-laden air, which was cutting through the forest as if the trees were insubstantial ghosts. It helped, but only a little, and within a quarter of an hour the left side of Torbyn's face was stinging with cold.

Like the others, Torbyn pulled his pack more snugly on his back, hunched down, and tried to hurry through the grim wood. Every few minutes, he cupped his hands in front of his face and breathed into them so that his breath warmed his hands and the lower part of his face. He began to wonder if the honor of being chosen to accompany the king was worth the discomfort.

Thoughts of home — a cozy two-storey house near the city wall in Pirren Glanwyn — came to him. The sky was getting dark, evening hastened by the storm; by now a fire would be burning invitingly in the hearth at home, water boiling to make tea, his wife sewing and his daughter coloring or playing with blocks. He tried to shake the thoughts from his mind. Only partly successful, he stumbled forward through Dankenwood.

He lost track of time. Evening had almost become night when the party entered a clearing in which stood an ancient, dilapidated building, a layer of snow veneered on its roof. It was small, no more than a hovel. No light showed from inside, but even so it was perhaps the most welcoming sight Torbyn had ever seen. The king strode up to the front door and knocked. There was no response. Drawing his sword, the king pushed the door open. No sound greeted the intrusion, and gratefully the party tumbled inside.

There were only two rooms, if they could be called that: a kitchen of sorts at the rear, and a larger living area at the front. In the middle of the latter, inexplicably, lay the carcass of a deer giving off an odor that indicated that it had been dead for some time.

The floor was dirt, and there were holes between the logs from which the hut was constructed: holes that were now mostly blocked with snow. Only a small amount of light filtered into the building through the single dirty window. One of the party stepped forward and, with Michael's permission, lit a candle that stood on a small table in one corner. The building was deserted, but the carcass indicated that it must have been occupied fairly recently. There were no cobwebs and no small animals' nests, as would certainly have been the case had it been empty for any length of time.

Grateful for the shelter from the blizzard, the party sat down wherever convenient in the large room. Two of them made their way to the kitchen. There was no palatable food in the pantry, but the fire was serviceable and there was a pump for water and a large black pot for boiling. They set about making a kettle of tea while they gnawed hungrily on their rations. The carcass was dragged outside: much though they wished otherwise, its decay was too far advanced for it to be eaten.

The gloom outside deepened. Inside, two more candles were lit; then someone began to tell a story, and soon the difficulties of the day were forgotten. One by one, they fell asleep.

Torbyn was unsure what woke him. He stopped and held his breath, certain that there had been some sound just at the edge of consciousness. For several seconds he heard nothing, but then, just as he was about to release his breath, he heard a movement over by the door.

There was only a little stray light in the room: all he could see was that the grayness was slightly darker near the door, as if someone were standing there. Then he saw the door open, slowly and without a sound.

Outside, the storm had stopped and there were gaps in the clouds through which stars shone. The moon appeared from behind a cloud and suddenly lit the scene brightly. The light limned the silhouette of Qivir in the doorway. He was there only a moment before he stepped outside and closed the door behind him. Torbyn shivered. Into his mind flashed the image of the momentary apparition just before the young elfling was killed. He swallowed twice and then, without exactly being aware that he had done so, he made a decision.

Quietly, he got up and crossed to the door. He opened it and peered outside. There was no sign of the king's minister, but he could see tracks in the fresh powder. He stepped outside and closed the door behind him. The night was bitterly cold, and he flexed his fingers to keep the blood circulating. He began to follow the imprints in the snow.

The minister had gone only a couple of hundred paces. He was standing in a glade with his back toward Torbyn. Qivir was talking, but it was several seconds before Torbyn could make out the words. What he heard chilled him even more than the physical cold of the night air. "Lord and Master, Lord and Master; It is I, your servant, Shadow. Make yourself known, I beg thee."

Three times the minister recited the formula. Then he turned and faced the place where Torbyn was hiding behind a tree. Torbyn stared in horror as the moonlight fell on the king's minister. Instead of a human face, there was an ugly grayness that seemed to swallow what little light there was. The gray face — if face it was — was evil-looking, with large pointed ears near the top of the head. Most terrifying of all were the two massive red eyes that seemed to glow with hatred in the gloom.

Torbyn could not help himself. At the sight of the creature he involuntarily stepped backward and yelped in fright. He was saved from discovery by the fact that at this exact moment a black lightning bolt rent the air. The accompanying sound was so powerful that he was knocked to the ground and it took him several seconds to recover.

When he did so, he peered through the trees to see the most horrific of sights. The gray, shadowy creature was in conversation with a black monster out of which evil radiated almost palpably. He could discern little of this new creature, but he had no need — there was only one creature so black, so lifeless, so base: Malthazzar, the Lord of Evil. As the creature spoke, black drops of drool dropped to the ground from the blackness that was its head.

"Why have you summoned me? You know I am not permitted to intervene."

"But my Lord, I wanted to tell you that all is going as planned. They suspect nothing. We shall be in Carn Toldwyn in less than a week, and once there I anticipate that we will destroy the Ruling Council within the hour."

"The Ruling Council! Bah! You know nothing, Shadow. It is not the feeble Council that concerns me. It is that human, the one who calls herself the High Queen."

"Sire?"

"You saw her, did you not, in my own castle?"

"So that was who she was. Indeed, Lord, I saw her. But surely she is no threat to you."

"But that she is, you fool! Olvensar, may his name be forever cursed, aided her escape from Sheol. Even now she is somewhere in this land and... wait! Fool! What is that over there?"

Terrified, Torbyn hugged the ground. But it was too late: the red eyes of the creature that Malthazzar had called Shadow were fixed on him.

"Torbyn!" Shadow exclaimed.

For a long second the three formed a silent tableau. Malthazzar broke the silence. "Shadow! I cannot intervene. You must slay him."

But before the creature that had been Qivir could move to obey the order, Torbyn heard another sound, a voice, from somewhere much closer. The voice whispered urgently, "Get up and run. I'll distract them. Head into the forest. Don't go back to the hut. I'll find you later."

There was no time to think. Shadow took a step towards him and Torbyn knew that unless something intervened he was going to be slain as he lay there, unable to make his muscles obey his brain's commands to flee.

There was a movement twenty paces away, not far from Malthazzar and Shadow. A creature stepped into the clearing, the starlight glinting from its golden, mouselike fur. The creature spoke in a voice that commanded attention and brought Shadow to an immediate halt.

"General Shadow of the Hordes! It is long since last we met!"

Shadow turned and a strange look, a mixture of lust and malice, crossed his gray face. Torbyn knew that he had seen that expression before, but it was a moment before he could place it. Then he realized: it was the look of one who has been beaten in battle but now saw a chance for revenge.

"You!" Shadow spat out the solitary word and then, in a second, all vestige of the king's minister was gone. His attire dropped to the ground and standing over it was a flickering shadow that seemed one moment to be substantial and next to be no more than an ephemeral gathering of quasi-darkness. A dark blade flashed evilly in its paws.

Torbyn had seen enough. Now that the creature no longer had his gaze on him, he found that he had regained the use of his muscles. He scrambled to his feet and began to run back towards the hut.

He had covered twenty strides before he remembered what the voice had said: "Head into the forest. Don't go back to the hut." Was it the creature with golden fur that had spoken? It must have been. But this was no time to speculate. He dodged sideways and began to scramble mindlessly through the trees.

Part of his mind was desperately asking questions: who was the creature called Shadow? why was Malthazzar here? why had Malthazzar said that it was "not permitted" for him to intervene? what was King Michael's part in all this? who was Queen Catherine? where was Sheol? who was the golden-haired creature? But there was no time to try to answer any of these questions; he just kept running through the trees, changing direction every hundred strides or so, distancing himself from the glade.

He had no idea how long he ran in this manner. Perhaps it was an hour, perhaps it was only half as long: the mind plays strange tricks in such circumstances. But eventually he could run no more. Out of breath, he pulled up against a tree and slowly, almost gratefully, slipped down until he was seated on the ground, his back against the trunk, panting to catch his breath.

He looked at the disturbed snow where he had been running. If anyone wanted to follow him, he had left an easy trail. All he could hope was that he had travelled far enough that Shadow (or whatever the chief minister was really called) would not come after him.

He rested for a while, listening uneasily for any sign of pursuit. At length his breathing returned to normal. Slowly, he got to his feet. He turned to the west, where the bright yellow star that seemed to hang over Carn Toldwyn shone through a small gap in the clouds. He set out.

The first light of the false dawn was in the sky behind him when someone spoke, so close that in his surprise he tripped forward and landed heavily in the snow. He turned to face the speaker. It was the golden-haired creature.

The creature extended a paw and helped Torbyn to his feet. The dwarf looked into the strange animal's face, but could not read its expression. The creature's whiskers quivered, flickering around Torbyn's face; then it said simply, "I am the dablik. Come! I will show you the way."

The dablik turned away, but Torbyn was too full of questions to be satisfied with this short speech. "Wait. Who are you? And what became of the king's minister? And where are we going?"

The dablik turned slowly back towards the warrior and now Torbyn realized that the creature was exhausted. The dablik spoke with slurred words: "We go first into the tunnels, and then to Carn Toldwyn, where you will tell your story. Now come, I am tired and we have far to go. Shadow will not permit King Michael to rest now. But I am so tired...."

The dablik turned away and began to limp through the trees. His paws hit the ground quietly but no longer silently as they dragged the snow in fatigue. His mind full of questions, Torbyn followed.

XXIX *Underground*

Anderskerrin slept long and deeply. When he awoke he was momentarily terrified as he became aware of the claustrophobic chamber that surrounded him, the dimly glowing rock crowding in on him from all directions.

Then he remembered where he was: deep in the bowels of the Third Land somewhere below the forest of Palindor, and on his way to Carn Toldwyn with his strange companion, the dablik.

The dablik was still absent, even though pangs of hunger told him that he must have been asleep for a long time.

The dablik had said that he wouldn't be gone for long. What if the dablik was lost? What if something had happened to him? What if he never returned? Anderskerrin felt an incipient panic; he swallowed and tried to suppress the disquieting thoughts. The dablik would be back soon.

He opened his pack and began to eat. But the state of his pack just added to his worries. How long would his food last? Worse, his canteen was already nearly empty; how long could he survive before thirst assailed him?

He tried to think of happier things. By now surely Hervân had wakened from her healing sleep. That led to more comforting thoughts. Iadron and Harsforn, and even the dablik himself, had seemed convinced that he had been chosen as a messenger to Carn Toldwyn. Chosen by the High Lord Olvensar no less!

And if that was true, then all the things that had happened so far — being saved by Treadlong in the forest of Reglandor; the escape from Pirren Glanwyn; crossing the border into Palindor; even the appearance of Iadron and Harsforn and the dablik — then all these things also must have been part of Olvensar's plan. And so there was no need to worry about the state of his pack, or what might have happened to the dablik. Because surely Olvensar's lordship reached even to the depths of the rock beneath Palindor.

Didn't it?

Torbyn followed the dablik for some time. He watched the creature's movements carefully. From the slouch of his shoulders and the uneven way in which his feet hit the ground, it was clear that the dablik was either utterly fatigued or injured or, perhaps, both. The dablik was leading them back towards Dankenwood.

Their progress became slower and slower, until eventually the dablik halted beside an outcrop of rock. He looked exhausted.

Torbyn asked, "Surely we can rest now? They won't still be looking for us now, will they?"

"You don't know Shadow as I do. And anyway, now that we've escaped, he and his party will be in a hurry as never before to reach Carn Toldwyn ahead of us. No, we cannot rest." Then, more to himself, as if he was trying to urge himself on, "At least, not yet. Soon, perhaps." He looked at Torbyn. "Come on; we must keep moving. Follow me."

The golden-haired creature rounded the outcrop and was suddenly lost to sight. Following him, Torbyn saw that there was a narrow passageway between the rocks, leading to some sort of dark cave or tunnel. He squeezed himself between the rocks — he only just fit — and found that they were in a narrow tunnel that angled steeply downwards into the ground. It was pitch dark, but he could feel the dablik touching him with a paw. "Down here," the dablik said, and moved off down the tunnel.

As they travelled downward, the tunnel walls began to glow dimly. Torbyn followed the dablik closely. They walked slowly, the dablik wearily leading the way for about an hour, when the dablik halted in a large chamber from which radiated six passageways. "It's no good; I must rest. Come, lay your head on my fur and let us both sleep."

The creature was too exhausted to say any more; it curled up in one corner of the chamber and in moments was asleep. Torbyn realized that he too had been drained by the events of the night. He cushioned his head on the dablik's soft fur. Within seconds, he too was asleep.

Torbyn woke feeling refreshed. The dablik was still asleep. Torbyn got up and crouched near the mouth of one of the tunnels. He wondered what they were going to do for food.

The dablik suddenly moved and, in seconds, was wide awake. The creature jumped to its feet and shook itself several times, clearing its head.

"My oh my oh my oh my oh my. We overslept!" he exclaimed. "Come, we must hurry, or the poor fellow will be in a terrible state."

He gave Torbyn no time to ask questions, and without so much as a single glance around the chamber to get his bearings, the dablik headed down one of the tunnels, his soft feet now utterly silent against the hard rock. Torbyn scrambled to his feet and began to jog after the dablik, his own footfalls echoing noisily down the tunnel.

They travelled in this way for several hours, Torbyn becoming more hungry with every passing hour. They stopped a few times to rest, although it seemed like the dablik halted only for his companion's benefit. Whenever Torbyn tried to ask a question the dablik merely said, "Save your breath; we're in too much of a hurry for questions."

Anderskerrin felt like he was going out of his mind. All sense of time had now left him. He had waited and waited until he wanted to scream out loud, "Dablik! Where are you? Help!" Only the fear that there might be goblins somewhere in the tunnels stopped him.

He paced around the small chamber for a while. Then he went exploring — only a small distance, and with his pack strapped to his back in case he got lost — but there were no points of reference. Without any distinguishing features to guide him, he soon became nervous and cautiously made his way back to the chamber, breathing a heavy sigh of relief when he found it once more.

Twice he opened his pack and ate when he got hungry. Still there was no sign of the dablik. Questions without answers arose endlessly in his mind: who was this dablik creature? was he really a friend? where had he gone? had he got lost in the tunnels? or, worse, was he now lying dead after some terrible accident? was there anyone still alive who knew where Anderskerrin now was? for that matter, where exactly was he? And so the questions and thoughts reverberated in his head, for hour after hour, without resolution.

Gradually, despair began to overwhelm him. He tried to nap once more. He might have nodded off or he might not, he could not tell. A deep melancholia gripped him.

Eventually, a new thought struck him. He had been afraid to make too much noise in case he was discovered by goblins. But even if he were to be found by such creatures, perhaps he would be in no worse a state than he was now. At least he would have company; and there was always the possibility that they would lead him back to the surface.

He tossed this thought around for some time before finally deciding that there was nothing to be gained by staying silent. So he began to call for help. "Help! Anyone there? Help!" He called out several times, then waited to see if anything would happen.

For a while, nothing happened. Then, with a sudden clutch of fear, he realized that he could hear a heavy, laboring footfall, still distant but coming unmistakably closer. For several seconds, a new terror gripped the elf. What made it worse was the knowledge that he had brought this upon himself.

For a desperate moment, he wondered if there was any way to escape the lumbering beasts heading his way. He pulled his pack on and tried to decide from which of the tunnels the sound was coming. But the echoing sound seemed to come from all directions at once.

Then, suddenly, there was a flash of golden fur and the dablik was in the chamber with him. A moment later the dablik was joined by a dwarf girded in the light battle armor of Reglandor.

Anderskerrin took a step backwards and pressed himself against the wall, afraid that the dwarf would strike them both dead. Instead, the dwarf simply gazed at the elf, seemingly in as much surprise as Anderskerrin himself.

Both looked at the dablik, who was wearing a self-satisfied smile. The dablik said, "Sorry for the delay; there was a spot of trouble above, good elf. But why were you shouting like that? We've been able to hear you for a good half hour."

"What? Oh, er, I was worried that something might have happened to you," the elf said, sheepishly.

"But what did you expect to accomplish by shouting like that?"

"I thought that maybe there were other creatures living in the tunnels, maybe goblins or something, and they would rescue me."

The dablik shook his head emphatically. "In the first place, we're too close to the surface and too far from the mountains for there to be any goblins around here; although I admit that the way you were shouting they might have heard you even in Mourn itself. In the second place, if a goblin had found you, you certainly would not have been thankful for very long. Have you ever seen a goblin, elf?"

Anderskerrin shook his head.

"Well, pray to Olvensar that you never do. Oh, don't get me wrong, I get on quite well with some of them in an odd sort of way. But for an elf like you, no..." — he shook his head — "...you'd definitely regret it. Now, much though I'd like to, I'm afraid we can't stop and chat all day. We must be moving. If this good dwarf could have a little something from your pack to ease his hunger pangs, then we'll be going. Don't worry, we'll be travelling near the surface before long and we'll be able to take a proper meal then."

Anderskerrin pointed at Torbyn. "But who is he? He wears Reglandor armor. Surely he is an enemy, not a friend."

"This is Torbyn. And he is not an enemy. We have only one enemy."

"King Michael?"

"No. Our enemy is the creature known as Shadow, who is Malthazzar's pawn. Michael and the other warriors are merely being used. Now, Torbyn is hungry. Give him some of your food while I explain."

Torbyn quickly ate his fill from Anderskerrin's supplies, the hefty dwarf nearly finishing the contents of the elf's pack. While Torbyn ate, the dablik explained his plan.

"I wanted to see how far Michael's troops had reached. But I got a terrible shock; something I had never considered. The leader of the party isn't the king at all: it's General Shadow of the Hordes."

"Who is this Shadow creature, anyway?" Torbyn interrupted.

"He's one of the most intelligent and cunning of Malthazzar's generals, and it is impossible to fear him sufficiently. He is a master of his craft. With him leading Michael's band, our task becomes infinitely harder."

"And what exactly is our task?"

"To reach Carn Toldwyn before the Reglandor warriors and prepare the Ruling Council for battle."

"But surely there are only seven soldiers in their party; six now that I'm here. It would be a very uneven match," said Torbyn.

Anderskerrin interjected, "I've been away from Palindor for many years, but you misunderstand the nature of the Third Land. If the members of the Council were to be defeated in battle..." — here the dablik interrupted: "Killed, not defeated; Shadow does not take prisoners" — "...then that would be no different than if all Palindor were defeated. Without leaders, Palindor will not fight. We are now a peaceful land. All your warriors need do is remove the Ruling Council, then Palindor will be under Reglandor's control, as in days of old."

"No," said the dablik, shaking his head. "Then Palindor and Reglandor would both be under Malthazzar's command, through General Shadow.

"Now, if you've finished eating, Torbyn, we must be on our way. Travel underground is faster than on the surface, but even so it's going to be a tight race. Once we reach Carn Toldwyn, we still need to persuade the Ruling Council of the danger that faces them, and then we must help them get ready to meet the warriors. There is no time to waste."

They got to their feet and, with the dablik in the lead, they set out once more.

XXX *Drefynt's Cottage*

It had been a week since Catherine had returned from Sheol, yet she was no closer to understanding her task in Palindor.

After she walked through the doorway in Sheol, she found herself in the shelter of the great granite slab of Toldwyn's Quoit atop Machrenmoor. She turned to look back at the doorway through which she had passed, but it had disappeared.

A chill breeze blew from the north, and the smell of snow was heavy on the air. She shivered. The sun was setting, and high over Carn Toldwyn the bright yellow star was visible against the darkling sky. She stepped out from under the shelter of the quoit and headed north.

Night fell before she reached Drefynt's cottage. She wasn't sure where else to go, and the Holy Gnome was sure to be able to offer wise advice about what she should do next.

She knocked on the cottage door hesitantly, unsure if she were doing the right thing. Lorin opened the door and gasped in surprise. Lorin looked older than the last time Catherine had seen her, and it dawned on her that perhaps time in Sheol was different from time in Palindor. To Catherine, it seemed like she had been gone only a week or so, but perhaps she had been absent from Palindor for many years.

"Oh, do come in, Your Majesty." Lorin bowed. "We thought you'd be in Pirren Glanwyn by now. What could've brought you back here? And is Sherna with you?"

With relief, Catherine realized that here too she had been gone only a short while. But in that case, why did Lorin seem to have aged so much?

"No, Sherna isn't with me. I was captured by Dark Knights in Dankenwood and have only just escaped from their land. Is Drefynt here?"

Her voice catching, Lorin replied, "Yes, Your Majesty, he is here. But he is not well. Since you and Sherna left us, he has done little more than sleep. He is in his bed now." She lowered her voice. "I am afraid his time is near." She brushed a tear from the corner of her eye. Then, a little more brightly, she added, "But he'll be glad you're here. Come inside and see him."

Catherine was appalled at this news. When she had left, it was true that Drefynt had been frail, but he had hardly been near death.

"Show me," she said, and Lorin led her to a small room on the upper floor of the cottage.

Drefynt was sitting up in bed, propped against a pillow. He looked at Catherine as she entered the room. She wanted to return his gaze, but found herself unable to do so. She couldn't look at her friend, who seemed to have aged fourteen years in as many days.

"Queen Catherine, you have returned. And with what news?" the Holy Gnome asked. His voice was dry and hoarse: the voice of a gnome near death.

Catherine sat beside the bed and took the old gnome's hand. It was sere, hard and papery, almost lifeless. She swallowed to keep from crying.

"Sherna and I travelled as far as Dankenwood. There I was taken prisoner by a band of Dark Knights. For the past few days I have been in Sheol, where I would have remained had it not been for Olvensar himself."

"Olvensar, in Sheol? According to all that I know, that is not possible. Are you sure, my child?"

It was the "my child" that sealed Catherine's conviction that Drefynt had not long to live. Never had Drefynt called her a child before. Even when she had first visited Palindor, when indeed she *was* little more than a child, he had always referred to her as "Your Majesty."

She tried to answer his question.

"Now I think about it, he never entered Sheol itself. But Fayorn was in Sheol — that was who the sage in the gray habit was. Fayorn saved me in Sheol and then was taken by Olvensar just before I was sent back to Palindor."

The old gnome asked weakly, "And my daughter? What of my daughter?"

"I don't know. She was not taken to Sheol with me. I don't think she was captured by the Knights, otherwise I'm sure I would have seen her there. And when I returned from Sheol late this afternoon I was alone on Machrenmoor, at the quoit. I don't know where Sherna is now."

"She is dead; I am sure of it."

"Dead? Why should she be dead?"

"Because of the words in the book."

"What words?"

Drefynt did not answer for a while, and Catherine began to wonder if the old gnome had heard her question. Then he said, "I was translating it, you know. The work was difficult. It is many, many years since I have used the Old Characters and the Old Words, but I knew that if I could translate the book, it would be perhaps the greatest achievement of my entire life."

"And did you finish?"

He shook his head. "I could not. The pain was too great. You see, like all the great and holy books, the book is prophetic; perhaps it is the very first and greatest of such books.

"All the known books of prophecy were stored at Perendeth and destroyed in the great fire set by Queen Cerebeth. But there was a reason that all the books were kept by the Holy Gnomes. Books of prophecy are both difficult to interpret and also very dangerous. It takes a great deal of training and skill and, some have said, a special gift from the High Lord himself to interpret such books properly. The Holy Gnomes always felt that such books were not for the common people, that they were too dangerous and too easy to misuse. Now I see the wisdom of such a policy. For the book I was translating is taking me to my grave."

Catherine hung her head, not wanting to interrupt her friend. She gave his hand a gentle squeeze, to show him that someone who cared for him beyond words was with him in his obvious torment.

Drefynt continued, "At first, the work was difficult but also enjoyable and fulfilling. I read prophecies concerning the establishment of Palindor as the Third Land, of the early battles among Palindor and Soltarwyn and Reglandor.

"Queen Cerebeth was prophesied. All of the prophecies were in the old style, verbose and repetitive and, to the uninitiated, impossible to interpret. But because I was reading of things that are now in Palindor's history rather than its future, I began to understand the way that the prophecies were written. It would have been almost impossible to understand a prophecy before the event to which it referred took place: the phrases were too ambiguous. It was only after reading so many prophecies that I began to become attuned to the book. By the time I reached the prophecy about you and Malthazzar on Machrenmoor, what would have been unintelligible rantings made almost complete sense."

Catherine was not sure she understood, but she nodded to encourage the gnome to continue.

"But I was a fool. I should have stopped translating then, satisfied merely to learn of things already past. But no, in my pride I wanted to translate the whole book. So I continued, and learned of things that were still to be. Perhaps if I had not become so engrossed in the tale told by the book, I would still have been safe. But the book's words, on the surface so obscure, were now plain to me, their meaning no longer hidden as it was surely meant to be."

"And what did you learn?"

"I read of you, and of Michael; I read of Sherna; but most of all, I read of myself. I am doomed, Catherine!" He clutched at her hand with a force surprising in one so weak, and a frightened look came over him. "My doom is that my daughter will be killed, and that I shall die alone and full of sorrow."

Several seconds passed before Catherine said, "But even if what you say is true, how do you know that these things will happen soon?"

"Because the book says that they will happen when King Michael, the Second High Monarch, comes to Palindor."

"But he has not come. Has he?"

Suddenly, Catherine was unsure of herself. While she was in Sheol perhaps the High King had arrived. A flash of jealousy caught her off-guard at the thought that a second High Monarch might be in the land.

"It's the star. The star is the sign of King Michael. But things are not that simple. Grave and deep happenings are afoot: even though the star has hung over the town for nigh on four weeks, yet there is still no trace of the High King, even though he was seen briefly after the star appeared. He is here somewhere, but no one knows where. Or why.

"But more importantly, we all misunderstood the meaning of the old prophecy that Michael would be the High King of War. We assumed that meant that Michael would lead Palindor in a war. That's not what it meant at all. Reglandor was once known as the Land of War. Michael is to be the High King of Reglandor, not Palindor. And he will come to fight against us, not with us.

"And there is something else. Never have I felt so alone. Always before when I have prayed to the High Lord, I have known his presence — ever since those days when you first visited us. Even if the High Lord chose not to answer my prayers in the way that I desired, still I felt his presence and knew that even in my weakness he loved me.

"But now, but now..." — a tear formed in one eye and began to trickle down his face — "...but now when I pray I feel nothing but an aching emptiness. He has withdrawn from me. It is the loneliness of which the book spoke when it described my end, I know it." The single tear multiplied; he withdrew his hand and turned away so that she could no longer see his face; his body heaved in anguish.

There was nothing Catherine could say, no words to comfort the poor gnome. It was fruitless to argue with him; in matters such as these, his knowledge was far superior to her own. If Drefynt said that he was to die soon, alone and despairing, there was no point in contradicting him, for it would be so. Silently, she lifted a prayer to Olvensar: "Comfort him in his hour of need, Lord Olvensar. Do not distance yourself from him, for he needs you now more than

229

ever." The prayer echoed in her mind. Whether Olvensar heard it she had no way of knowing.

She lifted herself out of her chair. Squeezing the shoulder of the sobbing gnome, she leant down and gave him a gentle kiss on his ancient cheek. Then she turned away and quietly stole out of the room.

Unlike the walled city of Pirren Glanwyn, Carn Toldwyn was open to all comers. The main entrance, such as it was, was at the south end of town, but most creatures arriving in or departing from Carn Toldwyn simply passed between town and forest somewhere along the eastern edge of the town. And so it was with the creatures who arrived more than a week later.

Apart from Drefynt and Lorin, still no one knew that the High Queen was living in Carn Toldwyn. She had discussed this with Drefynt, and together they had decided that it would serve no useful purpose to make her presence known.

As the days passed, Drefynt's condition worsened. So Catherine spent most of her time in the cottage, talking with the gnomes and helping Lorin look after her ailing husband.

She left the cottage twice. One day, she hiked to the top of Machrenmoor and spent the day in lonely contemplation in the shadow of the giant slab that crowned the quoit. It was the first time she had spent much time there alone, and she found it comforting in a strange, lonely way. The quoit looked like a large milkmaid's stool, the flat top supported by three granite pillars. A fourth pillar lay on the ground nearby. Asking Drefynt that evening, he told her that until Queen Cerebeth had ascended to the throne some thirteen hundred years before, the great top of the quoit had been held in place by four, not three, pillars. One night early in Cerebeth's reign, a great storm came and one of the pillars had toppled to the ground, where it still lay. Some said that it would remain that way until the day of Toldwyn's return, in the hour of Palindor's greatest need.

"And what do you think of that story?" asked Catherine, interested to know if the wisest of all gnomes gave credence to tales of Toldwyn's return.

"I think it's just a story, but stranger things have been known to happen. I've never seen anything in any of the Holy Books to suggest that Toldwyn will ever return. None of the prophecies ever indicated that he was anything other than a particularly gifted human mortal. His remains are buried below the quoit, and there I have every reason to expect them to remain until the very end of time."

Secretly, Catherine was disappointed. Part of her had been hoping that perhaps one day she might meet the great Toldwyn, and discover for herself how many of the stories she had heard about him were true.

Her second excursion was in the opposite direction, to the gardens several thousand paces to the north of the town. Before the time of her first visit to Palindor, the gardens had been left to run wild, and one of her tasks as High Queen had been to restore them to their former glory. She was pleased to see that they were still maintained; indeed, as she walked through them, admiring how even in early winter they looked fresh and attractive, she encountered no fewer than three of the gardeners who worked there.

But she returned from the gardens, as from Machrenmoor, no wiser about her part in the events that Drefynt was still sure were about to be unleashed on the land.

Catherine was mulling these things while sharing an afternoon pot of tea in the kitchen with Lorin when her thoughts were interrupted by a knock on the front door.

"I wonder who that can be," said Lorin, rising wearily and going into the hallway to answer the door.

Catherine heard a voice say: "May we come inside?" followed by the sound of several creatures entering the cottage. Something about the voice seemed familiar. She was sure she recognized it from somewhere.

She did! The creatures halted in the kitchen doorway. In a moment she was out of her chair and then awkwardly (for how else can one embrace a large dormouse?) she was hugging the dablik. "It *is* you! I never thought I'd see you again!" She completely ignored the two creatures who stood behind the dablik.

The dablik extricated himself. "Why, it's the High Queen!" he exclaimed. "Well, this does put a different light on things. You do keep turning up at the most unexpected moments."

It was perhaps not the most friendly of greetings, but that was typical of the dablik: his mind worked in paths unlike those of any other creature she had ever known. She felt an enormous relief at seeing the creature who had long ago saved her from the goblins under the Mountains of Mourn. If anyone could cheer Drefynt and explain what was happening, it would be the dablik.

"Into the living room with you all," said Lorin. "You're making the place untidy, standing around like that."

They shuffled into the living room and found themselves chairs while Lorin fussed over them. Catherine stared at the creatures who were with the dablik. One was a tired-looking elf, the other a fearsome-looking dwarf clad in light battle armor.

The dablik performed the introductions matter-of-factly. "Good Lorin, wife of the esteemed Drefynt the Wise, we three travellers bid you greeting and offer you our thanks for allowing us the honor of entrance to your abode. Permit me first to introduce myself. I am the dablik. I dare say you have never heard of me, but that is neither here nor there. For the fact is that I rarely spend much time above ground, and it is even rarer that I venture into towns such as this. I am here today merely as a guide for my two esteemed companions."

Catherine observed that the "two esteemed companions" shot a quick glance at one another when they were so described, and then both looked vaguely embarrassed.

"The dwarf dressed for battle is Torbyn, a member of the personal guard of the king of Reglandor."

A horrified look crossed Lorin's face, as if she suspected for a moment that her house had been invaded by the enemy. The dablik hastened to explain.

"Be assured, good gnome, that Torbyn enters this place entirely as a friend. Indeed, what he has to say may be the saving of Palindor. And as for my other companion, he is Anderskerrin, a brave fisherelf originally from the village of Penclaw in Palindor, but for many years now a resident of the Meadow of the Fire Mountain in Soltarwyn."

Catherine realized that gathered together peaceably in this small room were representatives of all three of the Lands of Abuscân. She wondered if such a thing had ever occurred before in Palindor's history. Not for a long time, she felt sure.

"And to you good creatures" — the dablik now indicated his companions — "I have the pleasure to introduce Catherine, High Queen of Palindor, and also the good gnome Lorin, wife of the Holy Gnome Drefynt of whom I have spoken."

Lorin bobbed her head lightly to the visitors, while Catherine made a more serious, formal bow.

The elf, Anderskerrin, seemed unsure that he had heard correctly. He addressed Catherine. "Excuse me, ma'am. Am I to understand that you are Catherine, the High Queen who rid our land of Malthazzar before I was born?"

Instead of answering, Catherine excused herself. When she returned moments later, there was a new quickness in her eye, and around her waist was a belt, in the center of whose buckle a white gem glittered with subdued fire. No words were necessary.

The elf bowed low, and prodded the dwarf to do likewise. "Please accept my apologies, Your Majesty. I did not know that you were in Palindor."

Catherine laughed. "You are forgiven, of course. Apart from yourselves, only Drefynt, Lorin and their daughter, Sherna, know of my presence here." She did not notice the look that crossed the elf's face at the mention of Sherna's name.

The dablik spoke once more. "And speaking of Drefynt, the tale my companions have to tell is for his ears also. Where is the good gnome?"

Now Catherine's sadness returned. She explained how old Drefynt now seemed, and how forlorn his spirit was. At first, the dablik seemed little affected by the news, but when she explained about the book of prophecies that Drefynt had been translating, he too seemed to feel a heavy sadness.

"Take us to him," said the dablik, "and my companions will tell their stories, for there is no time to lose."

Lorin led the group up the narrow staircase. There was not enough room for all of them to gather in Drefynt's room, so after she had informed her husband that he had visitors, she withdrew to the kitchen downstairs to prepare a meal for the guests. Catherine stood in Drefynt's doorway, where she could watch and hear what happened in the room.

A look of joy crossed Drefynt's face when he first saw the dablik. "You!" he exclaimed. But then, as if thinking better of it, the joy was replaced by the despairing sadness that Catherine had come to know so well in the past week. "But if you are here, then things are serious indeed."

"Yes," said the dablik. "I am afraid they are. We were hoping you would advise us what to do next. While my heart bleeds to see you this way, I am yet pleased beyond words that the High Queen is here, for I fear that it is only the intervention of a High Monarch that might stop the disaster which is about to befall Palindor. And now, I have occupied too much of your time. You must hear from my colleagues Anderskerrin and Torbyn. But be warned, good gnome, that the elf has words that will be hard to bear. I am sorry for the pain that you are about to feel."

There was a heavy silence in the room while Drefynt and Catherine digested these words. Drefynt spoke, his voice weaker than ever. "It concerns my daughter, does it not?"

No one replied immediately. The dablik nodded towards Anderskerrin, who eventually broke the silence. "Indeed it does, most Holy Gnome. Forgive me that I am the bearer of such news. Your daughter Sherna is dead."

A groan, a sound that seemed to hold all the pains of the entire world, involuntarily escaped Drefynt's throat. Tears welled in his eyes and began to course down his cheeks, mingling with his old, thin beard. Catherine too felt as if part of her had died.

"Continue, Anderskerrin" urged the dablik quietly.

The elf was unsure whether to obey. He looked towards Catherine for confirmation. Heavily and with infinite sadness, she nodded.

He told his story. How he had left Penclaw and crossed the Mountains of Mourn with Gondalwyn, a dwarf whom Drefynt had come to know well in years past. How the two of them settled in the Meadow of the Fire Mountain and there fell in love with the creatures who became their wives. The night in which the Fire Mountain spewed forth flame, sending him and Hervân on their journey south to Pirren Glanwyn. How they had arrived just in time to witness the coronation of the new king, King Michael.

At the mention of the new king's name, Drefynt's face became animated. He interrupted the elf. "Michael? Did you say that the new king's name is Michael?"

Anderskerrin nodded, and the gnome, although grief-stricken before, now looked bereft of all hope. "So I was right about the prophecy. Michael leads Reglandor, not Palindor."

Catherine felt an unaccountable unease as Anderskerrin confirmed the new king's name — as if, once, long ago and in some other place that she could not now remember, she had known someone by that name.

The elf continued his tale. He told the sad story of how the old king had come to be killed, supposedly by a female gnome from Palindor, and all in the room knew that it had to be a lie, that Sherna, the daughter of the gentlest and wisest of gnomes, could never have done such a thing. And then came news that was perhaps even more disturbing, as Anderskerrin described how the newly crowned king had marched out of Pirren Glanwyn and the city had been sealed after him.

"People were allowed to enter the city, but none could leave. We began to hear rumors that Michael had vowed vengeance for the death of King Glendour, and had pledged that Palindor would no longer be a nation of its own; that once again, as in the Old Days, the flag of Reglandor would fly over Palindoric soil.

"But I could not permit that to happen, not without a fight, so Hervân and I escaped the city. We hurried to the border, but it was guarded by soldiers from Reglandor. We managed to cross the River Chân, but Hervân was injured by an archer in the process. She is being cared for by a healer and a seer in the Mountains of Mourn. They brought the dablik to me, and he has led me here so I can warn the Ruling Council."

As the elf related how King Glendour was supposed to have been murdered by Sherna, Drefynt lapsed into a deep silence, apparently unaware of those around him. As Anderskerrin finished his story, there was no response from the old gnome except that the tears continued to trickle down his face. He stared unseeingly through tear-filled eyes at the ceiling.

"We should leave him, I think," said Catherine.

Quietly, they left Drefynt to his grief.

Drefynt barely noticed their departure. As Anderskerrin had been speaking, a realization had gradually stolen over him. It dawned on him, in an oddly detached kind of way, that he was tired of life. There was little point in living when a good gnome such as his daughter could be taken from him in such a meaningless way.

He remembered how he had played with her when she was a child; how her delighted laughter used to fill this very cottage. And even though she was now fully grown and the most widely travelled citizen of the land, still she always returned to this cottage, her first and most beloved of homes. With Sherna gone, what was the point of living any more?

Everything had gone so desperately wrong. King Michael was supposed to be the High King of Palindor, not King of Reglandor, intent on destruction of the Third Land. And his beloved daughter would never again grace Lorin and him with her presence.

The early twilight of the winter evening stole over the room, and the light from the bright star overhead flooded in at the uncurtained window. For weeks he had been trying to understand why High King Michael had disappeared so suddenly after his brief appearance on Penmichael Brea — but now he found that he no longer cared. He was tired; his body and his mind were both old; he had served Palindor once, long ago, in a moment of grave crisis; he had done all he could. Now it was time for someone else to take over. He was just too tired.

A shadow appeared at the bedroom door.

"Who's there? Who is it?" he asked, his voice feeble and cracked.

The shadow entered the room, and the light from the star shone yellowly on a form that was unmistakable. He should have been surprised, but for some reason it seemed perfectly natural that his daughter stood before him.

She held out a hand. "Come, father. Leave it to others. Your work is done. It is time."

She was standing several paces away, her hand held out towards him. He lifted his arm towards her, but he could not reach her. He got out of bed, then stepped forward and grasped his daughter's hand. A smile covered her face.

"I love you," he said.

It seemed a long time since he had said that. The words sounded good. He would say them more often in future.

Sherna turned away and, still holding his hand, led him to the bedroom door. Beyond the door frame was... not the candlelit corridor of the hall outside his bedroom, but, rather, a forest grove, in which he could see friends whom he had thought long dead.

She passed through the doorway. He turned for a moment and looked back into the bedroom. In the steady light from the star, he could clearly see the form of an old gnome laying in the bed, his face wearing a look of infinite peace.

Turning his back on the room, he stepped through the doorway.

XXXI *Confrontation*

Drefynt's death deepened the air of gloom. Surprisingly, his wife Lorin was in some ways the least affected. She had known the gnome for nearly three hundred years and lived with him for most of that time. "He was old and he was in despair. The news of Sherna's death simply took away his will to live. I too am old and tired, and I will not be long parted from my husband, of that I am sure."

The others were affected in different ways. Torbyn and Anderskerrin had never known Drefynt, but in their journey with the dablik they had come to look upon him as a sort of savior, someone who would have the wisdom to know what to do, who would tell them how they might defeat the foreign king who was intent on subduing Palindor. With Drefynt's death they seemed lost and bereft of direction.

The dablik was uncharacteristically quiet as they all sat in the parlor that evening, mulling over what their next action ought to be. Any attempt to engage him in conversation failed miserably. His brow was furrowed as he stared wordlessly at the floor. Every now and again he would lift his head to stare either at the star whose light streamed in at the window, or at Catherine, as if he knew that somehow the two were related and in some way held the key to the solution to their predicament.

As for Catherine herself, she was perhaps the heaviest hearted of them all. Only in the past few days had she begun to realize what Drefynt meant to her. And now, when she needed his counsel most of all, it was not to be had.

The news that Anderskerrin had brought, supplemented and amplified by Torbyn, demanded action of some kind. But what? The star hanging in the sky puzzled her as much as it had Drefynt. And then there was this matter of the new king, Michael. There was something strangely disturbing about the name "Michael". She recognized the name from the lines of the poem, but there was something more to it than that — a strange familiarity that she could not place. It nagged at her and would not leave her alone.

The night grew late. They began to fall asleep where they sat. Only the dablik remained awake as the clock monotonously ticked away the seconds, the minutes and the hours.

Dawn came, bringing a new day, and the creatures woke. Lorin busied herself preparing breakfast. Everyone was subdued, but some of the gloom of yesterday seemed to have disappeared. The dablik said, "We must go to the Ruling Council this morning. King Michael and his party could arrive at any time. I last saw them a couple of days ago, and if they've been making good time they'll arrive today. We lost half a day yesterday, talking. Now there's no time to lose."

They breakfasted hurriedly. Catherine asked Lorin, "How do we go about convening the Ruling Council?"

"We don't need to. Today is Gwenerday*. The Council sits in the Judgement Room this morning. We can see them as soon as we like."

Without waiting to clean the dishes, the party gathered outside the cottage. With Lorin leading the way, they made their way up the hill towards the castle.

The Judgement Room's antechamber held a small gathering of creatures who had come to lay their differences before the Ruling Council. A male gnome looked up as the party swooped into the room.

---

* Friday in our calendar.

Ignoring the waiting creatures, the newcomers headed directly for the closed oak doors that led to the Judgement Room. The waiting gnome jumped to his feet, annoyed at the intruders' lack of manners. "Here! You! You'll have to wait your turn...."

The elderly female gnome who led the newcomers stepped to one side, and her place was taken by a human woman with long, black hair; her eyes held a smoldering fire that gave the impression that it could flare into impassioned power at any moment.

The gnome looked at the human, and his jaw slackened in amazement. For around her waist she wore a belt whose large buckle held a white stone that glistened with a fire that matched her eyes. From the belt dangled a scabbarded sword which he recognized immediately: he had seen it many times, hanging in the Judgement Room. Aghast, he stammered, "Y-Your M-Majesty."

Catherine grabbed the handles of the huge oaken doors, swung them wide open, and strode imperiously into the Judgement Room. The rest of her party followed.

Inside, the Ruling Council was deliberating a case between an elderly dwarf and his wife's brother, who had moved in with them a decade before and now refused to leave. The dwarf, his wife and the brother had been sent to sit in the antechamber while the members of the Ruling Council discussed the case.

"I say...," started Ymyr, the leader of the Ruling Council, startled by the intrusion and rising from his chair behind the oval table at which the members were seated. His sentence trailed off into nothingness as he stared at the human who had stormed into the chamber.

A peculiar golden-haired creature who seemed to be with the motley party closed the doors behind them all. Ymyr slowly regained his seat as Catherine defiantly strode forward and stood opposite him. She drew her sword and held it with the blade vertical.

"I am Catherine, High Queen of Palindor. I demand to be recognized by the Ruling Council."

There was a stunned silence. At length, Ymyr said, "Oh..., er..., yes..., what? oh... of course...."

Catherine motioned to Anderskerrin and Torbyn to stand beside her.

"This is the elf Anderskerrin and the dwarf Torbyn. They have something important to say. You will listen to them without interruption. There is no time to explain. Just listen. Save your questions until they've finished."

As the previous afternoon, Anderskerrin began. He quickly related the events he had witnessed; then Torbyn took up the story, driving home the fact that the threat from Reglandor was both real and imminent. When they had finished, Catherine was dismayed to see that the faces of the members of the Ruling Council reflected only consternation. They had even less idea of what to do about the situation than Catherine herself.

Ymyr broke the uncomfortable silence. "I suppose it would be stupid of me to ask how sure you are about all this?"

"Yes," said Catherine. "It would."

"Oh, er, yes, I see. Well, er, are you sure that they will reach us so soon?" he asked Torbyn.

Catherine gave the warrior no chance to respond. She slapped the flat of her blade down on the polished oak surface of the table, so that its point was no more than an inch from Ymyr's hand. The sudden sharp sound reverberated through the room. Ymyr quaked visibly in his chair at the nearness of the lethal weapon.

"Haven't you been listening? You are the Ruling Council of Palindor. Yes, you! You are the creatures responsible for the defense of the land. Yet you sit here asking stupid questions. Of course the dwarf is sure! He escaped from the king's party at great risk to himself. The king will probably be here this very day. And didn't you hear? It's not just the king, it's one of Malthazzar's generals! A human king is one thing; a demon from the land of Sheol is something else entirely. If you don't do something, it is likely that none of you will live to see the night."

It was obvious that Ymyr wanted to argue. Perhaps he thought that this was all part of some cunning trap. After all, why should Reglandor suddenly invade Palindor now, after all these centuries of peace? He opened his mouth, but never had a chance to say what was on his mind, for suddenly from the antechamber came the sound of a skirmish.

For perhaps five seconds, no one moved. Catherine looked at her companions in horror. One by one, they realized what was happening on the other side of the doors.

The doors were thrown open, and into the chamber strode as fearsome a group as Catherine had ever seen. There was no time to count, but she already knew from Torbyn's story how many there were: four warriors, one chief minister and one other, the nominal leader of the group who (she saw to her surprise) was no more than a boy. King Michael of Reglandor led his party into the Judgement Room, his sword unsheathed and glistening, a bloody fire in his eyes matching the glow from the red gem that was seated in the center of his belt buckle.

Catherine took a step backwards, until her back was against the table. The last shadow of doubt had been banished. One look at that belt had confirmed it: this was indeed King Michael, the prophesied High King of War. But, as Drefynt had foreseen, instead of leading Palindor into battle as all those who knew the prophetic verse had expected, he was bringing death and subjugation to the Third Land.

The newcomers spread out, denying any hope of escape to those in the room. The Council members, as one, stood and moved backward until they were pressed against the far wall. All the members of Catherine's party scuttled to join them. Only Catherine remained where she was.

Michael stepped forward. He glanced at Catherine, then addressed the room at large. "I am Michael, crowned King of Reglandor. I reclaim the land known as Palindor for my realm. Surrender now and you will live. Resist in any way, and you will die! Who among you speaks for the so-called Ruling Council of Palindor?"

He looked at the cowering creatures, then spat on the ground. "Speak up! or I shall kill you, one by one, beginning with him," — he pointed his sword at the unfortunate Torbyn, who was trying unsuccessfully to hide behind Anderskerrin — "the no-good, deserting excuse for a dwarf."

Until this point, Catherine had been watching the young king, but now a movement by a short human who looked easily the least dangerous of the group attracted her attention. The human could only be the chief minister — the one known as Qivir — the one whom the dablik and Torbyn insisted was really Shadow, the most important of Malthazzar's generals. Shadow's face was furrowed, as if he were attempting to find a solution to a knotty problem.

His eyes darted back and forth between the dablik, who stood, uncowed and apart from the others near the rear of the room, and Catherine. Catherine realized that while Michael was undoubtedly here to subdue the Ruling Council, Shadow had a very different aim in view, and somehow it involved herself and the dablik.

There was a noise behind her. She turned to see Ymyr stepping hesitantly forward. The gnome bowed towards Michael.

"My name is Ymyr; I am chairman of the Ruling Council of Palindor. Surely there has been some mistake? This is not a warlike land...."

Michael shouted, "Mistake? Yes, there has been a mistake, and you feeble creatures of Palindor have made it. Now we are here to avenge King Glendour. We will march you all to Pirren Glanwyn and there you will publicly pay homage to Reglandor. Then you will be cast into dungeons, where you will spend the rest of your days."

"No!"

Drefynt's son Benglubber tore a decorative sword off the wall. In fury he ran forward towards the intruders. It was an act of madness. The warriors took a step forward to defend their king, but he merely waved them back with one hand while raising his sword in the other. Catherine waited for the gnome to realize the futility of his rash action and to retreat, but the thought that he was endangering himself never seemed to cross his mind. He ran headlong at Michael who, almost nonchalantly, brought his sword down.

The weapon struck the gnome heavily on the shoulder near the neck. The force of Benglubber's attack was such that his momentum carried him forward past Michael, who stepped easily to one side. Michael again raised his sword, now covered with Benglubber's blood. Benglubber plunged forward and crumpled on the stone floor, a red pool already forming on the flagstones. Michael lowered his sword. He did not need to strike a second blow.

It was obvious to everyone that Benglubber was dead.

No one moved.

There were enough weapons on the walls that every creature could arm himself. A dreadful choice faced those arrayed against Michael: they could fight and risk being slaughtered, or they could meekly surrender Palindor. Catherine grasped the hilt of her sword, ready to join the mêlée, should one develop. But it never happened.

"Enough!"

The voice was quiet but firm. Ymyr walked around the table, knelt and touched the body of the fallen gnome. Then he rose, stood before Michael, and dropped on one knee.

"One death is more than enough. We are no longer warriors, and there is no point in further slaughter."

He motioned for the remaining members of the Ruling Council to join him. With fear in their eyes, they shuffled around the table and arrayed themselves before the young king. One by one, they dropped to their knees. "We, the Ruling Council of Palindor, place ourselves and our land in your hands and request mercy in the name of Olvensar."

At this, Qivir stepped forward, fury on his face.

"No more!" he screamed. "That name is forbidden. He is gone! You will pay homage only to Michael and his successors. Your so-called High Lord has been defeated and his name shall be forgotten. Henceforth you will worship Malthazzar and his servant Michael."

Breathing deeply, he stepped back to his place behind Michael, a triumphant look on his face.

But now it was Catherine's blood that boiled. Images of Olvensar flashed before her: strange images that she could not readily place: in a garden, his ancient, lined face smiling at her; in some strange, gloomy building, his face receding into a swirling mist. She took a step toward Michael and the minister, grasping her sword grasped tightly.

"No!" she shouted. "The price is too great. I will never worship at the feet of the Dark One." She pointed her sword at Shadow. "You! I challenge you! Come fight me!"

The minister's face twisted into a hideous grin, and Catherine realized that he had laid a trap and somehow, monstrously, she had fallen into it.

The minister turned to Michael. "Your Majesty; she is the only one who refuses to accept you as the ruler of the land. I would be glad to dispatch her for you."

Michael shook his head. "No. I am king. It is my job."

He pointed his sword at the inert form of Benglubber, and addressed Catherine. "This is what happens to all who raise their sword against me. Do you really want to join him?"

"I have no wish to fight, but I will not let you banish the High Lord's name from this land that I love."

"Foolish woman."

Michael walked forward with his sword raised, until the tips of their swords were touching. "You give me no choice."

For the first time he looked properly at Catherine's face — and with a shock he recognized her. It was the woman he had seen in the necromancer's pot back in the palace in Pirren Glanwyn. Her face was full of power and fire, her eyes arresting, just as he had seen in the pot. But the pot had shown him that he would defeat the defiant woman.

He taunted her: "Recant and I might perhaps show you mercy, old woman!"

"Never, child!"

She drew her sword back to strike, but as she did so Michael said simply, "Then die!" He lunged.

Their swords clanged loudly as Catherine deflected the blow.

A surprised look flickered across Michael's face. Always before when he had struck with his weapon, the blow had gone home and killed instantly. Yet somehow this woman had been able to deflect his stroke. He took a step back, then came forward and struck again.

The same thing happened. She interposed her own sword and the weapons met as equals. Michael's blow once again failed to land.

Catherine saw an opening and prepared to strike.

"No! It's what Shadow wants."

It was the dablik, speaking for the first time since he had entered the hall.

She hesitated and, in that moment, the king's sword once more chopped downward. She barely had time to dodge the blow, and the point of his sword cut through her tunic near her left shoulder.

Now there was fresh blood on the tip of Michael's sword. The sight emboldened him. Michael struck with a rain of blows. Some she parried and some she sidestepped. Twice, he let his guard down enough that she had a chance to land a blow of her own. But with the dablik's reminder echoing in her head, she refused to take advantage of the opportunities Michael gave her.

Time and time again, Michael's sword flashed downward; time and time again the blow failed to strike home. The young king became more and more angry, and his slashes started to become ragged in his frustration.

"You will die, Catherine!"

This time it wasn't Michael who had spoken, but his chief minister. The distraction was enough. For a single dreadful moment Catherine's concentration wavered.

Michael's sword came down.

Catherine desperately tried to parry the blow, but she was too slow. Michael's sword caught at Scalmyùt's hilt, and the weapon flew out of her hand, skidding across the smooth flagstones and coming to a stop in the puddle of blood that was slowly congealing around Benglubber's body.

Down came Michael's sword again, and as she twisted desperately her ankle slipped beneath her; it twisted, and she fell clumsily to the ground. In a moment, Michael was standing above her, his hand raised high, ready to strike the final blow.

Their eyes locked.

For a long moment no one moved. The moment stretched out interminably. The expected death blow did not fall. The two monarchs stared into each other's eyes. Each of them saw something strangely familiar in the other's eyes. Neither of them could quite place it.

"Do it," urged Qivir, breaking the spell. "Finish it now, King Michael. Kill her, and none will dare stand against you."

Catherine said, "He's right. Kill me, Michael, if that is what you really want."

But still Michael did not strike.

He looked puzzled. He said to himself, "The necromancer's pot predicted this... but... but there's something more...."

Into his head flashed the memory of the elf child's death at the bridge over the Findell. Just as then, he was filled with a strange kind of certainty that something was very, very wrong. And this time he could do something about it.

Infinitely slowly, he lowered his sword to his side.

"Kill him, you fool!" urged Qivir.

"No. I will not."

Michael looked at Catherine, spreadeagled and at his mercy. There was something about that face....

"I... I know you...," he said haltingly. "Who are you?"

"Kill her! Now!" shouted Qivir. "Don't think! Just do it!"

Michael ignored him.

"And I know you...," Catherine said.

And in a flash, he remembered. He knew!

"You're my mother!" he shouted.

Qivir screamed wordlessly.

Of course! Of course! That was it! It all came back to Catherine. She raised her hands, not to ward off a blow, but to touch her son. "Michael! Michael! How could we do this to each other? We aren't enemies! You are my son; I could never hurt you!"

"Nor I you, mother."

"You pusillanimous fool," said Qivir through gritted teeth.

Michael turned to the minister and pointed his sword at him. "It's you! Everything here has been your doing!"

"Sssss...." the sibilant sound hissed through the minister's teeth.

"Who are you?" Michael continued. "Why did you want me to kill my own mother?"

Qivir seemed suddenly to flicker, alternating between the shape of the chief minister and a dreadful gray creature with blood-red eyes and pointed ears that lay flat against his rodentlike head.

With one eye on Qivir, Michael helped his mother to her feet, by which time the transformation was complete.

The creature opened its mouth and in a horrible, grating voice said, "I call on you, my Lord! Come! They are yours for the taking!"

As soon as the words were out of his mouth, the Judgement Hall began to shake violently. With a clatter, weapons jumped off the wall and fell to the ground. Catherine and Michael grabbed the table for support. In the commotion, the dablik dropped to all fours and padded across the room until he was facing the fearsome creature that the minister had become.

"No! You have lost, Shadow, as you always will. Your treachery has won you nothing. Begone; return to your evil master; spend your days with him and return to this place no more."

Baring pointed yellow teeth, an evil grin suffused Shadow's face. "I have no need to leave to join him, for my master is here."

He bowed, and all turned to see, advancing towards them from a corner of the room, the black form of the Lord of Evil.

Malthazzar strode to his general's side.

Shadow said: "Master; I could not make them destroy one another, but now there is nothing to prevent you from destroying them both yourself."

But Malthazzar, strangely, did not immediately advance on the High Monarchs. Instead he said to Shadow, "Fool! I gave the job to you."

"But, Master, I thought you would be pleased to finish the job yourself. I thought that was why you gave me instructions that I was to cause them no harm myself. I thought...."

"You think too much for one with no brain! I made an agreement that neither I nor any of my emissaries would cause harm to these pathetic mortal creatures. That was why I told you to make them destroy one another. Idiot!"

Malthazzar turned away contemptuously.

"But, Master... I am sorry, but this is too good a chance to miss. You have them in your power now. Take them to Sheol; they will be safe there. No one can take them from you there." With a glint in his eye Shadow added, "You could even throw them in the Pit."

After a moment, Malthazzar said slowly, "Aye; perhaps you are right."

He began to advance towards the High Monarchs.

Outside, the sun was at the highest point of its low journey across the sky. Its weak light lit the landscape with a cool, wintry, stark, gray light. But suddenly, all the citizens of Carn Toldwyn were arrested by a yellow light — a light brighter by far than the sun — that blazed into brilliant existence. The star that hung high over the town at night had suddenly flared so brightly that it far outshone even the noonday sun. All was suddenly, brilliantly lit with a warm yellow glow.

"It's moving!" one creature said to another. And sure enough, the pinprick of light that was the source of the yellow glow was rushing downwards, hurtling towards the ground.

Silently it fell from the sky, faster than any stone; in a moment it was gone, passing noiselessly through the roof of the castle, its light suddenly no more.

In the Judgement Hall, Malthazzar was standing above the two High Monarchs, his hands raised in the air.

Then, suddenly, the air was filled with a brilliant yellow light. But only for a moment. The light disappeared as suddenly as it had come. But as it vanished, Malthazzar, a look of terror on his black face, seemed to shrink as he backed away from Catherine and Michael.

There was silence in the room. Catherine leaned against the oak table, her ankle painful where she had twisted it. Michael stood at her side. But Malthazzar now ignored the two humans. Standing not ten paces away was an old man dressed in shabby clothes, a dark, angry frown on his face.

"I see into your heart, vilest of beings," the man said.

"No! No! I wasn't going to do it," replied Malthazzar.

"Don't waste your lies on me, you contemptible creature. We had an agreement, you and I, and you have chosen to disregard it. There is no place for you and your kind here, Malthazzar. Leave this place, and take your servant with you, before I lose my temper and forget how to be merciful."

Almost whimpering, Malthazzar nodded. "Yes, yes."

Shadow stepped to his master's side. He whispered: "Lord, why not have it out with him here and now, once and for all?"

"Don't be stupid!" Malthazzar's furious response echoed around the walls as he turned on his general. "We will meet at a time and place of *my* choosing, not his! Come, before he changes his mind and punishes us. Here his strength is too great."

"But...."

The others never heard the end of Shadow's protest. Malthazzar raised his hands, dropped them suddenly, and with a loud thunderclap and a flash of black light, the two were gone. Only the acrid smell of brimstone hung in the air to show where they had been.

Olvensar walked slowly towards Catherine and Michael. "Come! It is time to leave this place. Oh; you are hurt?"

Catherine nodded. "I twisted my ankle...."

Olvensar held out his hand and momentarily touched the High Queen. Catherine realized that it was the first time that the High Lord had ever touched her. With the touch an urgent tingle passed through her entire body. As the tingle died away, the pain disappeared.

She bowed: "Thank you."

"But what about him?" Michael, sword still in hand, pointed towards Benglubber's body. "Can you revive him?"

"Can I revive him? Oh yes, most certainly I *can*. But *should* I revive him? that is the question you should ask."

Michael waited for the old man to elaborate. Several seconds passed before he realized that the old man had no intention of saying anything further and was instead waiting for him to speak.

"Well, will you then?" Michael said, almost crossly.

"No. It was his time to leave this place. And now it is your time also, Michael Fowler. And yours, too, Katrin Fowler."

The room around the two High Monarchs receded into a gray mist. The whirling mist hid everything from them, until their whole universe was filled by just the three of them and a moist, cool, gray air. It lasted only moments, before a light breeze blew up and ripped apart the cloud that had enveloped them.

The air felt suddenly warm and clean. All around them were vibrant colors. They were standing next to a pond that reflected a sky of purest blue and around which grew a grass greener than any they had imagined. Out of the center of the pond a tree grew. Hanging from the tree was a single yellow-orange fruit, looking like the most delicious and desirable thing in the world.

Michael looked around in wonder as Olvensar addressed them. "Michael, you have a life to live. One day you will return to this place, but until you do, remember that you carry with you a great gift, for you carry the favor of the High Lord.

"And as for you, my child" — he turned to Katrin, who with difficulty turned away from the tree to look into Olvensar's face — "as for you, once before I gave you a choice; do you remember it?"

Katrin nodded. "Yes; I could choose to stay in Palindor or to return home to my parents."

"Now I offer you a second, more difficult choice. Do you remember what life is like in your own world?"

For a moment, Katrin struggled to remember her life in the world of humans. There was something ominous about that world, something that she could not quite remember. Then she *did* remember. A grief bore down on her with a weight that seemed palpable. In that world she was dying: a tumor was growing inside her head, and soon she would die. That world was full of sorrow, grief, illness and death.

"Yes; I remember, my Lord."

"Then I give you this choice; you may return to that world, or you may remain here with me."

Katrin opened her mouth to speak, the choice obvious. But then she closed it once more. She held out her hand to Michael, who took it uncertainly. How long would she live in that world? Not long, of that she was sure. But even though her few remaining months might be filled with pain and sadness, still that was as nothing against the joy of being with her son.

"I thank you, my Lord. But there is no choice to make. I must be with my son."

"Are you sure?"

"Yes. I am sure. I love him."

She said no more. There was no more to be said.

"Then until we meet again, I bid you farewell. You have my blessing, Katrin. And you also, Michael. Farewell."

There was a splash, and both son and mother turned toward the sound. The fruit had fallen from the tree, into the pool.

The ripples encircling the point where the fruit had entered the water moved outwards, growing as they did so. Within seconds, they had crossed halfway across the small pond, but had grown into waves the height of a child. Another few seconds and they were taller than a man. And then, before either of them could move, a wave towered over them, peaking at the very edge of the pool. It crashed down towards them, and they ducked to avoid the force of the water.

They were drenched. But there was no longer any trace of the garden. They were standing in a narrow, terraced street; a gray, dispiriting drizzle filling the air around them. The sidewalk was so narrow as to be almost nonexistent; a row of granite-faced cottages stood tight against the street.

Michael pointed. "Look, Mom!"

One of the houses had a window box. Amongst the geraniums that drooped miserably in the rain nestled a single yellow-orange fruit. Mother and son looked at one another. Michael let go of his mother's hand and picked up the fruit. He handed it to his mother, who looked at it for several seconds before plunging her teeth into it.

Once, long ago and in a different world, she had tasted such a fruit, but never before nor since. In a few moments it was gone, only the stone left. She dropped the stone into the pocket of her raincoat.

"Are you all right, Mom?"

Katrin nodded. "Oh yes, Michael. I'm all right. For the first time in a long, long time, I'm as all right as it's possible to be. Come here; let me hug you."

She held out her arms, and as the rain came down mother and son clasped each other tightly.

Colophon

The main body of the text of this book was typeset with the pdfTEX digital typesetting system. The typefaces used are mostly from the Latin Modern family, set at 11/13. The paper stock used for the body of the book and for the cover depends on the particular printer that created the book you are holding.

The VEDIT PLUS text editor was used to create the original text.

The cover was created with the Scribus desktop publishing system, in conjunction with the GIMP and Inkscape programs.

Computer processing for this edition of *Shadow* was performed on an Intel 64-bit quad-core system running the Kubuntu 8.10 64-bit distribution of the GNU/Linux operating system.